IN AMBER

a romance

Edwin Ahearn

I

Cantello, known as *the Peerless* wears like an unseen but not invisible mantle a refreshingly straightforward self-recognition, in which there is no thread of arrogance or its mirror-cousin, vanity. We, too, know him very well; has he not, with minor variants, hauled us through a hundred improbable adventures, spare, weather-beaten grumbler, ravaged, reluctant hero, solitary brooder in a barbaric world, scrupled but resourceful, grudgingly tender, ruthless at need, flippant over principles, yet in time angered by relatively abstract injustice, his claim of perfect selfishness hardly compatible with a slow-roused aptitude for altruistic sacrifice — a boondocks Hamlet, Sydney Carton repackaged, Bogart in buskins, snarling his indifference, even while stationing himself in the doomed rearguard, that others might live. Age cannot wither Cantello nor repetition stale his redemptive gesture, being our own unmaturing dream of enlightened self-immolation, our unguessed depths and that-within-which-passeth-show, suffering through Stendhal, brooding in Bronte, terse with Hemingway, misunderstood everywhere until too late — not quite too late. To see through the trick does not diminish its effect; that stream runs too deep to be deflected by dowsers.

We omit, or take as read, any detailed account of Cantello's formative adventures, his epic if somewhat meretricious trek across the reeking Wilderness of Arrans, the death-duel with his most ruthless enemy and, to date, only love, the alarming and alluring Sorceress of Synta, his ingenious escape from the thoroughly unpleasant bog-folk, aided by a powerful device obtained from an Eremite in Racq, chief city of Eremia; all this exciting comic-book rubbish is a waste of time for serious folk, though it did, we judge, help develop Cantello's self-reliance and disdain of the conventional, introduce a streak of irony in his iron.

But the times, otherwise why bother with them, are becoming unsafe for any voice of dissent; authority, as personified by the usurper, dark, suave, sardonic Corvan (another member of the stock-company, at once familiar), is increasingly oppressive, increasingly bad-tempered, as the time nears when he can consolidate and legitimize his power, ill-gotten, worse-wielded.

THE STORY SO FAR:

At Hallabreg (heartbreaking Hallabreg, once gay with pennons and melodious with laughter, its weathered stones now grimmed under the institutionalized glower of ever-suspicious tyranny) Corvan is on the point of establishing as legal fact extinction of the proper ruling house, hence his own lawful succession.

The true king, Dairemid, died (in fact, was poisoned) some eighty-three months ago. Had Corvan's efficiency equalled his ambition, he might have made himself king first go; the same fate as her father's was plainly intended for the eleven-year-old princess, Idomela, but friends contrived to rescue and deftly vanish her, and the usurper, bound to preserve the appearance of legitimacy, having put out that she had been kidnapped (which no one believed), declared a Protectorate, ruling through a spineless High Council.

The constitution stipulates that seven years must elapse before royal death can be presumed: Corvan, bastard son of the former king's late brother, has followed the letter of this law, but used the time in consolidating his de facto rule. As in a massive and unceasing search for Idomela, publicly advertised as a scrupulous effort to restore the rightful heir, but with covert orders to trusted lieutenants that the girl, when found. must be bundled away to an obscure death. Routine procedure in such cases would be to issue yet-more confidential instructions to even-more innermost confederates, to murder the murderers, and loudly announce that the second bunch came just too late to save the victim, his cousin, from traitors. Maybe so, but impenetrable secrets as part of the tale's texture must, for the sake of plausiblity, remain unpenetrated.

If Idolema, by luck, with many narrow escapes, aided by the resourcefulness and sacrifice of her father's diminishing remnant of loyal friends, has indeed lived on — which her cousin's restless, and indeed expensive ransacking seems to make more likely — the ever more distasteful rule of Corvan would persuade her allies that her reappearance, for some an end in itself, offers the last chance for restoration of the less onerous government of her father's day. But as the seventh year wears away belief is general that unless an Idomela can reveal and declare herself before the legal span has elapsed, no hope will remain: soldiers and ministers will take new oaths to Corvan, and his grip on the power will become unbreakable. The trick, then, for the Loyalists, would be to keep the princess concealed, unveiling her in one swift *coup d'oeil*, so abruptly and so publicly Corvan could do nothing but add his reluctant voice to the chorus of astonished gratitude for her survival — if she has, as I say, survived; drama too decrees that some information must be obscured, to be exposed in proper temporal sequence; God, for whom all time, present, past and to come, is as a single instant, can have no notion of narrative.

Corvan, equally, can do the sums, and, as time grows short, makes plainer than ever that he has not yet been able to hunt down the princess, by renewing and redoubling his efforts to do so. For him, some hitherto-reliable but suspiciously sycophantic prognosticators pronounce her dead, but Corvan, irascible under all the layers of silken imperturbability, has never been keen about even pleasant surprises, and spares no effort to forestall the disaster of some fairy-tale resurrection. The terrible companies of his minions, under the guidance of the Baron Nidlaam, extravagantly cruel founder and captain of the Black Guard, widely known as Lord Coldiron, quarter the realm without rest, using bribes, threats, whimsical loppings of, at the least beastly, fingers, even the occasional didactic execution, with the object of prying loose some word of Idolema's current whereabouts. At the same time, knowing any challenge to his power must come in the place of its proclaiming, Corvan, somewhat at odds with the desire to have his self-coronation witnessed by a throng drawn from all quarters of the realm, attempts to seal his capital in an impenetrable ring of defenses.

Hallabreg, though many miles inland, is a seaport on the Great Hallas, lying against the steeper southerly hem to its wide bowl of river-valley, the city walls gently lapped by enclosed and ordered pasture and growing-land, with tamed woods and pleasant rills. Beyond its back-fence of rocky heights, the Myrin, lies a belt of wilderness, in part featureless and barren, elsewhere forested and mountainous, stretching to the fringes of the fertile and populous southward provinces. In remote parts of the southernmost region of Tarne, her mother's homelands, Corvan guesses, Idomela, if alive, must have lived out her hidden exile.

Self-sufficiency is a relative term; even heroes must eat. Cantello is a skilled hunter and of course knows the edible, curative, lethal, or merely decorative properties of every growing thing, yet late winter is a lean period for living off the land, and in chill and windy March, leaving his solitary domicile at the very hem of the wild lands, he makes the long ride down to smoky Ault — Lesser Ault, a mere townlet, eight miles to the east of Grosault, a teeming city — to purchase supplies. For the sun, struggling up still trailing frayed ends of restraining mist, there is no apostrophe.

His first thought, just before this story begins, was to obtain what he needed from the Hammits, a numerous and amiable farming family he has considered friends for many years, and who owe him a favor or two. He has nothing like an assured income; as tales, by omission, imply, most questing, often expensive to equip and maintain, is of its nature *pro bono* work (a term Cantello would brusquely reject); opportunities to change the course of history, or to pluck back civilization (as one has known it) from the precarious edge of ruin are not on offer every day, or month, or year, and while he routinely declines small fees thrust at him in attempt to engage his services in some trivial affair, he has no false pride about asking friends for help. But when he went downstream to the Hammit lands he found his friends gone, their small knot of dwellings abandoned, though recently, to judge from many signs. No one living nearby could tell him anything — or would tell; as with much in the realm, a cloud of fear blurs all outlines.

Consistent with his slow-kindled nature, Cantello's concern is deeper than he lets be seen. He does not intend the disappearance of his friends to remain a mystery. In the meantime he is obliged to barter for his necessities, and in Ault to accept the food-merchant's drastic undervaluation of some quite good gems, the end of his tithe in a substantial treasure he'd recovered for its owner some years ago. Not quite angered, he is permanently puzzled by inconsistency; his name, when recognized, is respoken, as always, with a respect approaching reverence, but for his commercial dealings, awe does nothing to deflect — perhaps rapacity is overstatement; a shrewd business instinct, then.

At the last, when the price of sack of potatoes is set at a pearl which might buy a smallholding, his protest wins him a spare fistful of silver coins in grudged change, and after loading his pack-pony Cantello decides on a mug or so of beer at Ault's one hostelry, an ancient, sprawled, decaying house just short of where the brief street of shops meets the main highway.

There for the first time in years he is to meet a man he has continued to hear of, legendary Tarbul, once and for decades most celebrated of warriors, some of whose fame, the sword-fighting part, Cantello has succeeded to. It is the innkeeper who points him out, much altered, seated over a pewter tankard at a table in the farthest corner.

Hailed, Cantello bows courteously, determined to treat the man with the respect reputation deserves. Encounters with rival and would-be rival champions can turn stupid; more than once he has had to deal with purposeful provocations from a young or not-so-young heroid out for fame, but Tarbul, nearing, it must be, eighty, with his shrunken frame and knotted hands, is clearly no threat — except that Cantello has heard his name linked vaguely with those fatuous, unteachable and perennially endangered Loyalists — not unlikely; while his renown, a generation ago, was for unparalled proficiency rather than deeds of enduring value, and Tarbul has never been associated with any particular cause or point of view, his career and eminence began in service to the king who was great-grandfather to the fugitive princess. The mere possibility makes him a risky drinking-companion in Corvan's realm, where to be under suspicion is a wildly contagious disease. The innkeeper, having brought together old hero and younger, ostentatiously has nothing more to do with their meeting, sending the gaping straggle of a pot-wench to serve them.

There is, moreover, a troubling texture in the manner of this meeting, as if Tarbul has expected him; he speaks Cantello's name in gratification rather than surprise, and even the gesture with which he bids the serving-girl bring beer for the newcomer has an elusive whiff of prearrangement.

His manner of discourse is calculated, too, but in a different sense. When Cantello, for the sake of comfort, hauls off his boots, Tarbul, as if reciting a lesson, says, "What, after all, are boots, shoes? Protection for the feet, am I right? Anything more is mere ornament — " and it quickly becomes apparent that no subject can be introduced or discussed without a brief and unilluminating defin-ition. Not, as Cantello has witnessed among the learned, so as to delineate, avoiding cross-purposes; it seems to him Tarbul is acting on the choice, as a replacement and consolation for his largely out-lived fame, of a role for which he lacks intellectual capacity, that of the wearied titan in ripe and contemplative retirement.

"You have heard of the wilder-hounds?" Tarbul asks after some more trivial talk of things long past.

"Heard of them, and heard them baying by night, once or twice, though none has been seen so far south as my dwelling."

"A weapon," Tarbul notes. "Weapons, rightly considered, are, of course, only a particular type of tool, purposed to kill, and an animal you train is just such a tool."

"An unwieldy one, once let loose; I prefer to have weapons I'm less likely to find at my own throat."

Tarbul makes a humming noise. "But it's said there is a trick about their training — that they will never attack a traveller on the road, and that the officers of the Guard possess some means of mak-ing them docile, a secret command, it might be."

"A trick liable to be lost, living in the wilds. They are sure to breed, and their pups cannot be trained."

"Only males, it is said, have been released."

"They will breed with wolves, being half-wolf themselves, or with feral bitches."

"You question the policies of our king-to-be?"

This was a bait. "I question nothing. I observe."

To explain more efficiently than under the restraints of believable dialogue: saying (not entirely without justice) that the untamed intervening wilderness has too often been the home and refuge of brigands and outlaws, Corvan has added to its hitherto adequate population of dangerous beasts by stocking the wild with large numbers of these wolf-dogs, dedicated killers, bred and brutally schooled, though their fierce nature needs little prompting. For the most part the training has aimed at instilling in the animals a ferocity far beyond the requirements of food or defense, a relish for killing more like that of humans.

"Old masters must always give place when new champions emerge — " this abruptly, and so much like a recited lesson Cantello almost looks back over his shoulder to see if someone is holding up a board with the words painted on it.

"New champions are fools if they think they have nothing to learn from their masters."

"So." Tarbul's pleasure holds no suspicion; Cantello has rarely found a man to balk at flattery, so long as it is of himself.

"But deeds I now must leave to others." Waxy-eyed, Tarbul looks all about him with the air of a man inspecting the architecture, carefully avoiding any suggestion of the furtive. A pale tongue-tip moistens brown lips. "Some people I know," he remarks, "know a woman, a young woman, who must be in the north, at Hallabreg, three days before the next half-moon."

"Old New Year. There will be many going that way, to witness the events at Hallabreg."

"And what of it, you say, a three-day ride, four if the horse is a very poor one. But — " already kept low, Tarbul's voice becomes a near-whisper, frayed with age — "this young woman does not wish to go openly."

"Not easy. Disguised, then?"

A shake of the head. "That, no doubt, will be watched-for, and the same vigil kept against concealment, as it might be, among goods or foodstuffs being carried north; every wagon is being stopped more than once on the journey, and forced to unload its cargo. She cannot go by road."

"Then she can hardly go by water, and as you say, the wilderness is deadlier than ever." Cantello is beginning to be impatient with this game, or with the demand on him that lurks behind it.

Contemplating his own misshapen hands on the table, the old man opens his mouth, closes it with a hard pursing, and begins again, dulled eyes coming up to meet Cantello's. "Properly accompanied, she might be able to cross the wilderness. Not a large escort; notwithstanding the hounds. There are still the patrols, but a small company might slip through them."

Noisily, Cantello pushes his chair back. "I cannot help you." (A hackneyed device, by now hardly more than a ritual gesture, with the forlorn hope of provoking some suspense, though no one among us older than nine is even momentarily taken in by Cantello's grimace of indifference.)

"I have a pie ordered, veal, or so they say. You will share it with me?"

Hardly turned for home under a brighter sky, leading the pack-animal, Cantello is halted, all-but surrounded, by a cohort of the Black Guard, eight heavily-armed, mounted men under a slender but wide-framed young captain. Not at all unexpected; Tarbul has warned him the contingent has been hovering in the vicinity, asking specifically for news of Cantello's whereabouts and doings. He even supplied the name of their officer, Suliwat, describing him as having a great shock of hair, but did not mention that the hair is of a raw red shade, giving him the incendiary look of a blazing brand.

Extravagantly courteous, Suliwat bows a greeting, and asks if he is not the celebrity they have sought. Cantello affirms it, meanwhile, as is his professional habit, running an assessing eye over the company. Not a real warrior amongst them, he judges; the Guard's way is to intimidate by reputation and the bristle of weapons, but they are recruited among the offscourings of impoverished farms, the dregs of Hallabreg, whence come brawlers but few champions; Cantello would bet on his chances against any one of them — against any three together.

Possibly he could rout the lot; he has won fights in the past against similar or worse odds. There are spatial limits to the number that can actually deploy against one man at any moment, and the rest, their prowess entirely a collective illusion, may quickly be disheartened by the defeat of three or four. For the moment, however, his sword dozes on; his personal code bars killing, or initiating hostilities, without plain need. Besides, while he might master, here he can scarcely kill or disable them all, and those that flee with tidings will make him a fugitive, hunted everywhere by larger and warier companies, uncaring enough of reputation or the conventions of combat to cancel him with an unwarned salvo of arrows.

"Sir," Suliwat announces in a ceremonial style. "Our master, the Regent Corvan, wishing the great and famous of the realm to witness his forthcoming elevation to the throne, extends his invitation to Cantello, to attend him at the palace in Hallabreg."

"I am flattered. Is there more?" — recognizing this as no digression from the Black Guard's war on elusive Idolema, but an extension of it; Corvan intends to deprive the fugitive princess of potential allies by gathering them within his sight.

"We are here, sir, as your ceremonial guard, and will escort you to Hallabreg."

"Forthwith? Out of the question. I have with me no clothes suitable for Hallabreg, still less the palace there. Corvan must be told, I'll come in good time for his crowning."

"The invitation of His Highness is meant to do you honor, but we are not to return without you, sir — " this with the faintest movement of an elbow, as if to free his weapon-arm.

"There seems little difference between an invitation and an arrest, then."

"Oh, come; kings, you know, and kings-to-be, will have their way. Clothing and everything necessary will be provided you."

"These purchased supplies must be taken home. Ride with me, and we can start for the capital at daybreak."

Suliwat shakes his head. "We cannot spare the time. For small payment, your goods, I'm sure, can be stored here at the hostelry."

And at this point, Cantello, with what he believes to be a departure from the truth, begins to improvise a strategy. "I have a young woman in my care; she cannot be left alone."

Interest, understandably, is prompt. "Where is she?"

"At my house."

"How old a young woman?"

"How old? Not my business. Too young, certainly, to be left by herself at the edge of the wild for weeks together."

"She is alone now, you say?"

"I was to ride back before nightfall. But — " with a rueful lower lip — "If His Highness, Majesty-to-be, is so avid for my company, we, as you insist, must not delay. Someone here will take a note to her, and she can go to other friends. Shall we ride?"

Here we may observe what, instinct for any flirtatious girl of fifteen, is hard work for Cantello, the craft of making a thing more desirable by offering and then pretending to withdraw it; he knows Suliwat's original commission must be overridden by what might be the chance of capturing the grand prize; ever since mention of Cantello's mythic young woman, the captain has been trembling like a dog scenting game, nostrils flared.

"We can spare that much time. We'll ride with you. Perhaps the girl can come with you to Hallabreg."

"I fancy she has small desire for such occasions, and less apparel."

"Everything can be provided."

"Not the desire. Perhaps she would come, but at the proper time."

"She has a name?"

"No doubt. I have called her Aria — " a touch of wasted art; *Aria* is *Melodia*, a euphonious anagram of Idolema.

Conducting his self-styled escort to where it might be done, to kill all nine, eight of them underlings, seems wasteful to Cantello; professionalism tries to keep deaths to the minimum necessary for a mission, and it is efficient as well as ethically preferable to silence the ones who give orders, spare those who merely follow, the reverse of what usually occurs in war. Here, he can see no alternative, if he is ever again to have any freedom of action; fortunately for principle, there are no innocents in the case; no one is conscripted to be a Black Guard, a force recruited mainly from volunteers eager to be given scope for a fascination with arbitrary violence or a confirmed relish for cruelty. Too, from the first, Corvan struck a mother-lode of apt material for his terror-bands within various dim dungeons and greasy cells for the condemned, and departing from his prevailing rigor in enforcing ever-more-onerous and numerous laws and decrees, lavishly used his powers of pardon — or indefinite stay — to fill the ranks of his Guard with demonstrably ruthless if often dimwitted butchers. As opposed to sentimental legend, last-minute reprieve does not generally convert the remorseless killer to one for whom life, all life, is a gift, precious and revered; since clemency, as extended by Corvan, *de facto* and *de jure*, is no more than a truce, revokable at the first sign of hesitation or distaste in carrying out the nastiest orders, those saved from gallows or block are, on the contrary, among the most reliable beasts in a beastly force.

In any event, Cantello's only practical plan for separating himself from the unwanted escort necessitates a single, swift, comprehensive stroke. For which he has the means long prepared, though he never envisaged this use of what was designed as a defense of his isolated dwelling.

The afternoon ride, threading among trees soon to leaf, on little-known ways sometimes discernible only to Cantello, is smiling courtesy on a shifting foundation of distrust; watched like a prisoner, Cantello still keeps his sword. Suliwat's orders, clearly, are to preserve, so far as possible (and, as we see, well beyond that limit) the fiction of a friendly but pressing invitation from the Regent; no doubt Corvan hopes that some of the past and potential notables of the realm rounded up for his kinging will accept the inevitable and thereafter belong by choice to him, a view all known history sourly supports.

Suliwat's lieutenant, Abant, is a big, broad-faced youngster with straw-colored hair that flops over his forehead, bulged eyes, and a quick, sly grin recollecting facile success with impressionable (or intimidated) girls, as readily discarded. An hour into the jogging journey, challenged, perhaps, by riding knee-to-knee with renown, he embarks on a lengthy boast, though not of his nocturnal adventures; it is the gory history of a recent encounter with what he calls "rebels," and Cantello translates into a couple of unlucky families caught still displaying the likeness of King Dairemid; in Corvan's realm, nostalgia counts as a form of insurrection. But there is the hint, too, never plainly spoken, that these rebels were in some way associated with those who keep alive the claims of Idolema.

After one flickering glance, Suliwat, no doubt deciding the tale might function to remind Cantello of his own peril, does not try to prevent either the main narrative or the numerous additions and emendations contributed by other heroes riding nearby; Black Guard, blackguard, braggard, this form of crowing takes pride in the greatest relish for cruelty, the most ostentatious outfacing of squeamishness, and competition is keen.

It is, after all, simply an account of the butchery of fewer than a dozen persons, either unarmed or armed with amusing inadequacy, ranged in age from less than ten to more than seventy, yet the details accumulate beyond the reach of coincidence, and with one bland question as to the general location of the killings, Cantello is darkly convinced he has no further need to enquire into the present whereabouts of his friends the Hammits.

Heartsick, sick with anger, he is at the same time dangerously glad to have the news given him with such callous openhandedness; had he found out in some other way he would have needed to track down and haunt this company, killing them one by one as opportunities came, but now he has all together in his grasp, condemned beyond the nag of any scruples; this sample of the Black Guard has loudly endorsed its own death-warrant.

So, at least, our dice must be loaded; the heroes we admire are no longer bragging brutes, arbitrarily favored, prevailing with uncaring force, deceit and trickery, though the demand for heroic goodness is a very recent and quite precarious one — is, or has been; the old indifference to virtue may, and especially in megaboom movies, be making a comeback — indeed, especially in newish countries like the United States and Australia, hero-cults have always flourished in connection with figures that by any standard ethical measure are murderous thugs — though no more so than Saul, or Achilles, or Sigurd, or Robin Hood before he began to be blurred-over with a Christian-Socialist wash.

Everyone's favorite Austrian fantasist, made puritanistically uneasy by our (and presumably his) persisting admiration for a reprobate like Falstaff, offered (imposed, rather) the quaint explanation that our moral demands bounce off his rotundity. The fretful absurdity of this theory can hardly survive the observation that we have exactly the same sort of virtue-be-hanged regard for the slender Till Eulenspiegel, and the positively emaciated Mr Punch; the truth is these lords of misrule appeal to something far older than an attachment to the grey rewards of hard work and keeping to the rules; they represent the comedic survival of the primitive hero.

The primitive hero is heroic because he's one of us, and because he's effective; within those simple bounds he can be, and often is, a bully, a cheat, a ruthless opportunist, even a dedicated genocide; he possesses unfair advantages — invulnerability, magically enhanced strength, magically effective weapons, gods or God ready to intervene on his behalf; fair play doesn't enter into it.

In the change from these objectively quite appalling figures to the more modern notion of a hero who, for all his physical and intellectual gifts, is also *virtuous*, the Arthurian chronicles — those of Malory's Christianized King Arthur — are the essential document, wherein a Brythonic war-chief, struggling against Roman or Germanic invaders, completes his transformation into the chivalric and even Utopian ideal, becoming a repository of all the new-fangled virtues — all except one, and as with his henchman, that single flaw is his undoing; Lancelot's sweet adultery means tragic failure in the Grail quest, Arthur's early lapse from chastity provides the bastard nephew-son that will be his death. But now, with Arthur and his teeming literary progeny for model, we must make the hero's cause a recognizably just one, give him compassion and humility to go with a merely human prowess (and with a new scorn of unfair supernatural edges). Still, there can be no warriors and no tales of adventure without fighting and killing, and it is sound strategy, therefore, somehow to remove those who serve evil from the circles of pitiable creation, to make them Morlocks, orcs, devout Nazis, snot-dripping predators from deep space, to be slaughtered without guilt, allowing us to sweat through perils, indulge our taste for blood, and still retain our humanist credentials. The story picks up pace quite soon.

"You sir," Suliwat tries, when Abant's ghoulish eloquence runs down, "It is said that you have some great tales, as yet untold, or only half-told."

"Let them remain so. In youthful obscurity one strives for fame, as in ill-earned renown, he yearns for obscurity."

"Ill-earned? Was vanquishing the witch-woman of Synta not worthy of praise? Or recovery of the lost Spalestone?"

"First manhood is a dream, it changes with waking." Cantello recognizes some dishonesty here, making use of what he claims to reject; without his fame such gnomic utterances would bring mockery, not grave attention.

Always climbing, the way takes them past a hamlet, mournful and wholly deserted now, most of the wooden dwellings tumbledown or sagging, thatch of their roofs stripped away, perhaps by decades of birds, foraging for their nests.

"What place was this, sir?"

"I have never known its name, or whether it had one. There are other such places, and the remains of many single farmhouses and barns, gradually being digested, among the trees and undergrowth."

"Farms, here?"

"The trees, you will note," Cantello informs the skeptical Suliwat, "Are nowhere old growth; they have reclaimed the land since men relinquished it. These lands once bore both crops and herds, but they were laid waste during the Paranopan Wars, and after that were the Three Dark Years — "

"Were there Three Dark Years? I have heard that's only a tale."

"Plenty of people still alive remember them — Tarbul, who won his first fame in those wars, would remember, though they could as well be called the Three-Year Winter; in the third year, the Great Hallas at Hallabreg was frozen from bank to bank the fortnight before midsummer's day. Only in the farthest south could any food grow and ripen; many starved."

"You spoke with Tarbul at Ault, sir? Did he have any news for you?"

"He talked about Nidlaam's hounds."

"Ah. What did he have to say about them? — " a quick change of direction, the bleak opportunism of Suliwat's calling; they must suspect Tarbul of having some knowledge of Idolema, or other connection to the Loyalists, but, lacking evidence, perhaps the old man could still be arrested and made to suffer, for a seditious dislike of royally-sanctioned killer dogs.

Very soon, it is not going to matter what Suliwat believes, whether he believes anything, whether he has friends or had them, hopes, ambitions, desires for a family, remorse in any form, memories of childhood, spare boots, diaries, all futile promises of and provisions for persistence, their uselessness exposed, in a moment itself of no use.

Still, "We agreed, Tarbul and I, that the wilder-hounds are an idea of breathtaking splendor, daunting, perhaps, to the faint-hearted or the unwarlike, but excitement for the adventurous — and who but the adventurous should be found in the wilderness; it is no place for children, the elderly, any such foolish enough to be found there can hardly complain if they're eaten by dogs, can they?"

Suliwat has a struggle with this ecomium, practically certain of ironic intent, although to say so might reflect on his own enthusiasm for all of Corvan's works. "Who," he demands, "In these times, has an honest reason for going into the wilderness?"

"Herb-gatherers, who may cure our illnesses, trappers who supply our furs. Of those who fled there, not all were outlaws or smugglers; there have always been men seeking solitude — but I hardly think they'll wish to brave the dogs."

"Was this what Tarbul — " Suliwat begins, but the riding, emerging from among dense growth of spindly trees, is in sudden noise at the edge of water, the strong mountain stream, Hantrey, here a smooth, swift race, spilling from a massive and ancient dam and broadening to perhaps forty paces width, before sliding to headlong, roaring descent over jagged falls.

"My house — " Cantello indicates below, on the other shore by the foam-streaked backwater beneath the falls; a sprawling and apparently haphazard stone structure, originally and continuously built and occupied, he explains, by a growing family of dye-wood gatherers, broom-makers, quondam millers, and occasional traders in pelts, whose dwindled fourth-generation remnant dispersed to seek better fortune elsewhere some thirty years since.

Though this history suggests uncertain business instincts, they can hardly be held responsible for the disappearance, earlier, of the region's farms, which doomed their mill, a ruinous remnant of which can be discerned just upstream above the house. The clan obviously included some skilled stone-cutters and crafty if eccentric builders, and when he first came here, beyond ousting the various creatures of the wild which had taken up residence, Cantello's labors to make the place habitable again were slight; fireplaces are well-placed and well-constructed, available supply of firewood practically inexhaustible, and the steep-pitched slate roof required only a few patches. There is an internal well which Cantello has capped with a simple hand-pump, and if that grudged and panted, as it had near the end of a hot, dry summer, down a steep bank hacked into irregular, root-edged steps is an unfailing supply of water.

Nothing can be seen to move, no smoke comes from a chimney, and Suliwat, raising his voice over the noise of the falls, remarks that there is no sign of habitation, of this girl of Cantello's.

"She may have left. She came to me unlooked-for."

"From where?"

"I never asked."

"There is a decree, sir, you must have heard; it is no longer lawful to take in a stranger with unknown purpose — " petulantly, and impatient Suliwat wants to know how they are to pass the river.

Clearly, not through the turbulent waters opposite the house, down at the foot of the falls. Farther down, perhaps three miles, twisting and jostling in a narrow ravine, the stream is crossed by a rudimentary bridge of great antiquity, hardly more than a huge toppled slab of stone, with only the faint weather-blurred memories of adze-marks to show it was once shaped. But Cantello's dwelling is best reached, he points out, by crossing the swift water here above, where footing is sure, the shallow race, seldom rising to knee-deep, except during heavy rains, or in the spring thaw, when the deep basin above may for a while fill and overflow the dam, though most of the time any excess is diverted into a steeper, narrower side-channel, feeder for the mill-race, for which this entire construction was evidently devised.

For the main channel, flow is regulated by a pair of sluice-gates in the dam, heavy timbers wound up or down on worms by means of a cast-iron wheel, an arrangement which Cantello, working in late summer, when the water was lowest and current the least, has put in repair, and, to an extent, redesigned. Now, the sluice-gates are mounted additionally on a lengthwise pivot, and held in place by the pressure of water, but simple disengagement of a catch will allow the timbers to turn like louvers, releasing a sudden great flood. Amounting, when, as now, the dam is near-full, to an eight-foot wave or wall of water, brief but devastating, a surge more than sufficient to scour away anyone caught in mid-crossing, and hurl them over the high falls onto sharp, expectant rocks.

Noting (not falsely) that the water-level of the race is a trifle high for safety, Cantello explains how the sluice-gates can be wound down somewhat to reduce the flow. "I have only to scramble out on the dam."

"Can we not all cross along the dam?" frown deepening.

Suliwat obviously fears being tricked in some way, fears ambush; he keeps scanning the fringes of the circling trees. wondering if an enemy might be lurking. Cantello's tactic is to play on those suspicions. "The footing is too risky for horses. But, yes, that would be simpler, if you tether your mounts and cross on foot. For that matter, there is no need for your whole force to pass the river; some may remain here in charge of the horses — "

"No — " whatever of many fears may come uppermost, Suliwat is not going to divide his small company, sending half on foot into unreconnoitered territory. Conditionally he assents to the initial proposal, but Abant, who has an interest in machines and mechanisms, will acccompany Cantello, and what must be a contagion of curiosity has another of his men dismount to go with them.

An ineffectual precaution, since the uneven, dilapidated, here and there weed-grown walk crowning the dam necessitates single file. Behind, the water-level is high; the true spring thaw, when the snow melting on the mountains turns brooks into torrents, streams to floods, is still some weeks away, but already the melt-off from the foothills has arrived.

Reaching the controls, most of the way across, Cantello, watched by Abant, bends to the massive iron wheel, and gives it three wrenching turns, gesturing to draw attention to how the closing slots between timbers reduce the flow.

"Your men can cross quite safely now."

Abant nods, and shouts the same information to Suliwat, waiting below, and Cantello has his hand resting lightly on the lever to unlock the sluices.

"Come then — " Abant gestures for them to return to their horses.

A shake of the head. "I must open the sluices again, after the crossing. Otherwise the dam becomes dangerously full." Led by Suliwat, the men of the Black Guard, one by one, are filing down into the shallow water.

"We'll be coming back this way before long," the pale-haired, pale-eyed youngster objects. Below, all but two of the seven are in the water, and Suliwat is barely half across.

"That family that lived downstream," conversationally. "The ones you butchered — they were my friends."

Strangely, this brings a slow grin. "Nowadays, a man has to take care where he makes his friends."

"Or his enemies," Cantello agrees, and with a great heave pulls up his lever. Water leaps from the dam, and to sudden shrill cries from below of panic, Cantello turns his back on Abant, and with a few bounds reaches the other shore, in fear, not of his two remaining enemy, but of the chance that if he fights Abant in the narrow way atop the dam, the other will be able to escape, regain his horse, and carry off news of this affair.

As hoped, the two do follow, swords out. Cantello draws, wards a reaper's mow from Abant, and swiftly kills the other, dark and wiry, somewhat older. Pulling his sword free, he again parries, then with a slash comes near severing the youth's sword-hand.

"You are diverted by pain and slow dying," he snarls, as Abant bends at the waist, trying to staunch the blood with hands hugged to him. "I wish I had time and stomach for the entertainment you merit."

In terrible agony and equal fear, Abant still manages to squeeze out the inevitable, "I only followed my orders."

"Liar." Cantello kills him.

Below, the approach to the falls is washed clean, but Suliwat, his horse gone, has in some way succeeded in grasping the roots of the big waterside willow, and hauled himself up the bank. Cantello, descending from the dam, goes swiftly to where Suliwat has now struggled to his knees, weighs the possible profit in interrogating the man, decides he has insufficient interest in the plans and strategies of the Black Guard, and kills him with a quick thrust to the throat, just as the man's mouth was forming either "Treason" or "Traitor," it is impossible to be sure which. Or "Treachery."

An uneven and twisting old stair, part crumbling brick, part mossed and often slimy stone, descends past the site of the mill, through clouds of drifting spray from the thundering falls. Filled with the elation that always comes with killing (both just and justified, mind), Cantello goes rattling down to the level space, mainly herb-garden, next to the house, and finds to his astonishment that he has not lied to his late captors; there is a girl, a young woman, here, small, slender, the sex not for an instant in doubt, though she is dressed as a boy.

There are also two young men, both well-armed, muscled and bellicose, and to complete a curious tableau, a tall woman verging on the elderly, whose severe hair and taut lips, as well as her station, just behind the young woman's left elbow, proclaim a traditional function laughably incongruous in this place and time, certainly incompatible with how her charge is dressed. Except for this lady, all Cantello's visitors have their principal weapons at the ready. *For the sake of a more effective curtain, material information is being selectively withheld. Everybody does it.*

II

He knows both, one well, the other chiefly in the inherited traits of his famous family. Both seem at first a little put out, in the way of youth, that they have taken no active part in his annihilation of Suliwat's force; had Cantello known the younger was here, he might have found a way to let him take a hand in the revenge he was certainly owed; he is Sab Hammitt, younger son of Cantello's dead friend, and in an unwonted display of emotion Cantello seizes the boy in a hug. "It is good you are alive; I heard — "

"I believe I am the last of us; I happened to be out looking for strayed animals when they came. Or so the story then was to go; the truth is I was carrying a message for the southward Loyalists. When we returned, there was nothing left."

"As I was told."

Sab is a brawny seventeen, a couple of years younger than the other, whose far more illustrious descent makes him ally rather than friend; he is Tarfal, great-grandson in direct male line to Tarbul, and his mother is a baron's daughter (that anyone still functionally alive can have a *great*-grandson ready to carry and use a sword seems unlikely, but Tarbul, married young, was a grandfather before he was forty). The young man possesses the lithe and effective sinew of his lineage, as well as its long, bland face, and its some-times touchy pride.

"You did not expect us? My great-grandfather intended to speak with you about our plan."

"Your plan?" Their objective, and the presumed identity of the girl, are not hard to guess, but Cantello judges there must be some hundreds active in the Loyalist conspiracy. and cannot believe those astute and resourceful plotters, confident as they might be about enlisting Cantello to their side, would entrust execution of any plan to these two youths unaided.

Sab reads the thought. "We were to have had more men, my father's, among others, but the Black Guard has been everywhere --"

"We believe," the other interrupts, "Someone in many of our secrets has been either bribed or tortured to betray us — we could no longer tell which men were safe to approach."

"Of those left alive," bitterly.

"My uncle, Taremin, with some of his best men," Tarfal contimues, "intended to be with us, but has been too closely watched. My father was to have been at Mitfell with his following."

"And?"

"Like you, he was invited to Hallabreg, unlike you, he has gone with his insistent escort. All the House Tarbul is under suspicion — or rather, they know where our sympathies lie, but cannot yet prove we have given aid to the Exile."

"With common folk, no proof is needed — " Sab.

"My great-grandfather — " after a long look, hardly of sympathy — "was permitted to plead age to excuse his attendance; my grandfather, whom they overlooked or ignored, has ridden to the camp at Mitfell."

"Then — ?" with a gesture to ask why the girl was left behind. A generalized answer is readily available; Cantello knows and has small use for Darval, second and only surviving son of the old master, who picked up some of his father's skills, but is an irresolute and stupid man — made stupid, that is, by a lifelong overindulgence in wine and strockan.

"Because of the dogs, he was obliged to go most of the way by road, and we had no means of getting the Exile undetected past the patrols. My great-grandfather told him go, then, and he would find Cantello to help us."

To do, that would be, what his own son feared, take the girl across the wilderness, evading or outbraving the dogs.

"He was to find and speak with you, sir."

"He started to, but only today. I cut him short, told him he could expect no help from me."

"Yet you fought and destroyed Black Guard." They have gone inside now, and are gathered in Cantello's largest room; some-one has quickly kindled a brave fire in the great, gaping fireplace.

"I had reason to." He takes Sab by the shoulder. "Those men killed friends of mine, and boasted of it."

Sab's eyes, round in a flat face, open wider. "Were those the very men? And you have killed them all? Then I have no reason left to live."

"You have every reason. To live and marry, and father sons, so that Hammitt's name can survive."

The lad tears away from Cantello's grip, grimacing. Perhaps in anger, but his eye has met the girl's, and despite rough male cloth-ing she is very pretty, manifestly beyond his reach. Her name is given, provisionally, as the Lady Moriana, but Cantello, like you, is in no doubt why she is here, why these young men are here to guard her, why there is a mature woman of watchdog aspect to haunt her.

Also of some birth, Nila, apparently an impoverished relat-ive to the Earldom of Tarne, and she is the one to take up what she perceives as the challenge of Cantello. "No help! Is it any wonder this realm to be is ruled by dogs, where men can say, it is no bus-iness of mine — men once counted among our best."

He chuckles at her fieriness. "How will anything I can do make it better?"

"You have already," Sab says, meaning the killings.

"A private settlement of accounts with some bullies. More can always be enlisted."

"Not long ago," Nila, "we had a king who did not rule through bullies."

Such frank talk is now rare, even reckless; there have been too many betrayals, denunciations of friend by supposed friend.

"Untimely death," Cantello, with care, "years, and the blos-soming of our Regent, have all lent virtues, not all of them earned, to the memory of that reign." Here, the girl looks up sharply, lips par-ted, but she does not speak.

"Dairemid ruled, always, with justice," Tarfal protests. "My kin were at that court — "

"I knew of men at that court — not all young men, though all with young wives — who suffered abrupt misfortune when they failed in generosity towards the king's wide-ranging appetites, loss of their posts, breaking of their families. In this, the king only fol-lowed the example set by his father, Dairo, whom now we call the Good. Other men, perhaps — " with a complicit look for the two youths — "before letting themselves be too angry, should ask how much envy is in their condemnation; still, it is not the most admir-able use of unquestioned hereditary power. Then, too, for example, there was the execution of the man Tremary, when Dairemid was too ill-tempered to hear the evidence that exculpated him."

"My father did public penance for that."

Her father — the girl's quick passion is there, and Cantello bows a deference, to feelings rather than rank. "And he gave, did he not, generous compensation to the widow, found her a strong new husband and father for the son; she pronounced herself, and may well have been, more than satisfied. Still, unjust executions are hard to set right with the principal victim; unearned mercy is less awkward to explain."

"No one calls my father perfect. But Corvan — "

"I'll concede that Dairemid's worst moments only approached the daily routine of the Bastard. `Not as bad' makes an uninspiring war-cry." Cantello may be making an enemy of his rightful ruler, and needlessly, since, like us, he knows how this debate will end, and has small hope either of them can survive the desperate course it will commit them to.

His late friend's son takes up the theme. "The crimes of Corvan as Regent already include many murders like that of my family. Even so, you must see that Corvan as anointed king will see himself as beyond all law, and be far worse?"

"No doubt."

"If you had the power to prevent that — "

"Who has that power?"

"Some of us are ready with our lives."

"Is that all? Your lives? Nothing is easier than dying. Give me a guarantee that my dying will make it a better world — not perfect, but unequivocally better — and I'll gladly give up my life, what is left of it."

"Gladly?" — the girl questions this.

"By habit, by teaching, we think of life as hugely valuable, but much of it is tedium, or worse."

"But to be surrendered, even so," the girl says with the glint of irony, "for nothing less than certainty."

"It's a fair price; I don't like to be cheated."

Here, Tarfal begins a youthfully earnest estimate of possible success; Cantello's elimination of Suliwat's cohort has provided some breathing-space, though he concedes that the recent activities of the Black Guard have thrown the original plans into a muddle.

"And time is growing short," the other contributes, and again stirs Cantello's sympathy; it is the plaint of a youth events have taken out of his depth, two youths forced to make their own desperate decisions. "We could not wait any longer, if we were to make for Mitfell."

"What use is Mitfell?" Cantello. "We would still be a day and more short of Hallabreg."

"*We* would, you say?" — though quiescent, the girl has missed not a syllable, and stoops like a falcon on the pronoun.

"Whoever managed to get there," Cantello explains, but is disconcerted by the girl's new look, almost of complacency. Perhaps, after all, she was not offended by his reminiscences of Dairemid —

or she may be strategist enough to banish personal feelings from her calculations.

"There should still be at least eighty good fighting men gathered there," Tarfal claims. "Enough, it may be, to — "

"You believe Nidlaam has failed to notice this gathering? If it has not already been surrounded and overwhelmed, it must by now be surrounded and guarded — the wiser alternative, if the expectation is that the Exile will make for there."

"Mitfell cannot be surrounded, because of its situation," Tarfal argues. "Yes, the Guard is keeping watch, but Nidlaam knows that an attack on that fastness, even at odds of five or ten to one, will cost him many lives, with no guarantee of success."

"A good place to defend," Cantello concedes. "But what use are eighty men, or twice or five times that, once they set out for Hallabreg and its defenses? However," he can't help observing. "Its existence, the presence of so many skilled swords, might make it a good decoy."

"A decoy!" Young Sab manages to find offense in this. "There are men and families who have risked death for seven long years, and expect to be a part of the return of Idolema."

"Battles and wars are sometimes won by men who stand and die, without a hope for themselves. This is what we mean by *serving* — " unasked, a sour note comes into Cantello's voice. "Taking up causes is risky in ways we never count on."

"What about failing to take them up?" Sab, hotly, and the girl, assessing deterioration, holds up a hand.

"I would like to speak with Cantello alone."

This causes doubt, but the two youths are persuaded to go and capture Cantello's mount and pack-animal, forgotten on the far side of the river, and lead them through the water above the falls, which by now will be safe to cross. Still a little dubiously, they go out, Sab all shoulders and elbows, Tarfal with his somewhat self-conscious, upright gait.

"I say, alone — "

"My lady — " Nila, seeing herself like shadow or footprint, immune from attempts at banishment, is remaining in near attendance, and displays alarm, but the girl is implacable.

"I am grateful for the solicitude of your kinsman — yours and also mine — but it is not needed here. My Lord Cantello — " bowing her head to him — "is famed as much for his courtesy to women; it is well known that he was chivalrous even with the Lady of Synta, who sought to bewilder and destroy him. We are to discuss policy, not dalliance. If. It. Were. Otherwise — " giving each word separate emphasis — "that would be my choice, and my right. Leave us."

"My lady," nearly grovelling; plainly this is a tone Nila, and quite possibly the girl herself, has never heard before; only days from a throne or an early death she is establishing the logic for either.

"Leave the bag with me, the kidskin."

"My lady — " Nila, plainly, dislikes this.

"On the table."

Nila, with the nearest approach to rebelliousness she can now command, makes a disapproving mouth, as she finds the bag in question, small but evidently heavy for its size, and does as she is told.

"Thank you — " the girl is incontrovertibly dismissing the older woman.

Having got her way, she seems for a moment in doubt how to begin. Looking about her: "You seem comfortable here. No woman?"

A jut of the lower lip. "I sew on my own buttons."

"What is this?" taking a curious object from the mantel to examine.

"Amber."

"That I see." It is a light-struck handful of great clarity, and caught in its honey depth is a perfectly preserved wasp, slender and elegant, iridescent wings spread, the mere thread of a waist joining its two dark, menacingly effective halves.

"I have never seen such an insect."

"They are now happily rare. That is the notorious Assassin Wasp, also called Queensbane, since one brought about the death of Queen Kalatane. The stings of only one can cause agonizing death to a child, the old, or those peculiarly susceptible, while anyone unlucky enough to disturb a nest is certainly doomed."

"But this?"

"I picked it up in the marshes, many years ago. It was dull when I found it, but went everywhere with me for a year in a bag of bran, till it became as you see. Embalmed, perhaps for eternity, we can admire the grace and beauty of the wasp, as is hard when it still has power to hurt."

"Then this," replacing it, "would be the Lady of Synta."

Cantello chuckles, but has been momentarily troubled by the girl's penetration. "It is a creature trapped in amber, that is adequate for me."

She gathers herself for business. "The man who wants nothing is difficult to recruit. I can't threaten you with dire things if I come to the throne without your help — I don't believe you would care." A deep breath, and a tentative smile: "Would you wish to spend a night, or some nights, with me, if we could pry Nila loose?"

"Naturally I would — " though what must be meant as an offer, its brisk manner, has startled and faintly dismayed him; not a trace of added allure goes with it, and the only suggestion of relish is in her cool calculation of his.

"Each of us — " with a hint of satire — "Can be the other's trophy; I shall be bedding with a hero, as all women daydream, and you, if we live, will have a royal prize to boast of. Or not to boast of," she amends, perhaps in warning.

"But that prospect, my lady, would not make me work harder for your coronation."

"Why not?" flushing a little. "I would make myself your whore, and even royal whores expect payment."

His smile has a gentleness she has not expected. "I do not doubt your toughness, madam; there is no need to shock me."

Nevertheless, as such overtures virtually mandate, he is making a fresh inventory of the girl, a lovely throat, very slender but the hips in man's breeches inviting, softly hollowed flanks, the firm buttocks a pleasing pair of handfuls for broad hands like his — hold it; this sort of voluptuary detail is inimical to our genre, where we're supposed to swathe our women in flowing things you can not-quite see through, and keep any desire vague and high-minded. But Cantello, not the author, is responsible for this breach of tradition; his celebrated *gentilezza* with women is all the more admirable considering the strong erotic component of his nature. The truly heroic part of his celebrated youthful exploit was the hard-won victory over his own appetites; so many years later, he is still troubled often by memory of those serpentine arms tugging him closer, the transports he broke free of. Which all subsequent couplings, and there have been more than three or four, have been inadequate to efface.

This girl easily reads his reassessment. "Because you would not want used goods for queen, or that you would want to keep me for yourself?"

"I have never asked for a woman to be entirely mine — not since I was a boy."

"More than a boy, surely? You were full-grown when you went on your quest to Synta, no?"

He grins, wondering again at her cogency; she is, if sums are right, all-but eighteen, and despite a grave air, looks less. Living as she has, in hiding, or passed off, probably, as a succession of farmers' visiting nieces and the like, can hardly have encouraged any bookish tendencies; where she is has been reached intuitively — and the reflection becomes the thought that she may well be equipped to become a very good ruler indeed.

"Pardon me," she says, after much fencing with eyes. "It is only vanity that makes me set the price for my embrace so high. I am an untaught idiot for bargaining. I still hope for your help."

"If I decline to assist you, you will still go forward?"

"As I must."

"With the two boys."

"They are strong, and willing." This with a shrug in her voice, as if acknowledging hopelessness without an alternative, and resistant Cantello, who has provisionally decided not to let her collapse, sobbing, into his arms, is touched instead by the entire absence of self-pity.

"More than willing, perhaps, but ardent feelings are no substitute for skill, much less good judgment. What is their plan?"

"To get me to Hallabreg. To Mitfell, at least."

"How?"

No answer, she has none. An immense gulf of silence.

"Very well — " with that resigned grimace we all know so well — "I'll lead you; they'll make a mess of it without me. But I must be in charge, and everyone without question follow my orders. Including you, my lady, so long as we are in the field."

"Of course." Her eyes are quiet and level, and he has the strong feeling she made a rapid policy-decision not to kiss him, as was her first impulse. Impressed, Cantello is also saddened by the self-control here; her destiny demands forethought, but something other and more personal than prudence has shuttered up the girl's natural spontaneity — wait: within established and readily-known limits, a dash of torment (hi there, old friend) can add piquancy, but here we may be bumbling into more complexity of character than a simple quest plot can sustain.

She indicates the kidskin bag. "You must have charge of this, too."

By the weight, and the slight chinking as he picks it up, it is, as he anticipated, gold coins, perhaps eighty to a hundred pieces, up to five hundred marks of money. He grins, and though her answering smile claims to, is not certain she understands what amuses him.

There may be payments, bribes, even, to be advanced," she over-explains. "These are best handled by you."

"As you say." He knows she has known enough tactfully to avoid offering him any payment, not whether she believes he would accept it by this indirect route. "Where does this money come from?"

"Mostly, as I understand, from the Baron Falnis, who has Loyalist sympathies."

"With a strong castle, and a thousand armed men. No doubt he is at Hallabreg for the crowning; he will be baron with his revenues no matter how it turns out. Only fools choose sides."

Cut, cut now, to discussions (entire cast) of dangers to be faced and choices to be made; Cantello has been hailed and his primacy accepted, except by Nila, who continues to protest his first (and obvious) decision, to omit her from the wilderness party, where the girl will require the protection of swords, not chaperones, and the swords not need another to protect.

Tarfal: "My great-grandfather has advised on how to deal with the dogs; a hunting-pack, he says, rarely launches a mass-attack, against which, when it does occur, there is no real defense. When, as more usually, they come at you singly, it is a mistake to strike at them — "

"He told this to me," Cantello interrupts. "His method requires a cool head; to make no attempt at evasion, but stand in their path, and impale a dog with a sword firmly held — or let him impale himself, it would be; they are trained, we hear, to go straight for the throat. Your great-grandfather may have worked out the best among counsels of desperation; he has reached an age, may his name live, where no one can reasonably demand he try out his theories for himself — "

"He reached that some years since," Tarfal, with a smile.

" — but I would rather know more about how the Black Guard protects itself in the wilderness from the dogs; there is no doubt they go there."

"The officers are taught a secret word of command," Tarfal asserts.

"I have heard," Sab argues, "they have some device to tame the dogs,"

"I've heard both," Cantello says. "One does not exclude the other."

It is Nila who points out that if the latter is true, the thing might be found on the body of Suliwat, which they have with difficulty borne down from above the falls, and dragged out of casual sight by putting it inside the little court and herb-garden beside the house.

Suliwat carried written orders, in which Cantello finds himself mentioned by name, described as `not among known or guessed traitors, but not easy to command; extremely dangerous, his fighting fame deserved,' and there is the description, `the King's guest,' last word heavily underlined. Pencilled beside this, the words `full file' seem to be Suliwat's own estimate of forces needed for the non-arrest; earlier, less formidable names have `2' or `3' next to them; his original force was evidently some forty men, whittled down by providing these escorts to the eight now accounted for.

Sab says, "Nothing here about the dogs."

"You think they would ever write it down?" Tarfal rebukes him, with a patience more ostentatious than is needed; there is a hint of the patronizing in his dealings with Sab, whose lineage is pure farm. Yet he has inherited the straightforward, word-thrifty intelligence of his parents, and if he does not respond to the other's disdain, it is not because he fails to recognize it.

Hung on a bloodsoaked lanyard around Suliwat's neck Cantello finds a narrow metal tube, with its flattened end very much like a whistle, but when he cuts the cord and blows into the pipe, nothing is heard but the faint, high rush of air. Nevertheless, he puts the thing in his pocket, together with the papers. Small money found on Suliwat Sab scatters, saying, "It will take more than a dying to purify such wages." The young, young women in love, young men gesturing at life, are often sincerest where most artificial (these interjections, and even comments on the interjections, have to be put up with as the Voice-over of God, or a regional substitute).

The girl has come to the doorway. At evening of a drear day, the sun has found the edge of the clouds, and struck by late, ripened rays, she seems a source of light herself (we defy augury). "Who was doing the whistling?"

"What?" Taking the little pipe out of his pocket, Cantello again tests it. Again, he hears only a thin hiss of air, but the girl visibly clenches her teeth, and puts hands over her ears.

"Stop it," she implores.

"What do you hear?"

"Don't you hear it? A whistle, a piercing whistle."

She is the only one for whom there is such a sound, but Cantello does not doubt it is real. He understands. At fifteen he went to spend a half-year learning shadow-art, weaponless fight, from Maxan, the great master. His house was in the eastern hill country, and each evening from nearby caves, hordes of bats emerged. The first night there, when the house-dogs began to howl, Maxan's daughter, who was Cantello's own age (and for whom he contracted a passion never exposed), explained, "It is because of the bats." Cantello, who had noticed nothing, said, "The rush of their wings?" and she said, "The squeaking — don't you hear it? Neither can my father. His ears are good, but the sound is very high."

"But the dogs hear it?"

"Oh, yes; dogs hear sounds we can't." And women, young women, some that men can't, Cantello concludes.

"What makes you grin?" Sab asks, sulky-faced. From earliest childhood, he has never been one to deal lightly with the fear of being left out of a secret.

"Let us give this refuse to the river," Cantello says. Its flow is too free to be polluted by carrion, and when the body, like those of the drowned, is discovered, nothing can connect the deaths to this particular place.

"Clearly, we cannot make a start tonight. Yes, our time is short — " forestalling a protest from Sab — "but there is nowhere to find shelter in the wild, and the moon, if we see it, will be like a nail-paring."

"But that will still be true tomorrow night," Tarfal points out.

"There is a man who lives at Senningtop." Cantello has heard and believes that few dogs are yet encountered this side of the Senning, a rough stony ridge running northeastward, above a half-day's march, he estimates, for this company.

"The smuggler, Dernak — " face darkening, the girl looks up sharply from the plain food Cantello has provided from his meager stock.

"I did not say I liked him, but he'll do as I say, and give us shelter for the night. You know the man?"

"I know him well, with his brood, and would not willingly renew the acquaintance." She is disinclined to expand, but Tarfal explains: a year ago, the impoverished widow to one of the Loyalist plotters had been seduced by reward-money; she was in no important plans, but came near confirming for Nidlaam that the Princess Idolema was alive, and concealed somewhere in the far south. That news, the young man said, was start of the Terror there, the burning of hamlets, executions and torture. With the Black Guard steadily closing in on the families that had given her shelter, they decided Idolema must be hidden for a time among the smugglers at their encampment, not Senningtop, but another in southern Tarne, very near the frontier, across which, at imminent need, she could swiftly be — in a word — smuggled. Giving this account, the young man is taut with some strong feeling kept in check. "This was arranged and done without consulting the House Tarbul," he adds.

"Among Dernak's clan, I heard, often enough, about their home at Senningtop," the girl says. "I was supposed to be with them only a few days, but those who left me there were taken by the Guard. They suffered more, but it was a bad time for me, and weeks before my friends came for me. I feared no one would ever come; Dernak, or Dernlo, his son, told me all my friends were dead or captive."

"Many still alive were watched night and day," Tarfal says, as if defending himself. "When the news at last came to us, we could not risk leading the hunters to where you were." She has been told this before; the repetition is for Cantello.

"But they did not mistreat you, Dernak's brood?" Among felonies, smuggling has very often been regarded with levity, even affection, but these are, as Cantello knows well, not the impudent swashbucklers of legend, but dark and ruthless men, to whom murder, when expedient, is mere procedure. The Loyalists must have been desperate indeed to choose that camp as a hide for their treasure.

Hesitation, then a shrug. "They did not beat me; their own girls are beaten."

"Had they dared!" Tarfal's hand is at his knife. "Yet I was with my kin when we fetched the lady; Dernak and his sons became tame enough, after their shrewd fashion, as my grandfather knew they would, having dealt with them before."

Dealt is the right word, Cantello guesses, and strockan the commodity.

"You were never alone with them, unarmed." the girl says.

"This time, you will be with me, lady," Cantello says. Plain as the gun on Chekhov's wall, there's more story here, which, for structure's sake, is eventually going to have to be told, but Cantello, with nearer concerns, lets them be cagey, both girl and storyteller.

She says, "I do not want to go there, but I am in your hands."

Sab has been watching this exchange attentively. "Couldn't we try some other way? My father said it was madness to entrust the lady to such animals — last summer, he was on the point of coming to you for help, to be sure the lady would be released — they had crossed into Maegland."

"But that in itself was no bad thing," Tarfal says. Notwithstanding his own evident unhappiness with this episode, he is offended by Sab's criticism — or by the suggestion his clan could not deal with the smugglers. "The very reason these men were used, with the Black Guard everywhere in Tarne. Having guessed who the lady was, they demanded a handsome price for her return — for her keep, Dernak said, and my grandfather paid it. As he said, there was a danger Dernak might look for his reward elsewhere."

"It's a wonder he did not, through an intermediary," grimly. "Corvan could offer Dernak a price you could never have matched, a general pardon for all his crimes. Like Hammitt, I would not willingly have put such a prize in those hands."

"With all respect, sir — " Tarfal is now with difficulty holding down anger, "While we, too, were far from pleased, there were few choices available, to keep both alive, the lady and our hopes. Happily — "

Ignoring his courtly bow in her direction, the girl says, "And now we go to him again."

"This time," Cantello repeats. "You will be with me." He does not understand, but confidently exploits, the armor of his numinous name. "If we are to be at Hallabreg in time, we must start early; the weather is none too certain, and the going may be slower than I would choose. But there is a thing I need from Dernak — " what, he does not explain.

He does outline other considerations; the screen of forest and brush is practically continuous in that direction, and ponies can be used for baggage, as they can not for later stages, where the way will be rougher and cover hard to find. Hostile patrols should be rare so far afield at this time, and Cantello has little fear of early pursuit;

Suliwat, in his greed for a fame-making exploit when he heard of the (then imaginary) young woman in Cantello's care, neglected the elementary procedural precaution of sending a man back to whatever headquarters there are, to leave word of his intentions. The usurper's resources are not unlimited; the Black Guard is a formidable force when concentrated, but less so than its reputation, numbering only hundreds, perhaps three thousand at the outside; even the loss of Suliwat's small cohort must be significant for the watch on this out-lying sector. Corvan, while still maintaining vigilance on roads and better-known paths, will rely on his dogs to bar overland ways, drawing the bulk of his available forces tight around Hallabreg, and putting them in the streets of the city itself.

"And, bringing the lady to her city — " he raises his eye-brows in query.

"Yes, yes, there is a plan in place," Tarfal insists. "We have allies at Hallabreg. On the morning of Corvan's intended crowning — " but Cantello halts him with a gesture. There will be plenty of time to hear those plans if they can come safely to Hallabreg.

When everyone is settling to sleep, Tarfal has quiet talk with Cantello. "Your pardon, master, what was your father?"

"Was? Still is, so far as I know, a carpenter, a good one."

"And his father?"

"The same, I believe."

After a heavy pause. "You have no son of your own?"

"Not that I've been told."

The youth's nod of confirmation seems almost like envy, and Cantello is sympathetic. "Hard in either case: to make one's own way as the son of a nobody, or to live up to the expectations of one's famed lineage."

"I was merely curious," Tarfal says.

We are frequently warned of the dire consequences to our mental and physical powers if we fail to spend a third of our lives in unconsciousness; if true, this indicates an even greater difference between gifted men and the ordinary than appears, since many who have accomplished most in the world have done it on far less than a weekly fifty-six hours of sleep, hence, according to the narcomanes, operating at only a fraction of their capacity. Cantello cannot remember when last he slept as much as six consecutive hours, and normally makes do with four, often adding a brief midday nap. Though for a smaller proportion of his hours, he sleeps as cats do, with twitching ears, abruptly and completely awake at need.

At some black time, there is a disturbance, low-voiced but sufficient to rouse him. The youths, using their own bedrolls, have settled in the day-room in front of the dozing fire, the women in the larger bedroom across from his, and the first voice that comes indistinctly to Cantello is the girl's, murmured, but firm and assured; the words are not plain, but the tone unmistakable to anyone who has ever, in his arrogance, assumed an invitation never intended. Not illogically, Cantello's thought goes to the offer earlier made him; in the response, there is a note of aggrievement, and he catches odd emphasized words:

"...not good enough? when you...with the son of a such a man — " one of the young men, Tarfal, probably.

The slight yellow light of a candle or rushlight ebbs under and around Cantello's ill-fitting plank door, and a louder if not fully wakened woman's voice demands, "What is this?" — Nila. in sleepy outrage.

"Hush — " the girl, and it is impossible not to see her urgently indicating the door to Cantello's room.

The older woman does moderate her volume, and it is extraordinary how much can still be adduced from dark mutterings, Nila's icy courtesy and implacable affront, the intruder's unapologetic attempt at calming. There seems no other explanation than that one of the youths, and surely it is Tarfal, has tried to introduce himself to the girl's bed. Propped on a elbow, Cantello wonders if his intervention is needed, but Nila, now in a fierce whisper, has the situation in hand; scandalized, she tells the intruder to get back to his bed, and marvels sourly (and the sounds of feet suggest this is aimed at his defeated withdrawal) that he could attempt such liberties with the lady he is sworn to defend and assist.

Not, perhaps, so much of a paradox; Tarfal, with his baronial connection, may dream himself a serious suitor, but that would hardly entitle him to anticipate marital privileges; only a unique desperation, perhaps, the grim outlook for the immediate future, would cause him to forget the chivalry his chosen task demands.

Nevertheless, there is potentially a troublesome boil here, that demands early lancing. With care; a clumsy cure might out-ravage the disease.

The watchmaking delicacy of it is apparent as by first light all prepare for departure. Though avoiding any direct dealing with Tarfal, both women have decided to let the incident pass, yet the girl, at least, is owed some assurance she will not have more such attempts to fight off in the wild, this to be accomplished without the overt humbling of Tarfal.

Sab, it seems, slept through last night's alarums. That is well; there is in any event a potential for anger between the two, and Sab, Cantello guesses, would be outraged at Tarfal's nocturnal sortie, whereas believing the other committed to his own kind of ideal, storybook devotion to the girl, or to her cause, he can continue with the sometimes uneasy alliance.

Calling all together, Cantello — though there is one to whom this is not going to apply — reminds them of the hardness and danger of their road, the absolute need for discipline in their company. Nila's mouth opens, but the girl, who knows instantly that Cantello *knows*, puts a stilling hand over the older woman's. Only a complete and concentrated dedication to their task can see them through; "We can have no rashness," turning upon the young men, "no distractions.

"You have strockan?" face to face with Tarfal, knowing he has; it provides the final element in his amorous urgency last night; those who chew before retiring are often made sleepless by priapic stirrings, nocturnal visions of effortless conquest, voluptuous delusions of a reciprocal willingness.

"Strockan?"

"I am told that the House Tarbul always carries a supply when going abroad, for use in the case of injury or a wounding."

"A small supply. For easing pain," Tarful agrees, but his eyes darting from face to face betray that he guesses the real origin of this, and does not want it made open.

Cantello reaches out a hand. "I'll keep yours, for that purpose. In any other case, it merely muddles judgment."

The young man is reluctant, but Cantello not to be resisted; perfectly aware the leader knows about last night, Tarfal will grudgingly comply, to be spared further humiliation. Going for his coat, he hands over a pouch containing not what most would call a small supply, several curved pieces of the friable bark.

"Maelish," Cantello comments, much the more highly-prized of the two varieties of bark commonly (and illicitly) imported.

Tarfal nods. The chances are he has somewhere a stock of so-called twigs, slivers cut from the bark for chewing, but Cantello rests on an emblematic victory. An incomplete one; he cannot unmake the feelings that still float, affront on one side, resentment on the other — it is disturbingly possible that the young man, though embarrassed, still feels wronged, retaining the indefensible, ineradicable conviction that he is the victim of an invitation slyly made and cruelly withdrawn; as with dreams of danger or failure, the induced illusion itself fades by day, but the experience of it is as real as any memory.

He has a recovery. "As you say, master, the way will be arduous... " making it seem a question. His eyes are resting on Nila.

III

At setting-out, the girl, watching Cantello pull his door shut, says, "No lock?"

It is Sab who laughs. "Everyone knows whose house this is; what fool would rob Cantello?"

"Only a merchant," Cantello says sourly.

The decision to omit Nila is one already made, irrespective of any motive Tarfal might be nurturing; in the wild, presence of a chaperone would make no difference for the girl's safety — or rather, her absence would help it; three swords, only one tested in battle, might well be inadequate to protect one woman, how much more so two? Idolema has proclaimed that she knows how to use her knife, but she is no sorceress, and this would not be some minstrelsy fight where wisps of girls can use mysterious skills to overcome broad-shouldered warriors, but a brawl with broadswords, or a defense against the murderous jaws of charging half-wolves, where skill needs also the weight of muscle and bone.

It is very little out of the way to where, a couple of hours upstream, lives a fisher-family, dour but predominantly honest, who, with Cantello to daunt them, can be trusted to see Nila safely on the road back to Ault, or to keep her safe — as safe as anyone is, in these times — for the few days that must settle all their futures. None of these arrangements are pleasing to the woman, and it is hard to tell which causes her more pain, abandoning of her charge, or being deposited with people of no social standing — this Cantello somewhat ameliorates by telling her the fisher-wife is a noted fortune-teller, a trichomancer (one who reads meaning from the coiling hairs embedded on the surface of soap), who has achieved some remarkable results. About the other, appealed to direct by a Nila near tears, the girl, whom hereafter, when naming cannot be evaded, we are to call Idolema, could easily hide behind her promise to leave all such decisions to Cantello, but she does not, pointing out soothingly that the best service Nila can render is not to place added burden on men whose plain and overriding mission is more than hard enough. This argument is unanswerable, and remains unanswered.

For the first stage of the journey, following the river upstream, Cantello's own pony, unloaded onto the not-overburdened pack-animals brought by the youths, carries Nila — with further rearrangement, it would have been possible to provide a mount for the younger woman, but she insists she will walk, and when the start comes, does so with an easy, untiring lope. On the plain riverside path under a cool overcast, the girl at his side, Cantello sets a steady, unhurried pace, and after a mile or so Tarfal, leaving Sab to lead the tethered ponies, comes up to say, "If I knew what it was you wanted from Dernak, I might be of some help — with his sons, especially, I reached an understanding before."

Idolema (there!), expressionless, is keeping her eyes to the front. "We'll see," Cantello says. "We do not know what Dernak's mood will be."

"Mood! The only mood that clan knows is a desire for profit."

"Dernak," Idolema says, as if talking to herself, "Would, it is true, in ordinary times, sell his daughter or his grandchildren, for the right price. It may be otherwise now." Her cool opinion appears to surprise Tarfal, but surely the youth must recognize that everywhere in the realm, with lifelong lawbreakers no exception, people are making assessments; any who have the least inkling (whether hope or fear) that there will be an attempt to prevent Corvan's ceremonial accession are weighing their options; those asked to help, as well as those sworn to hinder a last-minute reappearance of Idolema are trying to guess what real chance she might have, and what, therefore, will be the personal consequences of their actions, rewards, preferment, perhaps a pardon for helping the winner, but for choosing the loser, loss of everything, not necessarily excluding life. If Dernak has made up his mind the girl has no chance, even Cantello may struggle to find the lever to move him.

The parting with Nila, when it comes, is not devoid of feeling. Since the assertion of rank by her charge, the woman has been subdued, not venturing any opinion, and now, abruptly, she is openly weeping; her sobbed question, where will my lady be without me? (though it goes with a sidelong glance for Tarfal) is easily reread as anxiety over what is to become of Nila. Idolema shows, without the smallest striving for an effect, what Cantello sees as a touching solicitude, thanking Nila for her attentions, reminding her she will have a secure place in the retinue if — she snags a moment on this, then finishes, "if Corvan's coronation can be prevented."

The young men, one (Sab) somewhat embarrassed, the other not much interested by all this emotion, are evidently only glad to cut away dead wood — like (almost exactly like) a storyteller, hastily bundling off a character he has invented but has no real use for. The leave-taking is set next to the stout stone riverside house of the fisher-people, whose distinctly cool welcome has been improved by payment out of the kidskin bag, and as the girl is bestowing on Nila a consolatory and reassuring embrace, watched from her doorway by the fisher-wife fondling unaccustomed gold, from the northwest, downstream, comes ambling a tall, spare and weathered man in drab and much-mended clothes, leading a shaggy pack-pony. Some twenty paces short of the other travellers, he pauses, squinting, and in a dark and sonorous voice announces as if to an audience, "Cantello the Peerless, not yet dead."

"Hodd," Cantello says, carefully concealing any surprise or possible pleasure. "You're in good time."

"I was coming to see you."

"Money all gone, or are you looking for drink?"

"Bored. Just back from foreign parts, and thought you might have a new way of trying to get me killed, everything in an uproar, what with the Black Guard everywhere, and our king-to-be rounding up all the heroes. I guessed he'd not find it easy inviting you to his party." His pale, shrewd eyes have swiftly appraised Cantello's company, resting a long moment on the girl, though with no hint of anything beyond mere curiosity.

"You were not invited to Hallabreg?"

"Not yet." Hodd has come nearer. "As always, it's the names they want, not the ones who do the work." With a long and strikingly well-kept hand he gestures inclusively at Cantello's companions. "Is it children only, this time, or do you have room for an old jackal?" His own age is unguessable and indeed unknown, somewhere between a ravaged thirty-odd and a fit sixty.

Tarfal, ready to be offended, opens his mouth, but decides against rejoinder; it may well be he knows the reputation of Hodd, styled Scorner, and fears being bested and even made to look foolish in a bout with words. Cantello's worthy, sometimes crucial companion in more than one of his latter adventures, Hodd has no noticeable convictions beyond the idea that he ought to be drippingly wealthy, made so in one swift stroke, since he lacks the capacity for any sustained effort towards that goal. The sardonic contempt for ideals, causes, is balanced by an infrequently stated but ferocious belief in personal loyalty, and his physical courage at times verges on the excessive — if courage is the right word for one who, in fighting mood, seems unable to imagine the possibility of his own death, this in spite of more than one grave wounding; his lean body is scarred, and he goes with the trace of a limp.

Hodd's qualities, cannily deployed, dovetail well with Cantello's more calculated skills, and he is useful to us, also, in a literary sense, as a foil for our hero, permitting us to see how Cantello's ostensibly parallel rejection of noble sentiments in his case overlays a profound moral sense almost unknown to Hodd; either man may unleash a withering sarcasm against some lofty aspiration, but there is the difference between ingrained disbelief, and a stubbornly persistent faith that has come to anticipate and so defang inevitable disillusion.

"We can make room," Cantello tells him, "for a tried sword. I see small chance of much money in it."

"Who ever got rich following a legend? I can give you a week, ten days, but if you're on the side I think you are, and if Corvan's coronation goes according to plan, I don't know you."

"If?" the girl queries, trying to assess this newcomer. Near her, Tarfal does not approve inclusion of another member, but for Cantello the coming of Hodd has lifted his heart; the man's tested value alters hopelessness to remote feasibility.

Hodd turns to the girl. "Someone," he says, "Must think there's an if in it, Hallabreg swarming with troopers and spies, barriers on all the roads. Outside Grosgault yesterday, the Black Guard went through my load twice over, to see how many lost princesses were hidden in my bedroll."

"If there is anything in that if," Cantello says mildly, "a man would be a fool to be lacking in courtesy with anyone who might be raised to the heights by Corvan's bad luck."

"Oh, if you want courtly speech, you can do a lot better than me, you know that. I say what comes into my head, but it doesn't spoil my bowmanship." He is still speaking more than half to the girl, and there is an odd kindliness in his manner, like a father asking pardon of a favorite daughter he has disappointed.

She decides to smile. "If we succeed," she assures him, "there might, after all, be some profit in it, for those who helped."

"A farm, my lady, a little farm, for when my nomad days are over, that's what I now wish for."

Cantello is genuinely amused. "What would you do with a farm?"

"What? What other men do, grow my food, raise my beasts, sleep in the same bed every night. There's a woman, a widow, by Hemholt ---"

"All the powers! You mean to marry?"

"What? Marry? Yes, when I need help dressing myself. I know this widow near Hemholt wants to sell her farm and live with her grown children, who must be singing for joy at the thought; she has a tongue that would skin a hedgehog. Still, her price is a very fair one, good land."

"Now there's something you know."

"So they tell me, so they tell me," Hodd concedes with a grudging grin..

Though the farming is new (and hard to imagine) the sentiment is not; as long as Cantello has known him Hodd has been on the point of settling down, but has never acquired so much as a dependable address; it is likely that the whole of his possessions are on the back of the pack-pony.

Meeting his companions, Idolema remaining unnamed, he anticipates Tarfal; "You have the face of your kin, the wrists too, I hope. Your granddad, they say, before he began to stiffen, had the best wrist ever seen behind a sword."

"Great-grandfather." Somewhat awkwardly, the young man acknowledges the family compliment.

"Will we get off this path soon?" Hodd demands. "Or are you looking for enemies?"

Cantello, leaving the river near a shallow, pebbled ford, strikes out northwestward, and the going is slower now, the growth denser over rough terrain, any defined track only intermittently visible. He leads, the girl where possible beside, elsewhere a stride behind him, Sab leading the two remaining ponies linked head to tail, Tarfal beside him, and Hodd, long-blade in hand, guarding the rear.

There is little discussion; it takes fully an hour to come to something Cantello has anticipated, the first questioning of his path-finding. A faint, irresolute drizzle is spinning from a darkened sky when they reach a small clearing. Ahead, growth seems to thin out on a gravelly rise, but Cantello swings to the right, and, "Are you sure of your way?" Tarfal ventures from behind. "We seem to be bearing easterly too much."

Cantello's restraint, challenged on such a point, is admirable. "There is some bare country I wish to avoid. We'll — "

An angry growl sounds, and Sab warns, "Dog!" — coming, large and dark, with headlong purpose down the littered slope. Without time to draw a blade, Sab, in the line of the dog's charge, shows both coolness and agility, bending forward in a lean, and only pulling back when the assailant launches himself; the spring misses completely, and the dog lands sprawled with an angry snarl, recovering, regathering with whiplike swiftness for a second attack. The normally placid pack-ponies jostle and whinny.

Cantello blows once into the little pipe taken from Suliwat's body. Instantly, the dog draws back, lowering to a crouch which ebbs into fully couchant; Cantello puts up a hand to restrain Tarfal, whose sword is ready.

Quiescent, with a powerful neck and massive jaws, almost a wolf-sized dog, he must be more than half Cantello's lean, muscled weight. Calling a word of caution to the others, Cantello gives the pipe two short, sharp puffs. The dog rises, as if prepared to accompany his tamers, eyes and mouth expectant.

"My guess would be," Cantello, even-voiced, tells his company, "That three blasts would release him, though I doubt he would attack us, even then. With a single blast — " giving it — "He would no doubt stay till we're out of sight, and then resume as before. There are limits to what training can do."

On haunch, the animal, filthy, brown hair matted, dagger teeth fencing its lolled tongue, has, nonetheless, so much the look of a biddable household or stable companion that the girl lets out a shocked cry when, at a nod from Cantello, Tarfal, coming from the left rear, kills but is chagrined not to decapitate the animal with a single backhand sweep of his sword, the cut landing too high on the neck.

"More wrist," Hodd comments succinctly. Apart from cocking his blade, his response to the dog's appearance has been no more than a cool interest, alert but unworried.

"My lady," Cantello, as dark blood gushes, "When you come to your power, if you want your realm to have any deer, or rabbits, badgers, otters, or ever again to be safe for gatherers of firewood or mushrooms, first task, an arduous and expensive one, will be to rid yourself of these beasts. Indeed, when they have hunted the wild bare, sheep, pigs, cows, travellers on the highways will be their next prey. We cannot always be ready with magic whistles, and if we could, they would in a few years be useless; the whelps these father will not be trained as they are, and will acquire only their sires' ferocity."

To all this she nods an understanding that in the circumstances amounts to an apology for her reproach, but then Hodd adds, as is his fate, one remark too many, an unnecessary gibe: "Aye, these will never be pets with pretty bows on their necks." Cantello sees both anger, and her mastering of it, sees the moral ascendancy pass to her, as, for the sake of their great object, she achieves a restraint the other has failed in. With Tarfal, however, resentment has returned; dispatching the hound, he had at once looked to Idolema for some word of praise.

Now both the youths are eager with conjecture, wondering whether a short note from the pipe would have the same effect on two, three, a whole pack of dogs. Cantello believes it would at least still them, but has no answer for whether they would allow themselves quietly to be killed, one by one. "If we do meet up with a pack, I would count it a victory to hold them and move on; we can't know whether they would calmly watch their fellows slaughtered; sight and smell of blood might be enough to break the spell."

He looks all round. "Let's not linger; there may be others nearby; their kind are not solitary by choice."

The girl says, "Yet I have heard you called `Wolf'."

Hodd barks a short laugh, but something about this, the intimate tone, perhaps only the suggestion of her interest in Cantello as a man, appears offensive to Tarfal, using a tough sheaf of last year's grass to wipe his blade with unneeded vigor.

"Among many things, madam." Cantello concedes. Ambiguous utterances, traditional device for deepening the nap.

"They called you Cat," Hodd recalls, "when you got in and out of the Mylsturm by night, with no alarm sounded,"

"I had more patience then."

Idolema observes this exchange with her head slightly tilted, curious about how it works, the easy friendship between the two men.

Though their alertness — or call it apprehension — is increased, the drearing day is condition rather than incident, while obstacles and the steady drizzle both increase; Cantello keeps an assessing eye on the girl as she tramps on, in his mind the probable full day in rougher country tomorrow. She does not complain, though sodden clothes and the steady upward tendency of their way make it a dogged business. Chiefly now they are among brush and great dark bulges of thorn, and at last, mid-afternoon, though gloomy enough for late evening, Cantello calls a halt beneath what seems to be the last stand of substantial trees, ancient firs on a cushioned ground laid down by their own dead needles.

"I must go forward alone," he tells them. "We have reached the country Dernak calls his, and he'll have watchers out — " bow-men. It would accord also with logic for the Guard to keep watch on the smugglers; no doubt there have been rumors about the myster-ious girl they had with them last year, but it is generally accepted that an attack on this encampment would be useless, unless in over-whelming force, probably several hundred men: the hillside beneath the dwellings is said to be an ants' nest of tunnels, well stocked with food and water, some guess with well-hidden outlets a half mile or more distant.

"Dernak's men will remember me," Tarfal says, once more ready to step forward.

"In good light," Cantello says, "I, too, would be recognized." He is unwilling to expose any of them, to expose Idolema, to the speculative arrow of a sentinel, nervous in the murk.

The solution is not hard, though it entails a certain amount of patience. Leaving the dog-pipe with Hodd, he instructs both youths to be vigilant, and gives them a probably unneeded signal, a bird-call, by which he can be recognized. Half an hour at most, he tells them.

A scan of the slopes ahead, broken skyline tufted with low cloud, quickly lets him decide on the likeliest hide for a watcher.

Using ground and sparse cover with no more than a fraction of the skill his legendary role makes him heir to, he is able to approach the place from an entirely unanticipated direction. Paradoxically, the watcher's laxness makes Cantello's task more delicate, since instead of looking out from his breastwork of boulders the man, roughclad and bearded, is reclining with a yawn against the bank of earth to the rear. Nevertheless, Cantello is able to get a hand over his mouth, arms pinned behind, an authoritative knee in the frightened man's stomach.

"I mean you no harm; I am Cantello — " and he steps back, knife in hand, assuming that name will keep the young man docile.

Panting down to calm, he identifies himself as Harbalad, husband to Dernak's niece; danger of betrayal by mere hirelings, as well as the instinct for extending absolute power, tends to make an enterprise like Dernak's a family affair, one over which he maintains the control of a proud-horned herd leader. Even with Cantello, it is only grudgingly that Harbalad confesses his chieftain is here at Senningtop.

Here, and when informed, boisterously welcoming; as Cantello comes striding over the final barrier ridge, he calls him `My great friend,' and showing his square teeth, dingy from strockan, in a huge grin, wants to know what service he can offer. "You are supposed to be at Hallabreg, for the crowning — " waving a mock-censorious forefinger.

"As I mean to be — " declining to show alarm at what is likely to be only a guess.

The encampment at Senningtop, actually in a slight saddle just off the summit of the ridge, is maturing into an unlovely fortified village; it began as a group of square tents, which, never dismantled, started to acquire wooden frames to make windows possible, and then solid walls, as spaces in the frames were filled with straw and mud; where possible these cabins expanded, or two or three were knocked together and roofed with turf; there are now about a dozen assorted dwellings ringed with a low wall, rough-built of big stones with no mortar used; chickens are in evidence and some milch goats, and there are small tilled patches suitable for raising potherbs and perhaps a few beans or carrots, but these are unwilling concessions; in general growing and herding are no pastimes for a smuggler, or his wife (Galda).

Their central agglomeration, smoky, dim and ungainly, where the picked bones of four or five cannibalized tents are still discernible, houses (at minimum) their married sons Dernlo and Dernfal, with wives and an undetermined number of squalling or sullen children, Galidern, the unwed youngest son, and a grown daughter, Galama, with a twisted foot and signs, in clogged speech and skewed eyes, of near-idiocy, although it is impossible to determine to what extent that might be the product of her mother's relentless bullying, often (according to Idolema's report) mounting to systematic cruelty, armed either with wounding words or a broad, singing length of supple leather. A stocky, dark-browed woman utterly dominated by her husband and treated as a servant by her sons, Galda in turn rules over daughter, daughters-in-law, grandchildren and menials of either sex with ruthless authority; in the nature of the family business there are extended periods when all the husbands (as well as her elder brother, Handor) are away, and Galda is unquestioned despot.

"But, my old friend, maybe this place will have to be abandoned," Dernak, with a shake of his unwashed head. "If the cursed dogs are starting to come south of the Senning; I lost a man to them last week. No kin, but a man is a man, and that's a bad way to die, and I have had to find a protected way back to the road — nine miles, shortest, it is. You came across the wild?"

"And killed a dog on our way."

"Ah, what it is to be a champion!"

"The dog was killed by one of the young men with me, Tarfal, of Tarbul's line." Tactics, not modesty; Cantello wants the man to respect his company.

"I know the boy. How many is your band, then?"

When Cantello tells him, "And Hodd Scorner?" Dernak makes a sour face. "Better have him keep a curb on his wit, my friend; there are men here quick to take offence."

"Then you had better remind those men that Hodd is skilled with more than sharp words."

Apprised of Cantello's needs, Dernak expansively offers an entire hut at present standing empty, says a fire will be built there, asks about food; nothing, he says, largely for the enlightenment of surrounding kin, is too much for his great friend to ask; he chuckles, gesticulates, in his mind has an arm round Cantello's shoulder — and all the time it is evident, in small, half-resentful glances, that he suspects, believes, is practically certain of what is in fact true; Cantello holds him in contempt; in the past he has made no particular effort to hide it.

He has made no mention of Idolema, but Dernak, ponderously casual, says, "There are some, even now, who believe Corvan's kinging will not be — that the daughter can yet appear. If so, through the years, she must have had many men and women to help her."

"As is only their duty, if she is rightful heir."

"Yes, duty. yes. But gratitude — to me, old friend, nothing is more to be admired in a king, a queen, you know? Gratitude, very sweet."

"I must return to my friends — " Cantello, standing, conscious of a tense watchfulness in Galda, and something sourer than that in the pale eyes of Surdane, the wife of Dernlo, heir-apparent here, a large, habitually angry man, who has been known to quarrel even with his father, but has now walked away as if preoccupied. Dernfal, his younger, more talkative brother, goes with Cantello, evidently to maintain his father's ostentatious parade of hospitality, but no doubt also to satisfy curiosity. Tall, twice a father, with a small, frayed wife like an anxious bird, he hardly seems older than Cantello's two youthful companions. *Note for rewrite: reduce these details about Dernak and his appalling kin to a quick impressionistic wash in muddy brown, streaked with emblematic gules.*

Dernfal prattles with his usual inconsequence as together they descend to where the others are waiting; of the realm at large, the wet spring, Corvan's impending coronation, the high current price of fresh fish, and the rumored appearance, in the far north, of speaking bears are given equal importance. When they reach the stand of firs, the encounter is oddened by Idolema; he of course knows her from last year, and nods with a familiar and somehow impudent grin, and a cheerful, "My lady." Seated, evidently chilled, she barely glances at him, and looks away, lips taut.

Nor does she rise when the others do, to accompany Dernfal back to the encampment. Cantello, not far from guessing why, takes stock: Tarfal is standing lopsided, miming unconcern, one hand draped to his thigh below the hip, Sab, having untethered the ponies, is undisguisedly puzzled, and Dernfal, opening his mouth for a bright comment, has to be silenced with one of Cantello's most forbidding glares. Idolema, palms pressed together between her knees, keeps her eyes down.

In a polite theatrical piece (*Mon oncle le fourgue*, ou *Le weekend*), it is still feasible, I suppose, to remove a superfluous character from the stage by having her callow brother come bounding through the french windows with a cheery cry of, "I say, anyone for incest?" Except in a drama about British POW's in a Japanese camp, as many as two too many might be acceptably shuffled off with the suggestion that a bit of bridge might be jolly, but even the most docile playgoer fidgets at a device ("The troughs are filled, my lord") to clear the stage of all but the loitering pair for whom we have planned a tête-à-tête, penetrating, passionate, scintillating or harrowing, as our abilities and the requirements of the piece dictate.

In this, the purveyor of narrative fiction, like the filmmaker, has all the advantages; the world is his stage; he can effortlessly clear the immediate scene of throngs, armies, teeming hordes, tracking them briefly in medium shot to demonstrate that they remain in the landscape, in character, part of the tale, and haven't merely gone backstage for a quick smoke and a dab at their makeup. In the current case, all Cantello has to do is catch the eye of Hodd, and indicate that they should go on, and he will follow with the girl in due course.

There they go, up the rough hill under a drear sky, Hodd, Sab, ponies, Tarfal in talk with Dernfal; here they are beneath the dark firs, dank and unhappy girl, solicitous warrior, seated together on a mossy log. The prevailing tone is brownish, muting the violet of her eyes almost to black.

"Cantello, forgive me. I should have told you," she says at last. "When you said you meant to come here, I should have spoken. It is not easy revisiting shame. Last year — "

"In the south, yes — " mere encouraging noise.

"I slept with Dernlo, as his concubine."

Cantello, as is his way, takes his time, weighing the circumstances, before responding. "You were badly placed, when your friends failed to come for you."

"And when we crossed into northern Maegland. At first, I was treated with all respect, whether or not they guessed who I was, but as more of my allies were killed or cowed by the Black Guard, Dernak complained that he and his following were bearing the whole burden of my concealment and my keep — "

"Your food alone must have been a crippling expense for him, lady." His sidelong allusion to her small, spare frame comes near raising a wan smile, but she is tense and trembling with remembered feelings. Note, here, that the ambient conditions have a part in her misery; strange that to be dryclad in pleasant range of a good fire might lessen recalled humiliation.

"When we slipped across the frontier, Dernak and his younger sons remained behind; Dernlo was the leader in Maegland, but his mother ruled the women, and she, I think, would as soon have handed me over to Baron Nidlaam, if she had dared. She fears Dernlo."

"She knew who you were?"

"They were never quite certain, and I never wished to confirm their guesses; as you have said, I might be seen as the price of a pardon for them. But as the days passed, and all the news we had was of the Black Guard making arrests and torturing suspects, my standing was less and less, and the men of the encampment more and more open about — their interest in me, in my body." Difficult for her to say, and Cantello catches a whiff of her lonely terror.

"And Dernlo claimed you?"

"I seduced him," with a flash of defiance. "Oh, I knew he was willing; he had often tried to watch me washing myself, and his eyes followed me, even when he was beside Surdane, his wife. I made him believe I admired him — he was less repellent than the rest, and no one would dare try for a share in his chosen pleasure. It seemed better to be the leader's whore than an unclaimed temptation for a dozen others in his band, who might well have been entertained by a full night of successive rape."

This, then, in a sense, is the origin of the precipitate offer she made to Cantello, who here, as not in his own case, admires the dispassionate calculation. Though Dernlo is taciturn, probably dangerous, and now to be disliked for new reasons, Cantello in the past has found him the nearest civilized of Dernak's entire kin — very much a relative term; say the least uncouth, able to assess risks and profits with a distance alien to his impulsive father, and willing at times to listen to and comment shortly on, if hardly to discuss, larger matters with no obvious connection to his trade, if always with the lurk of that massive underlying dissatisfaction with the world. "Surdane would not love you for your choice." An arid, intensely practical woman, never seen to smile.

"Between her fear of him and her own uncertainties, she did not object, not openly, and Dernlo protected me — as he would an animal, a useful dog."

"Was he, pardon me, in love, or did he fall in love?" This bears on present circumstances.

"Him? I doubt he ever could love, with the mother and the father he has. And I, certainly, never wanted love from him — and yet, there were times when — " and the angry completion is lost in an agonized mumble. "Never mind," she says.

Times when, despite herself, she was moved, brought to bitter pleasure by the man's loveless exertions — it is not permissible, with the forlorn girl who may come to be queen, to enfold her massively in consolatory arms, allow and even encourage the dammed tears to flow, but Cantello does reach for and take her chilled hands in his, incidentally noting with pleasure the contrast between his large, weathered, lean and sinewy thumbs and the delicacy of her kempt fingers, the hands small but capable, still pale, blotchless and unsnagged enough to have cast doubt on any past masquerade as farm-girl or the like. Consider, here: we tend to think of others as repositories of the information they exchange, but all this is at least as much creation as recital; both are being altered by what is said and heard (as that is irremediably altered in the telling), and by the subtle and complex action of each process on the other, the unspoken interaction of tone and expression that goes with it; recollection of life becomes life; a changed Idolema is touching and changing a new Cantello.

"How long did you have to endure him?"

"From when I first gave him his desire? Not a month, but it was endless in the living, a nightmare with no waking. He wanted, I believe, to father a child with me, but when his father came south to say Tarbul's company would reclaim me, he left me to sleep alone, without a word said."

"He was not afraid you would tell your friends what had happened?"

"The father, Dernak, came to me and advised me, advised me, that *for the sake of my future*, it was best to say nothing to my friends about my lost virginity."

"And you told them nothing."

"I was not going to begin a fight in which good men as well as bad ones would have been killed. But now, Dernlo may fear that if my time comes, I shall have him hunted down and executed, him and his father both." In this can be detected more than a hint of wistful desire for such retribution.

"They are not likely to earn a pardon by refusing their help."
True, unless they convince themselves that without it, Idolema must
fail.

"How can we trust them?"

With a wry smile, Cantello presses her hands. "Lady, forgive my presumption, did you ever give Dernlo any reason to guess
your disgust with him?"

"Plenty of reasons, if he had the eyes to see. He is blinded
by his arrogance."

"In this, all men may be; I think there is hardly a man so
crude, so brutal, so malodorous, so loveless, so unlovely as to doubt
that he, nevertheless, or that part of himself where his pride swells
greatest, is all that any woman could ever desire."

At last, the hint of a smile comes to the anxious face; she
gently withdraws her hands from his. "To judge by the pairings one
sees, for some women that must be true. Nothing else explains
them."

"But with Dernlo, I think you may be underestimating the
arrogance. It is just as likely he is certain you still want him — your
pardon, that you lie awake yearning for his touch — " (predictably,
she shudders, or cringes) " — He may even persuade himself that,
installed at Hallabreg, married for the sake of the realm, you would
bring him there to be your esquire, your furtive delight. No man is
safe from private dreams."

"Not Cantello?"

"I make use of them in others."

Her smile dismisses his sardonicism, but swiftly fades.
"Dernlo's are not as private as they should be. Somehow, Tarfal
knows — knows, at least, that I shared a bed with Dernlo; any of the
clan might have told him, Surdane, Dernfal, half a dozen others — "

Yes, fragments from last night's disturbance coalesce; *the
son of such a man* — Tarfal, genuinely incredulous that a woman,
after yielding to a smuggler's brutish offspring, could refuse one of
his standing and attractions. But Cantello rejects the rest. "Who

would risk carrying such a tale to one of his house? Dernlo himself must have told him — boasted of it, if they drank together, or used strockan together."

She flushes, but now with anger. "And hearing that I have known a man, he thinks I can be bedded by rote. Yet any woman promised or wedded to him he would expect to be wholly his."

"Lady," even-toned and determined. "For now, there is only one objective, whether or not it can be achieved. The part Tarfal plays may be one he does not expect. Be patient, I implore you."

"Where, in all the years, have I been otherwise?"

He stands, extending a hand. "Come, then. Once more, you have nothing to fear from any of Dernak's brood; still less any reason for shame. To me, it seems you chose wisely and bravely."

"I am shamed by lying, even to a Dernlo. Not that I ever lied about loving him, but my body did — "

"Madam. If a fool says to me, tell me I am clever, or your friend will die, and has the power to do it, then lying is both wisdom and duty." *His friend*, note, not himself, but if necessary he is ready to point out that her life is more, is the realm's hope for a more tolerable future.

Face bleak, she nods considered but not consoled assent, and stands, so they can go together up the hummocky slope. That's a wrap.

"And where is Tarfal?" The other two are waiting in the central room of the sparsely-furnished hut where they are to spend the night.

Sab says, "He went with the other son, Dernlo, for private talk. It seems, after all, that they are friends."

"Friends," Cantello observes, determined not to reveal his real and disappointed feelings, "are not to be despised. We have no shortage of enemies."

Hodd growls, "So long as the friendship is not the lamprey's for his pike."

Sab attempts a half-hearted defense; "He thinks the son easier to deal with than Dernak — more likely to give us what we want."

"Which is?"

"I thought, help."

Idolema protests, "We have food of our own."

"Way-food, lady," Hodd says. "An old traveller never passes the chance to save his hardtack." Cooked meat and a pot of steamed carrots have been brought to the hut.

"I will not eat Dernak's food." She does not, assuaging hunger with dried beef and staling bread, far from queenly fare. The rough table is too small for dining, and there are only two chairs; they make their meal spread out on the broad benches which run the length of three of the four walls, and double as sleeping-shelves (there are also two small adjacent spaces containing camp-beds).

Sab has after momentary indecision, taken his place next to Idolema. He, Cantello believes, is no less admiring than Tarfal, but could never dream any bridge across the gulf that divides his standing from what Idolema might come to; paradoxically this absence of any imagined pairing makes him, of the two, the more at ease with her, accepting that she is, for this brief time, one of the company in which he travels. He points out a defect in how the hood is laced to her cloak, which in heavy rain will create a small reservoir, eventually to be spilled in a sudden cold gush between her shoulders. Idolema laughs, and allows Sab to take the cloak from her to redo the lacing, which she watches with interest, making small remarks to draw the youth out about his various skills; for a moment they could be brother and sister.

"What about the other?" Hodd mutters, close beside Cantello's elbow.

"What about him?"

No answer; Hodd shifts, stretching out his legs and crossing his ankles. Eventually, "What makes him so angry?"

"I took away his strockan."

"And what else?"

"It's a proud house — but honorable, always."

A slight noise, like a suppressed half-sneeze. "When did you start taking blood for a guide? He'll betray us, one way or another."

Silence, and then Hodd turns sharply to look hard into Cantello's face. "I should have guessed, old fox. You know."

Cantello stands, and goes to the door, ostensibly to look out at the weather, and Hodd, recognizing he does not want to risk being overheard, after a moment follows him, with a needless question about prospects for clearing in the morning.

"I don't know anything," Cantello murmurs, startling Hodd with his anguished earnestness. "The boy is on a knife-edge, and instead of trying to help him, I must use that. He is both proud of and oppressed by his lineage, knowing that the fame of the House Tarbul rests entirely on deeds done before he was born, which he can never hope to match. The following generations have married well, held high office, wielded influence, but it all rests on the past prowess of a man near eighty — "

"Eighty-five, if he's a day. Or looks it."

"Tarfal, with his kin, has taken up the cause of Idolema, but now he is filled with forebodings. If that cause fails — and you know as well as I that failure is much the likeliest — "

"Would be, if your head and my hands were not part of it."

" — and that must mean, at the very least, end of his House as an influence — perhaps his disgrace and death."

"Well, damn, that's being a man, you have to make choices and take the pay they give; you and I, we face it."

"We may have less to lose."

"Our lives," Hodd protests, then makes a face. "No, you're right. He's just beginning. Still, he's not too young to know constancy. How old were you — " but Cantello makes plain he does not want any more about his own past deeds.

"He has had, besides, a falling out with — with the girl; she has reason to be offended with him."

"Wandering hands where they're not welcome?" Hodd needs only one guess. "Well, can you blame him? He's what, twenty? and whatever she may come to, that's a tasty rump, in those cursed breeches. She'll never harbor a grudge, you think?"

Cantello glances back to where Sab is, with appropriate gestures, explaining a point of wicker-weaving, at which his family was expert; she says, "I see; like two plain and one purl," baffling the boy.

"Though abashed, Tarfal, for reasons I more than guess, sees himself as the injured party; he may bear the grudge."

"A sulk he could sell to Corvan for a soothing sum, not to say, rank of his own winning in our brave new realm."

Almost a groan. "If there were time and leisure — but I have to choose now, and let him choose. Both you and I may be wrong, the sour old men, but — "

He is about to say that he can not risk their enterprise on his hopes that Tarfal will remain faithful, but in tales like these, revelatory patches of dialogue are commonly interrupted before too much is told; out of the damp evening Tarfal himself appears, and with him is Dernlo. Idolema's quick displeasure is quickly concealed, and she even achieves a distant smile, which does not encourage any approach, while Dernlo contents himself with an expressionless bow.

Cantello imperceptibly applauds her self-control, but his deep disappointment returns full force, and with it a familiar revulsion for his own unrewarding clarity, as he conjectures that Dernlo's dissimulation be no less than Idolema's; it is possible to imagine either the smuggler's son or the old champion's scion nurturing, each in his own way, improbable dreams of a crowned and grateful Idolema falling into his arms or his bed, but then each would recognize the other as a rival; together, an alliance could only, or almost only, be one of shared rancor — Tarfal's is plain, but could it be bitter enough for him to turn his back on his family, and on what anyone would call his honor? With Dernlo, Idolema may very well have underestimated his capacity for detecting her distaste for him; what Cantello told her about the blindness of arrogance is, he knows and knew, a half-truth; the world is instructed to fear the rage of a slighted woman, but scarcely less dangerous is the anger of a stupid man forced at last to recognize he is not the whole life of his chosen woman.

"Dernlo," Tarfal begins, and is distracted. "Is that boiled beef?"

"Bearded beef," Hodd says.

Ravenous, the young man fills a bowl, and sits at the table, shovelling down large chunks of the stringy goat-meat, while he conveys that Dernlo, who has been out scouting earlier (no doubt for ample reasons of his own), is confident the Black Guard is now giving up their widespread search, and is contracting back upon the immediate approaches to Hallabreg.

Here, Idolema, doing all she can not to make it pointed, gets up and goes into the little adjoining space assigned to her; Dernlo's guarded gaze follows her retreat, and his lips briefly, sourly bunch.

"Then you say journeys may be possible." Cantello.

"Some journeys," Dernlo shrugs dubiously.

"Using smugglers' ways."

"If there are such. If anybody could find where they are."

Hodd says, "If he's looking for bread, who goes to a black-smith?" but looks chastened when Cantello flashes him a warning glance. These are delicate doings, and all have been warned not to question what might seem odd in Cantello's revealed plans.

Once more not to linger over the questionable plausibility of extended dialogue, Cantello tells Dernlo (falsely) that he means to ask his father if he can provide or indicate a safe way to the fens, easterly of Hallabreg.

"Madness," Dernlo judges. "A day and a half, not less. Most of it where the Black Guard is thickest on the ground. Unless you go around by Mitfell — which makes it not under two days for the full journey — you would have to cross, or very near cross the Coldiron Vale, where Lord Nidlaam is. What good is the fen-country, anyway?"

"Many paths," Cantello replies, "Too many for all to be watched, lead to the very fringes of the city. We cannot hope to get there by either of the southward gates. If we had a month, we might round the Myrin at its westerly end, cross the Great Hallas, and find a way to reach Hallabreg over the downs."

"We have not four days," Tarfal says, having finished his meal. His eyes meet Dernlo's. "I have been told it is the way smugglers use into the city, through the fens."

Treated as a question, and Dernlo rather belatedly adopts an unknowing air. "Some do, maybe. Those scarecrows who follow Argenan — " his father's onetime pupil and ally, now his chief rival, known for supplying illicit wines.

Though outwardly tranquil, Cantello is struggling with this cat-and-mouse business; if a complex man, his nature is for straight-forward dealings, and the question is muddled further by a keen desire for failure — to be proven wrong about Tarfal. He told Hodd the youth was balanced on a knife-edge, and believes he still is, still with the ability to pull back from an inadequately-reasoned, irrever-sible treachery — which, however, Cantello is bound to make use of, if attempted.

"You were saying — " Tarfal to Dernlo — "The way to Mit-fell might be safe."

"Our way."

"What about the dogs?" Cantello asks, inching nearer an objective.

Between inarticulation and a desire to obfuscate, the answer is unclear, but Dernlo indicates that within a couple of hours, they could reach an old mining road, where none of the wilder-hounds has yet been encountered, and by means of various well-tried smugglers' bypaths, make their way to Mitfell in reasonable if not guaranteed safety.

"At Mitfell," Tarfal reminds, "Strong forces are waiting."

He is obviously prepared to be told that this way has already been rejected, but Cantello demands, "This is what, a full day's march?"

"Not more," Dernlo says. "Unless there is need to lie low, either in the farm country, or where the main road must be crossed."

Tarfal points out that southward from the fastness of Mitfell, almost to the valley where the broadening Great Hallas flows through the fens to the sea, the so-called Cloudway, an ancient path, runs on a sharpbacked ridge, where a well-armed company would be safe from assault.

Hodd has so far remained heroically mute, but now his disbelief boils over. "Anything moving on the Cloudway can be seen ten miles away. Nidlaam would have a thousand men waiting for them to come down where they can be butchered, or rounded up like sheep."

Tarfal, annoyed, starts to stammer something not fully logical about starting by night, but Cantello pounces. "You and Sab here were offended when I spoke of using the gathering at Mitfell for a decoy, but you must see its value now. If word can be carried there to do as Tarfal suggests, then Nidlaam, as Hodd says, will certainly concentrate his forces where the Cloudway descends to the plain, and our small party may well slip behind them, and be in the fens within an hour of Hallabreg."

This is a plausible mixture of strategy and nonsense; Cantello has no intention of attempting Hallabreg by way of the fens, nor of going anywhere near Castle Coldiron, but the lie, if it ever reaches Mitfell, should be harmless enough, so long as the

Loyalists led by Tarfal's kin don't decide on a pointless pitched battle at odds of one to twenty-five or so.

To Dernlo, he says. "You believe you can get to Mitfell?"

"Wait! — " the anticipated objection from Tarfal, who is, nevertheless, a little daunted by his own peremptory tone. "I mean, your pardon, master, but — I mean to say, you cannot risk a written message, and, nothing against Dernlo, why would my kin and their following act on word brought by a smuggler, no offense, as I say. If this is to be the plan, I must carry it to Mitfell."

"With Dernlo to guide you?" For Cantello, and he hopes only for him, the face of Hodd, at the same time wry and sadly resigned, signals the crux that is here; out of despair and a foolishly offended pride, a young man of numinous lineage has made his bad choice, and must be used to serve unawares the cause he has abandoned. "I was hoping he might be with us on our longer journey, but your father — " to Dernlo — "Can no doubt find us another man."

The smuggler's son shrugs. "I am to be paid for this?"

"Naturally — " before something heated about serving the cause of Idolema can come from Sab.

He does say, "This will leave us a sword fewer."

"We still have yours, and Hodd can sometimes make himself useful. The strength of our part is the opposite to that of numbers, that we can hope to go unnoticed. Challenged by any large forces, whether we are three blades or four makes little difference. Still, this would add fresh dangers for you — " Tarfal. Outside of covert conspiracies, this would certainly include the risk of travelling alone with Dernlo, as with any of his family, and Cantello is not without misgivings on that account; if it is possible, after all, that the young man has no thought of treachery — or is still struggling with final decision — he may not recognize that in Dernlo's world loyalty goes with profit, or is compelled; there are no steadfast allies. Hodd's eyes are lidded, and he might be contemplating his own aquiescent hands, folded on a knee, but Cantello can hear his sardonic rebuke, *A youth? any infant knows that if you choose a bed among snakes, you may get bitten.* True, but Cantello will not now or ever be free of the thought that his failure, largely for strategic reasons, to con-front Tarfal openly about his feelings and intentions may have helped nudge him into this dark and unwise alliance.

One that gives Tarfal no nightmares; he brushes off risks. "My only misgiving is, I shan't be at Hallabreg as part of our triumph. As you say, master, a cause may be served in unexpected ways. With luck, you'll be there," he tells Sab.

IV

Remarkably enough, Tarfal, when time comes, is ready to part from Cantello without a word about how Idolema's allies within the city have been prepared to receive her, conceal her for what brief time will remain, and have her revealed at the critical moment — that point in the ceremony when the traditional and legally required but normally rhetorical question is put, *Who knows of any impediment to this man's crowning?*

Agreed. time is running very short, but Cantello observes that to reach Mitfell in time to have any helpful effect on the dispositions of Nidlaam's forces, Tarfal and Dernlo must start out at least a half-day ahead of his own move. At first light, then, they are prepared, and Cantello is to go with them for the first, most risky stretch, over the open country as far as the mining road, to lend them, as he says, the protection of the magical whistle against possible dogs.

Led by Dernlo, the three of them descend from Senningtop by way of a tunnel, beginning as a cleft roofed over with timbers and concealed under earth and rocks, leading into what might be a natural cave, emerging at last into a sheltered gully, which allows them to come down unobserved to where cover can be found. Under early cloud and banks of mist, full light is still an hour away, and they are at once picking their way among dense, dark clumps of thorn more than head-high, yet Cantello feels powerfully the sensation of being watched — an instinct, it might be called, though probably no more than experienced use of the normal senses.

Rough at first on steep downslopes, the going levels off, and a taciturn Dernlo leads with the surly assurance of familiarity, Tarfal following, glum-faced, with many sidelong looks for Cantello.

"If we can succeed in our venture — " this may be the last chance for talk with Tarfal, and Cantello ignores Dernlo. whose tight mouth loudly conveys a preference for silence — "Mitfell, your contribution, the contribution of your house over all the years of concealment, will not be forgotten."

"Maybe," Tarfal says warily. "But to me it seems the champions, like my great-grandfather — like yourself, master; is it that they wish their deeds to remain unrivalled? they work always for a world where their skill will not be needed — a world without heroes."

"Those credited with feats of arms, perhaps, see that too much is made of them. Corimal the Great, whom Tarbul served in his youth, is additionally named the Just, not the deadly, and his chief minister is no less of a hero for being called Fedden the Peacemaker. Those fireside warriors who make the songs and tales where warlike deeds are praised and overpraised beyond all recognition may well have more skill than any I possess."

"Still," Tarbal says glumly.

"The best praise any hero can be given is not how many he slew, what odds he fought against, but what Kaorin of old chose for his epitaph; he kept faith."

This, imperfectly following what has gone before, is all-but an invitation, and the young man gives a probing sidelong stare.

"But with what?" he says. "The Black Guard keeps faith, in its own way."

Cantello allows this to irritate him. "An argument for young students of law, or scholars in the wonder-realm of words; in the real world any man knows the difference, it seems to me — " but he is forced to break off.

"Dernlo," a soft call. "Hold. There are dogs keeping pace with us — " three at least, warier than yesterday's lone one, a short way upslope, gliding menacingly through tall, tattered, colorless grass, seeking, perhaps, an opening among the bushes where the travellers can be attacked. Cantello has the pipe in his hand, and gives one short blast; at once the matted backs and then the ears of the dogs sink out of sight.

"Go on," he tells the astonished Dernlo, and as they resume, gives two quick blasts on the pipe. They are now on something resembling a path, perhaps an habitual route for deer or wild pigs, and after a few paces, with a rustle of underbrush and the pant of eager breath the hounds emerge to keep them company. There are four, single file, their leader a particularly large, shark-toothed and bloody-eyed specimen, docile now, but still a threatening presence.

"I would sooner have them with us like this," he explains, "Than have them to deal with on my return."

"Madness," Dernlo says in a forceful near-whisper, as if anything louder might break the spell. "How can you know they won't turn on us?" His bad temper less hides his nervousness than might have been predicted; the entire family is of course a blustering clutch of cowards, but Cantello would have expected the competitive pretense of boldness this fosters among themselves to carry over into the rest of life. But perhaps, he concedes, it is simply the dogs, not a threat a man is schooled for; Maxan, the great tutor of his youth, brave enough to go empty-handed against fully-armed men near twice his size (and to leave them helpless) had a paralyzing fear of scorpions.

This morning, not seeking it, Cantello is recurringly troubled by the thought, the vivid image, of Idolema, gasping and writhing under this muddy-souled man; as a strategist he still believes her choice was brave and sensible, but now the idea, in the specific case, pains and revolts him. With an unseen, self-mocking grimace he concludes that his growing admiration for the girl could be enough to make him despise her.

"I don't know — " belatedly answering the question; he wonders if anyone does; those who make new weapons are intent on destruction, and control comes as an afterthought; it may be the same with those who trained the killer dogs. "Except that we can't outrun or hide from these brutes; to keep them in our sight may lessen and certainly doesn't increase the danger."

Dernlo is not comforted, while Tarbal, his face set, marches on, carrying the sword that killed a dog yesterday.

The pace is a plodding one for all of their twenty-two feet, the dogs quiescent but alert, as if expecting a fresh command; it is possible that some more elaborate signal from the pipe might make them disperse, but Cantello, reluctant to experiment, is curious, besides, about what the dogs will do when they come to the old mining road; all accounts agree that travellers on established ways are safe from them.

There is a place where Dernlo, showing the way, has to stoop under the low branch of a sickly beech, then slither down a steep, gravelly bank to where a sluggish stream flows. Finding the gap he wants on the opposing bank, he giant-steps across the water, charges up the short, steep slope, and breaks through a screen of brush and bramble onto something more like a path. When the dogs follow, the burst of exertion has roused them, heads are up, ears forward, nostrils testing the air. Not liking the signs, Cantello gives another short blow to the whistle; once more the dogs begin to sink down, but the second, briefly jostled by the third, whips around with a snarl, and Cantello risks a sharp, peremptory reprimand, "*No!*"

A frozen moment, and then the bickering dogs subside on their haunches, patiently waiting for the next instruction. To what extent, Cantello wonders, are they *his dogs*, his as being the one with the whistle? If, for instance, while held as they are, another hunting-pack attacked the party, would these four turn on, or defend him and his companions?

"Shall we kill them?" Tarfal is ready and eager with his sword.

"No." They might kill two, but he still doubts the rest would remain passive once blood started to gush.

"If you know how, leave the curs," Dernlo says. "Once over the ridge here, and we'll be coming to the road."

This Cantello ignores, waiting till they have gone a few paces before giving the quick double signal for the dogs to follow;

interestingly, they maintain that distance, waiting when the men stop for a moment. slouching on obediently when they resume.

Their training, Cantello concludes, must have been a cruel business, to leave them at once so deadly and so tractable. When Dernlo brings them to what he says is the old mining road, made of broken stone, but now much overgrown, Cantello would scarcely have recognized it, the margins lapped at and overlapped by a wilderness that threatens to obliterate all trace of a made thing, but the dogs do, coming to a halt and not venturing on its blurred surface till he repeats the signal; the four animals stand uncertainly by as leave-takings are made.

For these times, when even innocent travellers on their own business cannot be certain the Black Guard will allow them to go unmolested, Dernlo's confidence seems excessive; he and Tarfal, he assures Cantello, will find a spot to slip across the main road this afternoon, and will reach Mitfell by nightfall.

"You understand the plan?" Cantello questions the younger man. "They are to stay clear of a fight, but be seen moving north-ward in strength."

"On the Cloudway," Tarfal nods. "I wish success to your own journey, master. We should all meet again at Hallabreg."

"At Hallabreg — " waiting for what does not come, an omission that sickens him in its apparent confirmation of his worst suspicions; surely if Tarfal believes, or even hopes that Cantello can bring Idolema to the capital, he would name Loyalists within the city prepared to give shelter and assistance.

Jogged on the point, he does supply names and whereabouts, first of a woman, "the daughter of the old steward on our estates," who had come north when she married a master-wheelwright, and then of Geddo, an officer in the Royal Guard — not the Black Guard, but a far older and more soldierly regiment, with none of the malodor that goes with Nidlaam's bullies. Beginning generations ago as company of one hundred picked men responsible for the monarch's safety, in its first year it grew, in the way of such things, to four hundred, and with ever-expanding responsibilities has by now become a well-trained and formidable force of something near two thousand.

Their strikingly handsome commander, Armid, Earl of Lasth, still no more than a young thirty-odd, popularity enhanced by his choice of a lovely and reputedly gracious wife, is a cognate cousin to the ruling house, but with no perceptible ambitions of his own. On evidence, lacking also any strong convictions; Cantello has heard Loyalists complain that Armid's passivity allows Corvan to parade him as a benign mask for his brutal reign. On the other hand, it is commonly rumored that he has quarrelled loudly with the Baron Nidlaam, and is contemptuous of his Black Guard; leading the only warlike force at the heart of the realm concentrated enough to over-match Nidlaam's, which way his allegiance, and that of his officers, goes must obviously be a critical factor in any attempt to supplant Corvan. Their ranks are conjectured to include many with Loyalist leanings, and plainly the rise of the Black Guard reflects Corvan's reluctance, perhaps his inability, to make the Royal Guard the instrument of his darker will. Though they have served Corvan and kept him safe for the past seven years in a day-by-day extension of their duties, the solemn traditional Oath of the Royal Guard can be pledged only to a lawful monarch, and Cantello has no doubt that delayed oath-taking, the step that more than any other will make Corvan's rule secure, is meant to be a central element in the forth-coming ceremonies.

While you, like Cantello, have never met the Earl of Lasth, like him you know him very well, competent, likable, guileless and guiltless, his vanity more dangerous for its diffidence, he is in a pos-ition to justify, even to congratulate himself, on any outcome, the recurrent man who, when unchoice turns to evil, takes a stand too late, and ends up discredited or dead, quite likely both.

Reflections that only confirm Cantello's mistrust of any con-tact with the Royal Guard; his suspicions about Tarfal are hardly needed to deepen doubts about the wisdom of entrusting Idolema's safety where allegiances are so unpredictable, and a wrong choice a decisive disaster; far better to astonish and challenge them with her sudden reappearance; once persuaded of her legitimacy Armid, popularity intact, will become the staunchest pillar of the new reign.

All this, by cast-iron convention, must be conceived as stampeding through the mind of Cantello, as in mere physical time he thanks Tarfal, and grasps his hand in farewell, detecting no sign of perplexity or larger regret.

Dernlo says, "You will keep the beasts with you? We don't want them on our trail, now they find they can go on the road."

"They'll stay with me." Tarfal, surely, is safe from Dernlo; if only he were equally safe from himself.

Returning, Cantello seeks out their host, who is at the shelter used for stables, seeing to harness repairs. His middle son Dernfal is nearby, sorting through scraps of leather.

"You should have made an early start on your own account, my great friend. Rain not much past noon, take my word for it." The morning has become cool but dry, and the sky has a scrubbed look, with high, streaky cloud.

Getting no reply, Dernak tries another line: "You are heading, what, north, north by west?"

"Well east of that. You will give me the key to the Old Water Run."

"The what?"

"You may have another name for it. The tunnel into Hallabreg. I need the key."

A forced laugh. "If I had it, perhaps."

"You have it. It is the way you use to take your loads of Paranopan silk and Maelish strockan into Hallabreg."

"Once, maybe," turning away to reach for a tool. "If I ever had the key it is mislaid, my word on it."

"It will be found again."

"How?" blandly, but he means, why should he?

"The gratitude you spoke of last night is a coin with two faces. You guess the purpose of my journey, and access to the Old

Water Run can make it less difficult, but I am Cantello, and as always mean to succeed. If, as you hinted, our rightful queen will have rewards for those who sheltered and aided her, what do you suppose there'll be for those who could have helped, but declined to?"

A long silence while the smuggler threads a rawhide lace to reattach a stirrup-iron. "It is a dangerous journey, now, more dangerous than ever."

"As you have often heard, I have overcome dangers before." Cantello knows he — hence Idolema — has never been in more danger than at this moment; only name has kept them safe; the encampment is filled with practised and kindless fighters, who could in concert, and if they believed it, overcome him. To the extent that Dernak is stupid, it is that shrewd species of stupidity which, where his own benefit, his own survival is the question, can always assess the odds; he may already have seen how impossible it is — that he, in effect, is asking that their queen, helped to a crown, will countenance his continued lawbreaking.

No, he had not yet struck the balance; in the man's face Cantello witnesses the moment of its arrival. Dernak's new grin is far more menacing.

"My great old friend, there are some men — let us say you had gone instead to Argenan — " the rival smuggler over in the west. "A rogue, so he is, a fool, you say, agreed, but a hard fool, who knows ways to stay alive, and he might think his best chance would be to kill you all."

"He would end with fewer mouths to feed, perhaps his own. He has, what, twenty men, two dozen? I have done well against worse odds — " (*But, o, vain boast! 'Tis not so now.*) — "and I am not alone this time; there are good swords with me."

"Hodd, and a boy?"

"A boy hungry to make his own name." Actually, while Tarfal's lineage makes certain that he has had some training, it is doubtful that Sab, however strong and agile, would be of much account in a fight against such killers.   — and they would not of course kill Idolema but save her to use for bargaining with Corvan.

But although the breath is laboring in Dernak's nostrils, as if the refreshingly simple idea of a death-fight has roused his blood, Cantello knows it won't come to that; if he has learned anything as a licensed hero it is that logic does not dictate whether men will dare to fight; alone among a thousand who saw some advantage in his death, he could still find a way to achieve ascendancy.

He speaks quietly. "Call your forty men to assail us. I doubt that forty would answer your call, but at least you and your sons can be first to die."

"You threaten me, when I have opened my hearthside to you?"

"You may not need to give any order, once your followers see how it is; There are men here, I guess, who would like to be leader in your place, men you have given little reason for gratitude."

Putting on the least convincing of grins, Dernak touches a tongue-tip to first lower then upper lip. "Last year — "

"For last year's services you were amply compensated."

"Well, but my eldest son — " and an astonishingly swift pounce puts Dernak's throat in Cantello's grip. A bradawl goes clattering to the board floor.

"Do you want to live?" Cantello hurls in the man's face, while Dernfal takes an ineffectual half-step in his direction.

"My friend — " a strangled croak. "We are friends, allies -- "

"My allies," slowly releasing the pressure, "Are respectful of our lawful ruler."

As Cantello steps back, so does Dernak, rotating his head from side to side as if confirming it remains attached. He attempts something between a cough and an arid laugh. "You come for help to outlaws — "

"Outlaws, I thought, were still men, not wilder-hounds."

"My old friend — " Dernak's climbdown is in jerky phrases, like the aftermath of a breathless fit. "Have I said I won't help you? You treat me as your enemy — " rubbing at his throat — "When we both have more than enough real ones. Haven't I given you food, shelter, one of my sons to guide your messenger? But that key you want — If I could give you the key you want," suddenly sullen, "Where would I be? As things now are, the patrols, the stops on the road, out of business."

"The key will be returned to you."

"To a smuggler, by the queen?"

Not a negligible riposte, a queen, moreover, who as a fugitive has thought enough about vengeance against these smugglers to suggest it might be in their minds. After a measured wait, Cantello says gently, "Then do not entrust me with the key — "

"If I had it."

"It will be found, I know, within the hour. Send another of your sons with us, to carry the key, and bring it back safe."

An open-mouthed stare. "Too dangerous, I cannot spare any more sons."

"The Guard will not detect us, and I have means of managing the dogs." His four earlier shadows, stilled with a single blast of the whistle, have been left on the far side of the little stream, well away from any route he will take now.

"Ah, but once out of sight — " Dernak's calculating thought is cut short by the rekindled blaze in Cantello's eyes, so to say, *Do you dare to impute a bent for treachery in me, Cantello, called Peerless?*

He does not (reminiscently feeling his throat). "I mean only to say, my son cannot make his way back all alone — across the wild, with the dogs abroad?"

"He can remain at Hallabreg, till it is safe to travel, or you make your next journey there — you must have friends there, confederates."

"They cannot help you — " very quickly.

"They won't be asked to. We have allies of our own." He wishes that was certain.

"My friend," shaking his head, "You know how to get your way. Corvan, though, and Nidlaam Coldiron — this may be your ending — believe, I'll mourn with the best on the day your luck runs dry."

"Luck — " an interruption comes, as Dernfal, ready, it seems, for his mid-morning babble, picks up the thought. "That's so, is it not, master? As much luck, and maybe more, goes into making a reputation as strength, or speed, or cunning. When you hear of the heroes of old, all the tales have luck in them, isn't that so?"

This sounds like a variation on the taunting Cantello has so often shrugged away, coming from youthful would-bes; but surely this tall, ungainly-looking mongrel can have no such high regard for his own skill with weapons?

"Perhaps. I have often been called lucky, but to me it seems I have had to work hard, harder than other men, for anything I have accomplished."

"So you say, master, but your legends tell it otherwise — there was luck in it when you downed the bog-folk, wasn't there. Or, again — "

"If a man is lucky — " with what he hopes is finality — "His luck is part of him, like swordsmanship, good sense, courage, strength, or even bad temper — " the addition an intended warning — "to be weighed in assessing him. Meeting such a man, I would be a fool to suppose I crippled his luck by naming it, to think that it might all at once fail."

"But doesn't it always fail, sooner or later?"

"Who would try to guess when? Tarbul is past eighty, and unscratched."

"Yes, but — well, we can talk more about this, while we travel."

"You're not going," his father says, to the immense relief of Cantello, who, after a full afternoon of Dernfal, would be inclined to cut his throat to stop his chatter. "Work for you here, those pelts to sort and grade. My good friend, you may have Galidern to go with you — " the youngest son. "He has been that way before, more than once."

"An unpleasant boy," Idolema judges, when told who will come with them. "His chief amusement was seeing his younger cousins, or his nieces and nephews, being whipped; he would, I think, plot mischief with them, then be nowhere near when it was found out. But he is his mother's favorite, hence an annoyance to his brothers, not to say his father, from whom she shields him. She will not be pleased."

"But she will never dare go against Dernak." Cantello half-questions.

"As you say."

"What is this Old Water Run?" — Sab is asking the question for all.

Cantello explains. Long ago, time out of mind ago, when the north was the land of the Wordless, the capital was at what is now the baronial seat of Tarnhombe. Hallabreg (not then with that name) was little more than a riverside hamlet, but after the conquest rapidly became a thriving port and chief city of the larger realm.

There was ample water from the Great Hallas, but it had an astringent taste. Those who had lived their lives there did not find it unpleasant — to them, that was the taste of water — but when the kings wished to move the capital to Hallabreg, they demanded a sweeter water — one, also, in which, as they were accustomed to in the south, soap lathered less grudgingly. For which purpose, a great aqueduct was built; stemming from the uplands of central Nid, it ran for many miles westward along the line of the heights behind Hallabreg, the Myrin, which range it finally pierced by means of a great tunnel, part cut, part making use of natural caves, to emerge high above the spires of the city, whence it descended by a multitude of lesser courses.

"But there is no such now — " Idolema, stuffing a pack which she insists she'll continue to carry.

"You say, lady. The aqueduct was always hard to maintain along its whole length, and quite soon it was discovered that the taste the kings and nobles found offensive in the Great Hallas was contributed entirely by one of its lesser sources. That stream was dammed and turned, and is now the Haelwater, which runs down to Halabad, where the sick and the lame go to take the baths and the waters; the Great Hallas now being good to drink, the aqueduct was soon neglected, fell into disrepair, crumbled, and is now forgotten by all but a few. Some centuries ago, the tunnel through the mountain, the Old Water Run, was closed with a massive gate of iron, though there is I think — " turning to the listening Galidern, to whom the historical account has come as unheard news — "a lesser gate or grille within it."

"Yet still heavy," Galidern agrees, "A hard climb to reach."

"Not hard beyond ordinary powers, since your father and others have taken pack-trains that way for many years."

"He never said so."

"Any secret shared by a dozen is known to more."

An exemplary expository passage, economical and lucid; please mark for re-reading at leisure.

When clear their course is to take them nowhere near the fen-country, Sab asks, frowning, "Why was Tarfal misinformed?"

Cantello is ready for this; he means to keep his suspicions within the smallest possible circle. "Not so much Tarfal, as Dernlo. I do not trust him. There was no chance to give our true intentions to Tarfal. But the false information they are carrying at worst can do no harm; a riding in strength along the Cloudway should indeed hold Nidlaam's attention in that quarter."

"If the tale ever gets there," Sab agrees, startling Cantello; there are limits to the boy's innocence, and it is to be supposed that he wonders why Cantello would send off Tarfal in the sole company of an untrustworthy and, in the ways of his family, a ruthless man, if Tarfal himself is not also suspect. However much he guesses, Sab is showing signs of petulance, and mutters, "Hodd Scorner is in your thoughts, the lady is in your thoughts — "

"She is not — " with admirable instinct, Idolema takes Sab's hand. "I know as much or as little as you about our plans, but I have given Cantello my trust."

Embarrassed, Sab mumbles half-apology. "I'm not questioning our leadership."

"When I was in Racq," Hodd mutters, as if reminding himself, while restuffing his pack. "There was a woman, a Hallabregger, though she's lived there years, told me she wanted to put down the whole story of Cantello and his adventures. I don't see how she can; didn't know one end of a sword from the other; she asked me whether a parry was the same as a sortie. Still, I told her all I could, and she wrote it down, every word. Mostly lies, I could see that's what she wanted."

"All the times I tripped over my own feet, and would have been cold meat if you hadn't been there?"

"To the contrary, I made you out to be twice your legend and some change. You never heard of such feats. I just pity the poor buggers a hundred years from now, told to take Cantello for their example."

"What we ought to do," Cantello concurs, "is write down our own account, all the mistakes, the boredom, the bad meals and worse resting-places — "

"All the damned fear," fearless Hodd growls. "They leave that out."

Idolema is regarding them with amusement. "It seems to me the two of you rejoice in danger."

Merits real consideration; Cantello discards an evasive or superficial answer. "So others have said, though I cannot see that in myself, knowing how much I love untroubled life and a comfortable bed, good food well prepared. But I possess a craft, or crafts, which make their own demands, and it may well be that to use them is a kind of satisfaction, the selfhood of a horse running with its fellows or a cat stalking game."

"Or a bedbug in an armpit," Hodd suggests.

"Such skills might be a burden."

He looks to see if she intends irony, and remains unsure.

Till now we have managed largely without the cheap atmospheric assistance (though often exploited by some of our most expensive novelists) of characterising the landscape in humanly expressive terms; these lands are largely empty, uncultivable, arduous for the traveller, but while Cantello is not insensitive to impractical aesthetic impressions, his normal attitude to country that must be traversed is purely utilitarian; novelistically fruitful assessments like brooding, melancholy, foreboding (none of which, to be truthful, would be rejected by an impartial observer) are not useful to him. Yet it cannot be doubted that the bleakness (borderline case) that lies ahead contributes to the grimmer mood of this new setting-out; Idolema, frowning, asks, "Is something troubling you?"

After a pensive moment, Cantello manages a small, self-deprecating laugh. "Only the world."

V

Scarcely acceptable to our sophisticated and originality-addicted selves, there's a lot to be said for the lapsed tradition, stretching at least from Homer to the brothers Grimm, of ritual repetition, setting sail on the wine-dark seas, journeying over hill and dale, conventions to sidestep the tedium of extended but in the end inessential description. Growing up, for our artistic experience, means learning to endure much boredom, for the sake of uncertain benefits — illusory ones at times, as with self-indulgent novels whose characters internally monologize for ninety thousand etiolated words on the desirability of visiting a fire-station. Yet this is not to condemn boringness as such; we should always distinguish between the trivial dullness of nothing to say, and the licensed otiosity of transcendent masterpieces — of *Canterbury Tales*, of *Parsifal* — where excess is integral, and perseverance imperially rewarded.

Remarks provoked by the echoing quality of the day's second start for Cantello; like him, the light is brighter now, and most of his company more congenial, or less grim for Cantello's own ponderings, but once more they descend into a cutting that becomes a roofed tunnel, once more emerging at last in a stony gully, and as before they are for this stretch guided by a son of Dernak, though the quick, ferretlike and inexplicably furtive manner of Galidern is nothing like the eternal half-suppressed anger of his elder brother. Galidern will be fourteen at midsummer, and seems both less and more, with his small stature, lean body, and almost elderly, wizened face. He is, by Idolema's account, his mother's pet, but while the gap of years between him and his preceding brother, the unnecessary Dernfal, suggests the phrase, it is difficult to imagine his crude father and the dour Galda renewing first passion to produce an unlooked-for, autumnal love-child.

He is wearing, on a cord tied round his middle, the big iron key that brought Cantello to Senningtop, and as soon as they are outside any observation from the encampment, Hodd, by prearrangement, seizes the boy from behind, and holds him while Cantello unties and pockets the key. The boy squeals about treachery and false dealing, but Cantello, not roughly, assures him the key will be returned to him when they arrive at their destination. Slewing sidelong glances suggest Galidern might try to escape and run back home, and it is Hodd who drily points out that while, able to find a way, they have no need of him, his best chance of escaping his father's anger (a condition likely to imply a hearty helping of pain) is to have the key with him when he returns. Sullenly, the boy shambles along with the resumed march, from time to time half-punching ineffectually at Cantello, complaining, "The key is ours. You have no right to take it."

Notwithstanding this presence as its continuing representative, to leave behind the oppressive shabbiness of the Senningtop settlement is for Cantello like finding morning after a night of bad dreams, and more so, he notes, for Idolema, less burdened on the march by her weighty pack than she was there with nightmare memories.

The way is harder, largely uphill in tendency, seldom with any clear way to follow. Cantello leads, and now there are benefits from his long association with Hodd, who has no need of instruction, waving the others to a halt when Cantello goes ahead to spy out the way ahead and scan for possible enemies, hound or human, moving on again at the leader's quick signal. Caution spends time, and Cantello, while trying to keep them concealed from any observation, sets as brisk a pace as he dares.

For which, when they rest for a while for water and a mouthful of food, he half-apologizes, largely to Idolema, saying that their goal must be reached by tomorrow afternoon, to have any chance of being in Hallabreg in time; tonight he means to spend in the shelter of some remembered caves. Dernak's predicted rain has not come, but its threat is plain.

"By Sowback Scarp?" Galidern says.   "No, the wilder-hounds have them now."

"Not those — " Cantello knows them, often used by the smugglers. "Higher up on the scarp itself, where no dog is likely to go."

"My uncle's man tried to save himself by leaping on a rock, but the hounds dragged him down, and ate his guts."

"Now that we know what they like, we'll know what to throw them," Hodd comments. "Smuggler's guts." The boy grins uncertainly.

In another half-hour, the gradient much lessened but the way no easier amongst patches of twisted and tangled growth, Galidern informs Cantello they must soon be coming to a kind of road, apparently another of the disused miners' ways; once grudging amounts of low-grade copper ore were taken from these wilds, but the find of much richer veins over in the east had made the task uneconomic. "We use it with our pack-trains," the boy says.

Cantello remembers the track. "It swings west too far."

About to go ahead once more, on a swell of rock that must overlook the cutting where the road runs, he sees hounds, a pack of perhaps five, balefully on watch. He reaches for the pipe, but before he can put it to his lips, the dogs, apparently of their own accord, sink to their haunches. Idolema is making a face, and the boy, too, has heard it, "Somebody whistled, very high." He has drawn a long hunting-knife, till now kept concealed. On quick reflection. Cantello decides to let him have it; the boy could not be foolish enough to attack one of the company, and is entitled to some small means of self-protection.

At a glance and a motion of Cantello's head, Hodd creeps forward with him, and their cautious approach to the road is in time to see a foursome of the Black Guard, jogging along on dispirited mounts. Hodd has unslung his short bow and nocked an arrow, but Cantello restrains him, content to leave them to their perfunctory patrol; they did spot the dogs, and their leader still has in his hand a pipe similar to Cantello's, but the depressed surface of the unkempt road is no vantage-point for observation, and they seem less than eager to encounter any possible enemies. One, the rearmost, with many wary glances back, is apparently grumbling about the `filthy curs,' till the leader tells him loudly to shut up.

Not far down, the roughly westerly course of the track bends rightward around a big rocky bulge; just before passing from sight the leader pulls up and turns to look back, the pipe at his lips. Not to be seen, Cantello and Hodd withdraw farther, and above them, not forty paces away, the dogs rouse, big heads turning this way and that, instinctively aware of quarry nearby. There is a low, anticipatory growl, as the two crouching men are seen.

At once, Cantello cancels what must have been the liberating signal with a short blast of his own, and the hounds, at least four, not more than five or six, sink back down. He fears it possible the patrol includes someone able to hear the whistle, but when he risks another cautious look at the roadway, they have gone out of sight.

"Two short and one long," Idolema supplies, asked if she heard the signal for release.

Sowback Scarp is an alien thrust of bare rock, varying in shade between a pale sand and a brownish mustard-yellow, and rising perhaps two hundred feet above the grey surrounding stonescape. The shallow caves at the base, most scarcely more than large dimples, are a dreary place under a newly threatening sky, indeed the littered and fouled domain of dogs, a dozen or more to judge by the droppings, though to Cantello's careful reconnaissance only two are now visible, one motionless by the opening to the deepest of the caves, the other, younger and less massive than most, pacing a restless circle nearby; this must, he concludes, be a sort of encampment, from which the dogs go out on their hunting expeditions.

To reach the place where they can climb to the higher caves without a long detour, it is necessary to pass in plain view of the dogs, which tense and growl as the humans come in sight. A blast of the whistle instantly stills the younger, but the one beside the cave-entrance is more reluctant to sink into his crouch, continuing to raise his grimy muzzle, moving his formidable head from side to side.

The reason is soon apparent; from the cave emerges the cautious head of another, smaller dog of other breed, obviously a bitch, and in the dim behind her can be seen the pulsation of a furry mass that can only be the numerous pups of her litter, suddenly deprived of her teats. Their many-voiced whimpering can be heard, making the large male increasingly restless.

For this once, it is not enough to still the wilder-hounds and move on. Keeping his tone conversational, still twenty paces short of the dogs, Cantello tells Hodd (who nods his understanding) he will stand ready on his signal to kill the younger male, while he himself takes the other. "Can you kill the pups, and the bitch?" to Sab. "They will learn to kill, running with the pack — " in explanation — "but cannot be trained; grown, they will be uncontrollable, and father or bear others like them."

Idolema says sadly, "They could be trained if we could take them away, trained as good dogs."

"Madam — " with the still-distant threat of exasperation. "The pups are not weaned. How — "

"I know. I only mean, it's a pity."

"I can help." Galidern, teeth showing, has his long knife out, and Sab now draws his sword.

The guardian dog has to be drawn away from the cave. Cantello reflects he might have chosen an easier adversary; other bitches, of course, might be running with the hunting-pack, but competition to mate with them when they come in season would be fierce; this must be the victor in many fights. Rarely, he knows, with any animal, are such conflicts to the death (the losers, it seems, follow some established ritual of submission) but it is hard to imagine these big jaws over the powerful neck and shoulders being parted short of death once they lock onto actual prey.

Nothing goes by plan. As he saunters closer to his uneasy opponent, about to sound the summoning signal, the untrained bitch sets up a loud, offended yapping.

"Shoot her," he raps, thinking the noise might bring a nearby patrol, and finds Hodd anticipating the order, with his characteristic economy of motion sheathing sword, unslinging bow, fitting and sending an arrow. The bitch is instantly silenced, struck near an eye, and going over with a jerk.

For the evident mate the point where tension between instinct and training snaps; he is up, turning to nose over the fallen animal, wheeling back to snarl, baring fangs. Against any instinct of his own, Cantello goes forward, not wishing to leave the animal space for a leaping charge; from the tail of his right eye he is aware that Hodd has turned his bow on the other, younger male.

With unexpected tactical acumen, the big dog leaps sideways and then forward, launched like the stone from a great catapult; Idolema lets out a cry, and Cantello's backhand slash with his sword is improvised, nothing like the still, receptive blade recommended by ancient Tarbul, fractionally late, finding flesh and bone as the teeth lunge, but fail to clamp on flesh. Hurt and writhing, the hound still propels him back. but he keeps his footing and his grasp on the hilt, and is able to thrust again, driving his sword full-length into the heart.

When he looks up from the animal's death, Idolema is regarding him with anxious concern, while Hodd is briskly finishing the other, crippled by an arrow-wound to the chest. Sab and Galidern, having finished the female with many hacks, are killing off her helpless litter, a dismal, unheroic business.

"There was no need," Galidern gloats when the last tiny whimper is silenced. "They could not live, with their milk dead."

"I hate to see them butchered," Idolema says. "But better this than leaving them to starve." The boy looks at her open-mouthed, as if she has gone into an incomprehensible foreign language.

"Other — " Hodd begins, and breaks off at a peremptory glance from Cantello; he had been about to observe that the remainder of the pack, when they returned, would no doubt find a use for meat freshly killed.

A victory not without its dangers, and unarguably prudent, yet the entire gory episode clings with the unwanted tenacity of some sticky and malodorous secretion picked up in the woods, as they clamber to the upper levels of the scarp, a stony steep, Cantello believes, no dog would attempt without great need.

"Or a great reward at its end," irrepressible Hodd suggests. "Smugglers' guts." Sab, meanwhile, another kind of casualty from the encounter, goes in a kind of lopsided hobble, scraping his right boot at each step.

The caves, when they reach them, are unoccupied, deeper than those below, and a great deal cleaner. With patrols in mind, there cannot be a fire, but sheltered from wind and expected rain, sleep will be possible — not a consideration with Hodd, for whom profound sleep is achievable in any circumstances, and, like his waking, instantaneous. That in mind, Cantello tells him to rest now, as soon as he's had some food; he will be roused at midnight to watch till near dawn.

"Watch!" he says. "It's going to be blacker than Nidlaam's heart." The sky overhead is, for now, almost clear, but lurking clouds promise to obscure the young moon when it rises.

Cantello nods. "But I'm not going to be surprised by chance visitors, man or brute. The rest of you, sleep with your weapons to hand." But he demands Galidern's knife, on the promise of its return on waking.

"You don't trust me," the boy complains.

"True," his hand still waiting.

With no other choice, the knife is grudgingly surrendered.

Issuing from a crevice between masses of yellow rock, the small spurt of an ice-cold freshet lets them wash away most of the blood and part of the grime, young Sab in particular scouring at his hands as if to obliterate memory, before settling to cheerless rations. Hunger stayed if hardly satisfied, the youth is not much behind Hodd in finding sleep.

There is a creaking rustle behind, and Idolema is there, wrapped, it seems, in a blanket; Cantello is curiously moved by the slight starlit gleam of her eyes, of teeth when she murmurs, "May I watch with you?"

"You would do better to sleep, while you can."

"But I can't. Two nights more, however it goes, and I shall have all the rest I need."

"And a soft bed for it."

"Do you believe that?"

"I believe we'll be in Hallabreg this time tomorrow."

"Master — if it goes wrong — if I am near capture, I mean to kill myself. Promise you'll help me."

"I cannot."

She gives something near a groan. "Is Cantello the Peerless sentimental, after all? You know that taken alive, I provide sport for Nidlaam; can't you help save me from that?"

"I mean only that so long as I am alive and able to act, you won't be near capture — this is not drink-shop bluster; Hodd would tell you the same; we finish what we begin."

In the dark the small sound that answers this is difficult to read; pain, recognition, wonder, gratitude, even exasperation, any is possible. She shifts, rearranging the blanket around her. Alarmingly, Cantello catches himself wondering what if any clothing she discarded before swaddling her young body, and tries to divert imaginings both crude and perilously tender by promising himself a whore in Hallabreg, if he can live that long. Two whores, perhaps.

"If I can come to the throne," thoughtfully, "It seems to me I may be a better ruler, for having known danger and hardship, slept rough and dined on crusts — there must be ten thousand who have never known anything better."

"Oh, more, lady."

"Of this realm, I mean."

"So do I.   Within a bowshot of where you'll sleep at Hallabreg, I could show you ten thousand who, like many others, are schooled in living without hope. Or take Galidern, here — "

"He could be trained otherwise, like those pups." The same note of regret is in her voice.

"Exactly. Some crafts do well kept in families, but Galidern will be a smuggler, live out his life in holes like Senningtop; it is all he knows, or can hope for. It would be good to have a realm where a laborer's son might come to keep his own shop — "

"Or a carpenter's son do mighty deeds."

He brushes that away. "Too often, our rulers — "

"Our rulers, what?"

Cantello had broken off in what might be tact, and now he reconstructs his thought less accusingly. "Rule," he concedes, "Must have display; it's true the people have always loved to see their kings clad, as Dairemid sometimes was, in rough clothes, digging with a spade, or joining the harvest-dance — "

"I know."

"But to me it seems that when they say, *just like ordinary folk*, it means the opposite; would they find such delight in these rare humble moments if they did not believe their royalty, when not on holiday, is of a different breed? — and that belief is surely confirmed by the silks and jewels, the banners and banquets, all that sets royalty aside from the ordinary."

"Which might be envied."

"Yes, but strangely it is possible to be gladdened by luxuries and splendors, without coveting them — to share them by being glad such things exist. The pomp and the glitter are only resented, I think, where display is offered in place of hope. Isn't that the real business of kings and queens; that they can stand for the hope of a better life, for enough to eat, something to own, impartial justice?"

"That's a great deal to ask of one feeble man or woman."

"But the throne is a great deal to give one man or woman, feeble or otherwise."

"To give? What about blood, the rights of blood?"

"Yes. No light thing, lady. Men, sane but soured men, may take incalculable risks in that cause, even in half-belief."

In the silence he can feel the stillness of her grave examination. Of herself, he believes, her proximity to and remoteness from these questions of rule — but then she says, "You are like no man I have known. You step outside yourself."

He shifts uneasily. "I have to be my own historian, or be swallowed up by a preposterous legend."

"Oh! — " not a response, but pure startlement; it has begun to rain, not the drizzle of before, but in large, slow, solemn drops, the individual impacts easily countable, and one has splashed on Idolema's nose.

They shift back farther into the mouth of the cave. He knows he should insist on her getting some rest, but is reluctant to lose her company; after some quiet time they move on to reminiscences about life at Hallabreg in more generous times; these memories for Idolema, no doubt guarded beyond any treasure, have in that process, many tellings, perhaps mostly to herself, lying awake, become more tales than pictures, stilled in repeated phrases, so that even the emotions they recall are recited rather than revisited; she speaks of holidays, special foods, riding for pleasure on a sturdy but spirited pony, shimmering frocks and long, perfumed baths...

Baths. Tactfully, we elide in these adventures details of personal hygiene or its absence; Defoe's hero, amid exhaustive domestic detail, never alludes to the subject (though his prototype, Mr Selkirk, must surely have mentioned it), and there are tales in which prisoners are kept tightly bound or securely chained for days and even years on end — true, they may be fed like invalids, but if other physical processes are not simply lost in the syntax, some distasteful imaginings may bother the thoughtful reader. Nor does it do to calculate how long our epic heroes and heroines may go without a toothbrush or a change of underwear; conditioned from infancy, you, reader, genuinely believe in the identity of plumbing with virtue, lack the objectivity to recognize that, while you might be now, you would not *then* have been offended by the background scents of sweat, decay and shit, not less than faintly eternal in everyday life for most past generations of even our civilized kind. A musty visitor from 15th-Century England, not recently washed or frequently laundered (dry-cleaning to him is for the sparrows, involving dust), may appall us, but he, equally (who, can, by the way, as you can't, read Dante, Virgil and Homer as well as Dunbar in the original), will be repelled, perhaps soon laid low, by the sulfurous, carboniferous reeks and hazes we have adapted and modified ourselves to — not to say the hoarsing chemical choke of fake pine, pseudolemon, simulated rose, our chosen, constant, intimate envelopes of washing powder residues, fabric softeners, domestic solvents, air-stalers, antisweats, petrochemically scented everything — oh, clean, sterile asthmatigens, carcinogens, granted, not bacterial crowd scenes — with which we cover and piously agree we deodorize the innate stench of everything, including our ravaged bodies. But while standards change, it has always been possible for decent people, brave people, admirable people to stink.

She says, "You are still young — "

"You cannot think so — " well short of twenty, she must see him as more than mature.

"But all my life I have heard of you; kitchen-girls would sigh about having once seen you ride by — and now — "

"Even now, I can still grasp a sword."

"I was going to say, you must still be in the dreams of young girls."

From anyone but a queen-to-be, he would hear this, or want to hear it, as provocation. "I know less than nothing about young girls."

"Won't you tell me about the Lady of Synta?"

"No. You must excuse me."

After this, talk flags, and in a short while he finds her chin has nodded down; he is able without waking her to swing her gently down to where the slender back is resting on a folded blanket; even in sleep she is supple. The imagined is dangerous only when permitted to pass into words; he turns to the contemplation of nothing.

VI

Baron Nidlaam — half-apologies, here, for abandoning what has been, so far, a strict point-of-view: events till now have been seen through Cantello's eyes, or from a spatial point somewhere about eye-level behind his right shoulder, and while we have noted feelings and the evidence of thoughts in others, the observation, barring general reflections stepping (like this) outside the frame, can only have been his. Quite a modern invention, and in many ways an admirable narrative strategy, but not holy writ, and we must not let our stylistic aspirations enslave us; a key scene set at Castle Coldiron, impossible for our hero to observe, is both useful to the plot and diverting in itself. Here goes.

It is, as you anticipate, a starkly intimidating fortress, hewn in dark stone, set on a bare eminence at the head of the vale that gives its name, the unfailing spring which feeds the moat and would keep thirst away in the unlikely event of a siege being a principal, though not the only source of the Coldiron River. Surly, impenetrable walls, ring after ring, enclose the adamant central keep, which supports the baleful spike of an unsleeping tower, known as Nidlaam's Eye. Yet with all the surrounding gloom and menace, the living-quarters at the heart of the keep, cunningly made so that tall windows high beyond the reach of any assailing give abundant light, are more in the nature of a splendid manor-house, carpeted, tapestried, furnished with an eye to ease rather than ostentation, cool and airy in summer, with ample well-wrought fireplaces ensuring comfort in winter. There is an orangery, with brilliant birds aflit.

The layout, in fact, is on archetypal principles, these apartments, with their well-stocked bookcases, tables and and sideboards equally so, handsome chambers with vast and sybaritic, silken beds, expressing the illuminated aspect of Nidlaam's hedonistic nature, while descending as in a dream, exasperating in its orthodoxy, through many levels and down steep and narrow stairs, we come at last to its dark side, the slimed dungeons and torture-chambers where too many have died in torment, what's left of them consigned to the collective oblivion of swift, black water in the uttermost depths.

Though irresistible, the Jungian paradigm is for us, not Nidlaam, since he, by no means a stupid man, imposes no censor's hierarchy on his sensations, and is no more ashamed of relishing the flogging, branding or spoiling of smooth young bodies, inventive torments, hilarious cries of agony or futile pleas for mercy, than of enjoying a well-cooked meal, the scent of roses, or an evening of traditional music, in which he is almost expert.

The Baron is, in his way, a near-match for Cantello. Not really as a swordsman, though in his youth he was among the best, and he is still formidable, the crushing strength of his big, square frame to a large extent compensating for any loss of speed or agility. Nor is he quick-minded like our hero, but where Cantello's ironic resistance to any idea of absolute good turns him, when roused to action, into a constant improviser, Nidlaam's massive, unctuous sense of rightness gives him a strategic head-start; his course is set, and the details take their place within a framework that requires no further consideration; in the sphere of action, even a faulty metaphysic, firmly grasped, can often outperform unresolved doubt; that's what makes bullies, despots, messianic frauds so effective and so difficult to defeat.

Nowhere in Nidlaam's household is there a mirror — that's probably untrue; there may be several in the servants' quarters, but none for him to encounter. Interpret that absence as you wish; though no Armid for looks, his bold and weathered features are not repellently ugly, and aging is not a question that dominates his thoughts; past forty now he will quite soon be looking for a wife to ensure the succession — to an earldom, if Corvan's gratitude keeps faith — but aside from that dynastic aim continues to feel no real need to marry; between helpless prisoners, the hapless wives and lovers of prisoners seeking release of their men (and, in some youthful instances, their women), biddable servants and adoring admirers, he has bedded several hundred, and has kept successively more than a dozen fairly long-term mistresses, of which at present he has two. Fair-haired, wide-eyed Fanda, who, although bred in the bosom of the land-owning but untitled class, affects the manner and dress of a fictional woodcutter's daughter or improbably cleanly shepherdess, has an air of lisping innocence at odds with her huge, excitable relish for tales, the truer the better, of lingering agonies and gratuitous cruelty; a quick visit to the torture-chambers, even for mere sight of the ingenious instruments, can flare her nostrils and moisten her ivory skin in preparation for madness of a very high quality, and Nidlaam has yet to discover some use of their bodies and her fecund imagination she is unwilling to try.

This evening, however, he is with dark, heavy-lidded Zembra, unruly daughter of an Eremian count, ambassador at Hallabreg, sent to improve relations between the two countries, in which Zembra has succeeded beyond the dreams of diplomacy; Nidlaam has no objection to her appetite for variety, since it helps keep him informed about others in the circle closest to Corvan, and her shrewd eye for personal quirks, combined with her engagingly imperfect command of his language, makes her an entertaining companion, whether upright or horizontal.

They are dining together in the Lesser Hall. In the Great Hall Nidlaam can, though seldom does, feed hundreds, but this place, though high-ceilinged, by night difficult adequately to light, sibillantly echoic, is less awing; the oak table, set transversely with the high-backed baronial chair at the center, easily seats a dozen, but with middle third bracketed by a pair of six-branched candelabra, it is intimate enough.

In her being here tonight, in his being here tonight, there is a suggestion of swagger; he could and probably should have ridden for Hallabreg to watch over final measures to ensure that Corvan's equinoctial coronation will take place without a hitch, but by leaving that departure to tomorrow hopes to convey the detailed farsightedness of his plans, and his complete confidence in their effectiveness.

"Armid," he tells Zembra, "Is fussing like a midwife over just where to set his pretty soldiers, and if I were at the palace Corvan would be popping in every ten minutes to remind me of something else I might have overlooked."

"Armid! He asked me to get him some bairnwort — " a rare but well-known herbal concoction from her own country, reputed cure for barrenness.

"Yes, Lasth still lacks an heir, not for Ilana's want of trying; she has tried with half Hallabreg." Untrue, but it amuses him; he once found Ilana desirable, but now sees her as an icy and humorless prude.

"Why does your king, your soon-king, come to you, and not Armid?"

"A question of trust; Armid's men will guard the coronation, but the Black Guard control access to it, and Corvan knows he can rely on me to be thorough. Armid's breed is dying out, there isn't going to be any place for them, those gentlemen who would rather lose the realm by the rules than be strong enough to keep it. Corvan knows that if we decide this or that measure is necessary, I'm not going to twitter over whether it is legal, as Armid sometimes has. Legal! those who have the power are the law. Besides, there are so-called Loyalist sympathies in the ranks of the Royal Guard, the reason the Black Guard was brought into being. All this is going to change when Corvan is crowned."

If she has heard most of this before, Zembra is discreet enough, or considerate enough of us eavesdroppers, not to abridge it, though she does poke a forkload of poached salmon at Nidlaam's mouth, much of which ends up on his chin. Laughing, he wipes it away, licks his hand, and reaches for wine. He enjoys Zembra's intermittent assaults on his dignity, and she has, under the careless manner, the tact of a diplomat's daughter, not to prolong her teasing beyond his allotment of good-humored tolerance. All women, in the end, are afraid of him, and he does not desire otherwise, though sometimes it irks him; beyond even most men, he is always a veil or two away from knowing a woman's true feelings, except when their minds disconnect and they are wholly consumed by physical ecstasy.

Yet, after all, to be loved is the desire of an idiot; other ambitions, for wealth, power, even knowledge, can be planned and striven for, success in them measured, but there is no method for winning heartwhole devotion, nor sure means of knowing if you have, and Nidlaam will waste none of his time or spirit wondering whether the woman in his bed feels genuine affection (as more than one, most lately lively Fanda, has gasped), simple gratification, or is perhaps pursuing an ambition of her own; no man has ever truly known, and the wise are content with what they are given, what they can seize.

With Zembra confusedly explaining a recent incident at court involving the discomfiture of one of the Council who no longer enjoys her favor, a newcomer enters.

Oh, but there are small parts; analyze, motivate, prep as you will, you won't make anything telling out of the anonymous servant who, arriving without biography, delivers a message, waits for an answer, and vanishes forever into the otherwhere. This one, a man, rather round-shouldered, has some misgivings (don't indicate, sir) about coming to the baronial dinner-table without food or drink to deliver, but manages without clearing his throat to get Nidlaam's attention, and tells him the guardhouse is detaining a young man who says he has urgent news for the Baron's ear alone.

"He has a name?"

"Tarfal, my lord."

"Um — " Rough-clad and with a way-worn appearance, the youth hesitates, and perceiving the reason Zembra gathers her napkin and starts, with her habitual fluidity, to stand. "I can — "

"No, no," Nidlaam protests, "You must finish your meal, we can talk in here — " indicating the adjoining room.

He notes Tarfal's gaze lingering, not on the bare shoulders and half-bare bosom (four enticing splendors) of Zembra, but on the cooked meat in front of her. "You are hungry?"

"I have walked from Senningtop today."

"From Senningtop — " while loading a platter with bread, thick chops of mutton, some small green apples from last year's harvest, cooked in sweet wine. "Without trouble from wilder-hounds?" A professional concern.

"Much of the time we were on or near what passed for a disused road — it was said the dogs would not attack us there."

"Yes," becoming loftily informative. "That was hardest in training the beasts, but we could not make them a danger to lawful travellers; it was only the open country we wanted to bar to the lawless. When we believed a dog trained, it would go hungry for two or three days, and then be set beside a road on which a kid was released. Any that attacked the kid on the road was whipped till it bled; one that did so twice, killed. My servants serve. And you met no soldiery?"

"I was guided by a man skilled in avoiding the patrols."

"Such foxes can be found, at Senningtop. He is now? — " giving Zembra's polished right shoulder a consoling kiss, then leading the way into the small writing-room, and placing the loaded dish on the high desk.

"Having food, I believe, with the off-duty guards, some of whom seem to know him."

"Hmm." Smuggling will never be suppressed so long as nearly everyone wants something smugglers can supply, but the band from Senningtop took on a changed importance in the south last year, when they are believed to have helped conceal the prize of prizes, the fugitive princess. Because of the surrounding wilderness, Senningtop is difficult to either assail or invest without a true military force, which the Black Guard emphatically is not; let loose in Hallabreg or Grosgault most of its rank and file could survive on casual labor eked out with shop-lifting, pocket-picking and petty theft, some with intimidation, but they have no real training for the shifts and hardships of a campaign; their chief virtue, unquestioning obedience, is not enough. Nevertheless, Nidlaam has until recently kept a close watch on comings and goings at the smuggler's encampment, till the gathering over in the west at Mitfell began to take more of his attention.

"What would you say — " Tarfal, given a nod, picks up and lunges hungrily at mutton, and speaks while chewing — "If I told you I know the whereabouts, almost to the half-mile, of a young girl who calls herself Idolema — that I could tell you the route she is taking, and exactly where she intends to be tomorrow?"

"I would say, you're going to tell me."

"Well, but first — " wiping his mouth with a cuff.

"No, no; first you are going to tell me, and without delay. You may have been told by my detractors that I actually enjoy inflicting pain. Believe it."

Tarfal at least affects unconcern. "You know who I am?" His uncouth assault on the food is in itself an unknowing statement; here is no peasant or laborer, no artisan, condemned in these surroundings to a desperate attempt at gentility, but one of Nidlaam's own class, unselfconsciously wolfing.

"Of course, you are the grand-nephew of Lord Lumatt, or Tarbul's distant sprig, if you prefer; the fame of one and the rank of the other has kept your clan safer than it deserves to be. With the proper persuasion, I believe any of you could have told me the whereabouts of Idolema, any time the last three years. Why now?"

"Circumstances can change; the old, sometimes, are slow to see it."

"Where is she, then?"

"First — "

"No, first is your information."

"Once told, I have nothing to bargain with. A shopkeeper has that much sense."

Abruptly, Nidlaam's face is very near Tarbul's. "Don't toy with me. If you and this Senningtop guide of yours simply disappear, there will be no questions; those who cross the wilderness often do, nowadays. As for bargaining, you have nothing to bargain with; I can make you any promise you want, and change my mind after you tell me what you know. Far better to tell me, and hope for my gratitude."

Recognizing, evidently as a novelty, his weak position, the young man tries a comradely smile. "The girl," he begins, and once committed, reveals all he knows about the proposed (and supposed) route from Senningtop.

"With Cantello?"

"And Hodd Scorner. The hero alone is arrogant enough, but together they know everything."

Nidlaam makes a mouth; he has just today received news about the disappearance of an entire file of the Black Guard, with one of his best young officers, said to have been waiting to waylay Cantello and escort him to Hallabreg, but has not known of any connection between this mystery and the elusive Idolema, last reported with any credibility well to the south in Tarne, and expected to be making for the encampment of so-called loyalists at Mitfell; not a man troubled by nerves, he is tweaked in the depths of his soul by the fusion of legend and legend, the undead princess and the undying hero.

"Hodd has been a good left arm for Cantello — " Nidlaam has already rung a hand-bell, and is making his plans for the morning — "but when the body dies, the arm dies with it. You wish to be a part of Cantello's capture — his death, as it will certainly be; his pride will kill him."

"No."

Smile. "But you want a share in the spoils. Amuse me — what was this bargain you thought you could make?"

"I desire to lead the Royal Guard."

A grunt, half laugh. "That force has a captain."

"Armid the handsome. He can remain titular captain. They need a real fighter as leader in the field."

"Tell me about your famous battles, old warrior; they seem to have escaped my notice."

Tarfal flushes with anger, but before he can launch an answer, the summoned officers of the Black Guard appear, led by the reliable Glake, captain of the hearth-company. Nidlaam issues his instructions; making for the fen-country, avoiding as he must coming too near either Castle Coldiron or the frequented and well-guarded immediate approaches to Hallabreg, Cantello is restricted to the narrowest of possibilities; either passing near or within the fringes of undense forest, he can easily be waylaid. More than a hundred of the men now guarding Mitfell, companies of those riding the main road, with Glake's company from Coldiron, can all be assembled in ample time; since Idolema, according to Tarfal, could not have left Senningtop before noon today, and has a rougher journey than the youth's, mid-afternoon is the earliest possible time for their arrival at what will be by then an inescapable trap.

Nidlaam emphasizes that if the travellers are first spotted by any small band, no attack is to be attempted until overwhelming force can be collected, as is only prudent when dealing with men like Cantello and Hodd Scorner.

Glake's thick eyebrows rise fractionally, but his smooth, dark features show no particular emotion. "Cantello will not be easily made captive; we may well have to kill him." A short, unhandsome man, he has an appetite for torment and death to match Nidlaam's own, but Glake interests Nidlaam by deriving no pleasure from these tastes — or betraying none, masking all private feelings behind his impassive face and always-immaculate appearance, the calm, attentive competence his men follow unquestioningly, though without real admiration, nor anything like affection.

Nidlaam gestures his lack of concern. "So long as he does not escape. But no bows — I want the girl alive, if possible."

"She can be captured," Tarfal breaks in, and wins a hard, cold stare. "I mean, with Cantello and Hodd once out of the way."

He is conforming to the ancient rule, that traitors win contempt, not least from those they aid; Nidlaam's own future is with Corvan's victory, and he would shirk nothing to advance that cause, yet he, seldom repelled by any man's deeds, is very nearly shocked by Tarfal's indifference to the contemplated death of not only a hero of glittering renown, but a man, two men the youth has travelled with, shared food and dangers with. The other, the farm boy, is more understandable; possibly he was better-liked or more trusted in the company, and he is, all said, of no rank or renown.

When the soldiers have left to prepare for the morning, Nidlaam, having told a bored Zembra to wait for him in bed, if she prefers, picks up the question of the reward asked by this young weasel — too young, he suggests for the post he is seeking.

"Armid himself became Captain of the Guard at twenty-three."

"Yes, but Armid earned it. He had something the late king, Dairemid, wished to borrow, and lent it with generosity and grace."

"Money?"

"His betrothed. The revered countess-to-be was then eighteen, and already greatly admired, `an apple-blossom trembling,' as the court bard had it. Evidently she trembled enough and in the right places to please the king in a variety of ways; Armid got her back in time for the wedding, and a captaincy for interest." Again, entertaining invention, or true enough, but not of Ilana, who did not come to Hallabreg or meet the earl till after he had his captaincy.

"Cantello spoke about Dairemid's appetites; I thought he was — "

"Was what? Our Cantello is no gossip-monger, and his history is safer than most."

"I thought he was merely making reasons not to work against Corvan's elevation. By remembering, or inventing, the faults of Dairemid."

"But he agreed to help the girl."

"He had to be persuaded — or it seemed so. He is strange."

"Yes he is, for his time, this late in the realm's story. Once, you could find such men everywhere — oh, not champions like Cantello, but fools who thought the world could be won back by arms and then governed by virtue, hard men soft at the center."

Nidlaam is wound up to declaim. "There is often too much softness in men, when the hard choices of government need to be faced. People at large, those without power unless in numbers, are much like children, ruled by fear where love fails, needing pain as well as feeding in their lives. How can it be otherwise? Men of birth and breeding are guided by ambition, by duty, and the hope of pleasures to come, but as the world is, most by far must serve without hope of improvement. Oh, religion has its uses, promises of a better world beyond the grave, but, like children, people become impatient for gratification this side of death — come to believe it their due. Yet rewards, for the most part, imply wealth, and wealth, except in children's tales, can only come to a few from the labors of many; unless we can make war and enslave an alien race, the common people must be kept subservient — and where the notion of duty fails, that can only be through pain and the fear of pain or death. No doubt there is unfairness, and what is called cruelty, but universally and infallibly benificent rule is a romantic dream with no real-life counterpart; all countries have in their histories, as we have, rulers called `The Just' or `The Good' — for the most part the second designates weak kings who enfeebled their realms with well-meaning half-measures and bedraggled indecision; even so, these styles mean no more than less unjust, less wicked, the standard being so low that one inattentive act of what passed for kindness — merely forgetting to have someone tortured or put to death — came to seem like a lifetime's saintliness."

You will perceive that Nidlaam is excessively vain; detecting, as he habitually does, the presence in Tarfal of an admirer, destined if not yet fully captured, he turns him into the mirror he does not own, preening even in the gaze of a contemptible renegade.

He is far from done. "Besides, why pretend otherwise? the power to decree pain, to bring about death, can be enjoyed for itself. Like trampling an unmarred swathe of snow, the whipping of a smooth young girl, torture and breaking of a boy, can be the most exquisite of pleasures, and to call that enjoyment monstrous virtually concedes the point; we don't bother with girlish labels when dealing with pleasures we fail to recognize; only what is secretly envied is condemned. Tell me you have never dreamt of having a fresh young girl completely in your power, to maul or to mar as you choose."

Tarfal is alert. "Speaking of such things, my lord — when this girl who calls herself Idolema is captured, before she is put to death, as I suppose she'll have to be — I must have the chance to enjoy her — a night, two nights, I doubt I would need a week."

"You *must*?" Nidlaam stares hard, then gives a loud, understanding laugh. "Young goat — you're willing to betray your house, because a half-budded girl refused you?"

"Who said she refused me?"

"Gave you no hope, it doesn't matter."

"Nor am I betraying my house."

"How will they see it — old Tarbul, for a start? Surely, the miraculous reappearance of Idolema was to be the crown and perfection of his life's fame."

"He fought always on the side of winners; he must see, as I have come to, that Corvan is our future, not Idolema — even if the girl really was Idolema."

This time Nidlaam takes the bait, or seems to. "There was a fool — a menial from the Falnough household, a lad of little wit, and less after we had taken and tortured him — who said he had heard the princess was dead; she, or an unrecorded twin, was alive enough the year after, when we ransacked all Tarne, and barely missed her. Still. after her capture, before her execution, it would be useful if someone of name, someone known to have spent time with the girl, could convince both her judges and the realm at large that she has been, from the first, an impostor." Note that he himself does not ask for new evidence from Tarfal, being indifferent to the truth, interested only in what can plausibly be asserted.

"Her judges? What judges?"

"Whether she is given a public trial, or merely vanishes, may depend on the availability of that very evidence. The only use of publicity is to strengthen the Lord Corvan's rule. As king, once a false claimant has been put down, he may well be inclined to mercy and reconciliation, even with the House Tarbul, given a sign of sincere repentance for all the assistance they have given his enemies."

"I told you, I desire rank. For myself."

"You probably desire life more. After she is shown to be a fraud, there are going to be some executions in this Idolema business. Your repentance is going to have to be convincing."

Tarfal still declines to display fear. "When it is known I played a part in halting Cantello's treason — "

"No, no, no;" almost shocked, "Cantello's reputation will outlast him: the realm still needs its heroes — " this apparent cynicism is another departure from honesty; in fact Nidlaam fears that Cantello's good name will survive any defamation, and any such attempt recoil on its authors. "He will be dead but never denounced; some tale of an heroic end will be put out, and the new king loudly mourn the passing of a legend. A week of mourning and a lavish state funeral, perhaps."

"But if Idolema is publicly tried, his aiding her is bound to come out."

"No. She will say nothing about it."

"How can you be sure? If she already knows she's going to die."

"Boy, there are ways and ways of dying. I find that after some experience of true pain, and having no hope, a person will do quite a lot for a swift rather than a lingering death. For the promise of a clean beheading, your Idolema will name the confederates we give her — after all, most will be beyond any harm, already dead — and keep silent about those whose names we wish to spare. You need to think about why you should be among the latter."

"Any testimony I give — " Tarful is tenacious — "Will gain weight if it is known I have been among the slut's lovers."

VII

Perhaps thirty tumbled miles from where Nidlaam's forces are waiting in confident ambush there is a reminder that the wilderness had its dangers long before it was stocked with killer-hounds or haunted by Black Guard. Neither of which has been encountered again, although the dogs down below produced a howling chorus to signal the end of the rain or the coming of dawn as the march resumed; perhaps they too were setting out on their day's exertions; it must be supposed that in the absence of any human prey, they hunt down anything they can find, not even scorning rabbit or squirrel, though the elusive speed of one and the swift climbing of the other might frustrate them; deer might be better quarry, for a cohesive pack, even or boars or bears, despite their weaponry.

Working past an extensive swathe of heavy, tangled growth, Sab, bending down a branch, snatches back his hand from the sudden strike of a viper coiled beneath; Hodd, behind, whips off the long-fanged head with a flick of his sword. At every opportunity for the next two hours Galidern expatiates, with a tone of personal aggrievement, on his extreme dislike of snakes, but reminded of their existence everyone is observably edgy about stepping blind into overgrown patches, or sidling past clefted rocks.

Everyone except Idolema, who from the first has chosen an emotionless mask of preoccupied competency for the physical business of their trek, without complaint, requiring no help, though not refusing it, as when Cantello clambers a steeper rock, and turns to offer an outstretched hand.

The climb is steady now, and ahead is the stark wall of the Myrin, almost black, but the loftiest of its sharp peaks away eastward still streaked with snow. About noon, Cantello indicates, somewhat leftward of their course, a tall spike of rock a little detached from the main mass of the mountains as they decline westward, scarcely needing to identify it; Ridderben, the height overlooking Hallabreg, familiar from its depiction on gold coinage, and on the Seal of the Realm.

Galidern helpfully supplies that if they were no more than a mile or so westward, the going would be easier on a well-marked track.

"Easier seen, too," Hodd says, and Cantello reminds the boy that any men seeking this company cannot, as with his father's ship-ments, be bribed to look the other way. The boy's wide-eyed over-innocence confirms what is pure surmise, but logical enough, and part of a lurking unease for Cantello; he cannot be the only one to remember the existence of the Water Run, nor to have deduced it has provided a covert way into Hallabreg; he will not lead the party to its opening without a thorough reconnaissance.

Nor is that all. "Let's get on," he says with unusual testiness.

Hodd, knowing him, asks, "What?"

"I feel we are being tracked."

"Near?"

"Not yet."

From the last place to give adequate cover, harsh and desolate country, Hodd beside him, he looks up to where the track leftward, climbing from below, broadens to a kind of threshold in front of the great iron bars that close the tunnel, easily visible from a half-mile distance. There, armed men are idling, Black Guard.

"What, eight?" Hodd says, after time to watch their desul-tory comings and goings; their vigilance has the perfunctoriness of those who lack belief in the likelihood of an enemy coming their way.

"Some others, the night watch, may be sleeping." They would not be visible from here below.

"Only two horses among them — " they are tethered nearby, dejected-looking mounts, heads hanging.

"For emergencies," Cantello says. "Or to carry reports. No doubt they all rode here, with others who led their mounts away; keeping ten or a dozen horses fed and watered here would not be easy."

As often when he knows there will be killing, Hodd is honing an angry contempt. "A stupid spot to stick not a dozen men, with no hope of aid or reinforcement — what if those gathered at Mitfell had come this way? As it is, if we weren't in a hurry, we could shoot them down, one by one, and waylay any who tried to go for help, or to give warning."

Cantello smiles grimly. "I think they have no real conviction this way will be tried, and know that only a small party could approach here undetected — when the camp at Mitfell breaks, any riding, if not immediately assailed, will be shadowed by larger forces."

Hodd makes a lemon-sucking face. "These bold Loyalists have a lot more loyalty than brains. What was their plan? If they hadn't found you, or Corvan had managed to bring you to Hallabreg? The girl would be wandering about with a couple of boys and a nursemaid, with the armed might of the Loyalists, all few dozen swords, sitting on a hilltop waiting for a sign from the heavens."

"Nidlaam has them in disarray, all the arrests and executions; they may have had a better plan. Only desperation brought them to my door. What do you think?"

"About what?"

"This," nodding his head forward.

"My good, great, honored friend — " Hodd slips momentarily into Dernak's fulsome style. "If, among the long chronicle of your virtues, there is one thing that might be annoying, it would be your habit of asking other opinions when your mind is already made up. You're the leader, no one questions that — have I ever?"

"My mind is not made up."

"Yes it is. You just don't like all the killing it means. There's no other way; they have weapons in their hands."

"Should anyone be as good at this trade as we are?" Resigned, he points out where the path that winds up to the enemy lookout continues beyond, turning a corner by a big bulge of rock. "We can make our way there without being seen; when we charge them they'll be looking in the wrong direction."

"For the first three seconds."

"That's enough."

"Plenty."

When they return to where the others are concealed, Idolema questions. anxiously, "A dozen? And you mean to attack them?"

"They are camped in front of where we must go; they won't meekly let us pass." Then Cantello perceives her fear is not for Black Guard lives. "There will be no good swords among them, no time for bows, and good room for us to work where they stand."

"And the slope in our favor," Hodd adds. "I give them half a minute."

The girl stares hard to see whether they are indulging in some obscure game; for those who have had no chance to see them in action, the confidence of master-swordsmen, of expert warriors, against heavy odds must always seem unreal.

Though Hodd has the added task of repeatedly pushing down the unwashed head of Galidern, with his not-uncommon urge to spoil concealment by trying to observe that he is unobserved, there is otherwise small danger in the stealthy move to where a dry watercourse allows them to climb to the upper path, above and around the corner from the bored and complacent watchers. Though little sign of worked stone can now be seen, this packed surface is actually where the former aqueduct ran; farther eastward steadily crumbling but still impressive sections stand like bits of a high, fantastic road, as a memorial to ancient craft, a defiant determination.

While Sab plainly cannot be denied at least the idea of a chance in the coming fight, both the older men, for whom untried allies are potentially dangerous clutter, wish it were otherwise, and Cantello finds no reluctance in Galidern to be excluded, though his knife is out.

As is the girl's. "Perhaps I may — " she begins.

"Stay here with the boy."

"This is as much my fight — more."

"Stay here," and, "Madam," he adds, without diluting incontrovertibility. "You will be told when it is safe to move. Except for your safety, nothing we do has any object. Do as I say."

Caught between annoyance and contrition, she stands back. Cantello has a glance for Hodd, who shifts the grip on his sword a fraction, and nods.

Still without any idea an enemy is near the Black Guard are astonished — like Sab — by the force and fury of the sudden assault, the two experienced swords racing down the slope with the youth behind, struggling to keep up.   Many men, if crudely, can when needed unleash a surge of all the force they possess; a far smaller number, with much training, completely control such power as they choose to deploy, but very few, ever, can do both, maintain skilled discipline over an eruption of unmoderated violence — and when seen, it has the savage beauty of a murderous, swirling dance (for further elucidation, the samurai films of Akira Kurosawa with Toshiro Mifume are instructive, but neither Cantello nor Hodd, as in silly American derivatives of the genre, holds his sword vertical next to his ear, nor wastes time and invites disaster with wind-whooshing displays of twirling); both men, perhaps, feel the need to expunge all memory of yesterday's ragged and inglorious encounter with the dogs. Four of the guard are downed in seconds, and their panicked comrades, though they wield their weapons, have no target, as Hodd and Cantello, precise with all their speed, sidestep, whirl, lunge with venomous accuracy, and whirl again.   With seven down, the remaining four, including three who were resting, and struggled from their sleeping-bags with the fight already lost, shrink back against the rock-face by the massive iron grille, dropping their weapons. Two at least are bleeding.

"Is this all of you?" Cantello shouts at them. The men shuffle and shift, exchanging glances, but no one answers. "How near is your main force?" Again, no answer.

One more attempt: "Are there others of you in the Water Run? — " but here non-comprehension becomes an element of silence; these men have no notion of what they are guarding.

He sighs. "They must be killed; we can't manage prisoners." The arithmetic is starkly simple, and as always he loathes the sums; three swords, four men to be watched, mainly by touch in the long dark of the Water Run, four more to bring to Hallabreg, where some place of concealment must be found, men who can at any time betray them with a shout.

Sab is shocked. "Kill men who have laid down their weapons?" He has yet to cross blades with an adversary, having been altogether bewildered by the rapidity with which Cantello and Hodd engaged and disposed of their enemies.

As with the whelps yesterday, Hodd is one with Cantello's reluctant realism. "What then? Let them go? We can't tell how close their friends might be."

The youth thinks it through. "Put them out of action?" he suggests. Meanwhile the four survivors fidget uneasily, exchanging sidelong looks, probably guessing the subject of this muttered debate.

"How?" Cantello. "Give them disabling wounds?"

"Bind them securely," Idolema suggests. Despite Cantello's strictures she has come down the path not far behind the fighters, carrying Hodd's bow, which he unslung and laid on the ground in preparation for the charge.

"And leave them here," Hodd says, in sarcastic agreement. "That's a kindness. We won't be coming back this way, and can't send help, if ever, in less than two or three days. We leave them here, two of them most likely to bleed to death, if, with the others, they don't die first from the weather?"

"And that," Cantello bleakly contributes, "might be the best of it. Chances are strong the hounds would find them, still alive, but defenseless."

"They're going to have a feast here, as is," Hodd says, "if the crows and ravens don't rob them." He wipes away the trickle of blood from a graze high on his cheek.

Idolema shudders, and Cantello abruptly wants her to acknowledge that as ruler, she will have to oversee executions as cold or colder, quite a lot of them, at the start, if she means to purge her realm of Nidlaam's bands of murderers. "If you come to have a realm, madam, its security will demand you hunt down these same men."

"Yes, and disarm them," she maintains.

"Do you suppose this is sport for me?"

As if in challenge, she returns his gaze, half-angry, lips par-ted. Then, quietly, "No. Do as you must."

Sab has looked away. "Come," Cantello says bitterly, an arm across his shoulders. "This is what make us the heroes of song; harsh choices. Men like these did not hesitate to butcher your mother, or even Fanda — " Sab's beloved younger sister, a born flirt at six, dead at ten; Cantello does not fail to recognize a certain cheapness in his appeal, but Sab's squeamishness is plainly diminished.

As with all aspects of the killing craft, there is a technique to executing those who are not defending themselves; be swift and resolute, avoid looking into pleading faces. Two, cowering back against the rock-face, are quickly cut down, and a third, wounded in the arm, attempting a belated escape, is, with a stride and a sweep, chopped down by Hodd. When the fourth edges then darts away in the other direction, Sab, who, protecting Idolema, has turned aside from the slaughter, wheels back like one reminded of necessary business, and kills the man with a strong thrust to the heart.

"Well done," Cantello says, bleakly enough.

"Is it?" the boy's face is filled with revulsion.

"I know, I know." It is that unchange Cantello is saluting; Sab would have come to despise himself for the hypocrisy of passive concurrence in a deed he still finds shameful. Almost at once, he is completely absorbed in a short lesson from Hodd, who tells him that when making such an underhand thrust, he must not be in the habit of bracing a thumb against his hilt, unless he wants it broken when he hits bone or, for example, a belt-buckle.

"Where is Galidern?" of Idolema.

"He crept away when your fight began."

Hodd looks up from instruction. "His father will be no end overjoyed when the boy creeps home without the key. If the dogs don't get him. *My great good famous friend* — now he captures exactly Dernak's querulous but blandishing tone — "*I did not lend you my son, forgive me, for the hounds to breakfast on.*"

Nevertheless, it is a serious concern, and Cantello risks a shout, calling the boy's name and telling him he will not be harmed. Nothing in the entire harsh landscape can be seen to move, except that high above a couple of carrion-birds are already spiralling nearer. "We are wasting time — " again with the conviction of pursuit.

Hodd bellows, "Don't be an idiot. You're forgetting the wilder-hounds." As if for apt illustration, a distant chorused barking comes to them in answer.

Cantello says, "I promised his father he would be safe."

Hodd starts a comment, then recognizes that with Cantello such a promise is not less binding when made to a man he despises.

But double reminder of the dogs has brought about the boy's shamefaced reappearance. He comes down the slope explaining that he had simply taken the chance to relieve himself. The wondering look he has for the huddled bodies, however, suggests he wanted to distance himself from a fight expected to end otherwise.

"Cut loose the horses," Cantello instructs Sab. "Running free will give them some chance of escaping the hounds. Horses cannot bring news," he tells Idolema, whose face has contrasted this sudden clemency with the litter of human bodies.

Seen close, the forearm-thick iron bars closing the Water Run are corroded and pitted by weather, many of the crossings mossed over, the gate good for perhaps another couple of centuries, so massively was it made. At some time after, probably when the great gate became too embedded ever to be opened, some of the bars were (no doubt, laboriously) cut away, and a lesser iron grille, still immensely strong, set in, closed by a tough bronze lock, the condition of which is worth a wondering shake of the head; a glance can tell that it has been kept cleaned and oiled, and therefore that this way is both usable and used.

The big iron key goes in smoothly and the lock springs open. Together, Hodd and Sab drag open the gate, which is head-high for Idolema, and almost square. Beyond, the dark mouth of the more than man-high tunnel is uninviting.

"You take pack-ponies through?" of Galidern.

"Some. Not all will go into the tunnel, not even following a lantern."

"There are lanterns."

"There were before," with some reluctance, indicating a niche near the tunnel-opening. The boy holds out his hand. "Now I get the key back."

"You get the key when we reach Hallabreg."

"I have no need to go to Hallabreg. I get the key now."

"Not if you mean to cross the wilderness alone; that I do not permit. Your clan must surely have a confederate in Hallabreg, where you can stay. The day after tomorrow, after the coronation, the roads will be filled with people returning home, as you then can."

"My father will be angry. You said — "

"Your father's anger — " Idolema intervenes. "Is not as bad as your mother's grief would be."

"The dogs are everywhere, more than ever," the boy mutters, as if rehearsing an explanation for his father. Cantello tries and fails to imagine a grieving Galda, but supposes even that grimness might somewhere have a pierceable underbelly.

Galidern's customary air of cunning has returned. "After the coronation?" he questions. "I thought you were going to stop the coronation."

"Oh no," Cantello promises. "There will be a coronation."

He brightens. "I have never seen one."

First thought on finding the cache of lanterns is to wonder where they might have been stolen; there are four of excellent make, brass with wicker-wrapped carrying-handles; all seem to be filled with oil. Taking two to the daylight, Cantello finds his steel and fools' gold, and as he bends to start fire, hears again the jumbled chime of baying hounds, no longer distant.

They are on the mounting path, the biggest pack yet seen, more than a dozen of the large and dirt-caked creatures, and as he sees them, their purposeful, low trot changes gait into a headlong charge.

Foolish as it surely is to impute a capacity for planned vengeance to creatures that are universally and mindlessly destructive, he knows with certainty these are the wilder-hounds that bivouac at Sowback Scarp, and have tracked the killers of their leader, his mate, and their litter for half a day, most likely delayed only by the difficulty of picking up the scent; the ferocity of their approach inescapably suggests anger at the thought of being thwarted in their revenge.

He has no confidence he can calm them with a blast on the whistle, and no inclination to experiment; with the nearest set of reaching teeth within yards, he jumps back, wrenching the gate shut, snapping the lock closed, snatching his fingers away from the bars as furious jaws clash; more than one of the pack hurls himself bodily against the infuriating obstacle. Behind Cantello, someone's voice is fearfully muttering.

Now he blows into the pipe, and achieves at least a pause; the growls and snarls subside instantly, but the great hounds are still restless.

Hodd says, "As well we wasted no time with the sentinels."

With the unstilled animals prowling and panting not an armslength distant, Cantello returns to the lanterns, striking and nursing a flame, till he has them burning at a low but steady level. He is to carry one himself, left-handed, Sab the other, while for safety's sake Hodd ties an unlit spare to his pack.

For the only time, Cantello sounds — if that can be the right word, when he hears almost nothing — the releasing signal described by Idolema, two short and one long blast. At once, the dogs are fully wakeful, and almost as soon a new note, a sort of crooning near-whimper, is heard in their voices. Their hunted prey clearly out of reach, they have turned to the Black Guard corpses. Not wishing to overhear the sounds of that feast, Cantello leads the way into the wide tunnel.

The route now is over stone cut and smoothed, cracked in places, and from time to time obstructed by minor falls from overhead, but plain going for the most part. This is the actual course where the water ran, and Hodd remarks, "However far it is, we know it'll be all downhill." The slope, in fact, is hardly perceptible, and there is time to marvel at the skill and persistence of the craft that made it — a blend, probably, of careful calculation with trial and error, though with small margin for the latter.

Sab has a point to make. "My father always said, it is the nobles, the lords and, um, the crown — " he pauses on this, unsure whether to insist he means nothing personal, but then goes heavy-handedly on — "That that's where we must look for the standards in our crafts. We have jewelers and weavers, workers in cloth, as good as in any age, and if great works in stone and iron were prized as much as suitings and gowns and trinkets, those crafts would also revive, would have to."

Idolema is markedly silent, but Hodd says, "Maybe they could start with little works, to practise on, while the craft is healing itself. A new palace or a bridge across the Great Hallas is no place for learning how its done." Ironic overstatement, of course; the realm has able builders; it is in scope, style, aspiration that the decline can be seen.

"Nor a hospice for sheltering the infirm and indigent," Idolema softly agrees. "Did your father also have ideas on the collection of taxes?"

"He thought the hard-working paid more than their share, lady."

"As I do. But I said, collection, not apportionment. Equity is hard to reach, whilst barons and earls maintain castles and armies."

"Divide and conquer," Cantello succinctly advises. They have no clue whether numerous enemy are in waiting somewhere ahead, and any plans beyond a conjectural entry into the city are sketchy to non-existent; this dark, whispering hole only feebly penetrated by the light of the lanterns is a strange place for debating future policies, and the three companions of Idolema no likely choice for a privy council. Three: to say four would take absurdity to excess.

Something, however, is happening to Sab. The family the Black Guard did all they could to extirpate, neither comfortably fixed nor desperately needy, counting on each harvest to see them through another year, was a tight-knit one, part, really, of what is almost a tribe, some seven or eight farming, milling and smithing kins, already much-intermarried, tending to find brides or husbands among their own fecund numbers. As parents, Cantello's friends the Hammits were notably attentive, but as often, affection carried a price, not intended; Sab's elder sister, denied even the chance of keeping company with a young man from outside the usual circle and considered unworthy, ran away, and now is lucklessly married with too many infants for her husband's income (she will now lack, also, the relief supplies of food or small sums of money surreptitiously supplied by her father). While Sab, growing up, seldom beaten, never discouraged from his unusual tastes for reading and knowledge (of the sun and stars, for example, or accounts of distant lands) without evident practical use, was often tongue-tied, sullen-seeming as he approached manhood, when the fabled Cantello came to see his respected father.

But that father, cheerfully opinionated, thoughtful beyond the scope of most who till the soil, would never have pointedly aired those views while journeying with one he believed to be his rightful ruler. As little as two days ago, Cantello surmises, neither would the son; some untraceable interaction between the brutal loss of his family and his participation in great events has made him expand into a new confidence. In the still-unlikely event of Idolema's accession, Sab's contribution should be worth at least a knighthood, and with some further seasoning, there is no reason why he should not after all be a valued advisor to the queen — in this fanciful conjecture, Cantello experiences an unfamiliar mixture of feelings, an element of dislike, suggesting the impossible; he is Cantello, needing no other rank, and envies nothing, no one. After all, that undertow of sadness (which addicts of die-cut novels with green-eyed Felicity, brash Alison, clean-cut Brad and brooding Jon in them may be trained to interpret in a sentimental-erotic way) might be only a natural regret that his friend, the boy's father, is not alive to witness the son's sudden growth.

Symbolic landscapes, where church spires (e.g.) or unstilled waters are meant to stand (or swirl) for some emotional process or spiritual condition, can be tiresomely coy and shamefully unsubtle both at once; it is with real reluctance that we must record here that the fitfully illuminated tunnel-roof just overhead abruptly vanishes, hewn walls expand into rough natural stone; they have reached one of the places where the builders made use of existent caverns, this one of unguessable height and considerable breadth, the lanterns being inadequate to permit any definite impressions. But it brings a feeling of relief from oppression, voices losing their edged sibil-lance, the air its heavy, boxed-in quality. The old water-course, cut and carefully smoothed, though here sometimes cluttered with heaped chalk dripped down from above, makes the way impossible to stray from.

"It's foolish," the girl murmurs, only for Cantello, "Impos-sible, but I keep thinking, what if the water all at once returned; we would have no escape."

Cantello, embarrassed to coin, determined not to utter a sententious phrase about their being swept along, as is, on the flood of history, gives a not-dismissive grunt.

"This," Galidern says hopefully, "Is where we stopped and had food before."

"Not that I know Hallabreg to say, know, street by street," Hodd says, as they share out their way-food. "But I can't guess where this tunnel comes out. On the slope, southward, of the Myrin, certainly, but that's not exactly waste-ground; you would expect a tunnel to be known to everyone."

"You know the Shrine of the Pure Water?" Cantello asks. "It was named for the place the water used to come gushing. The sun-ken garden surrounding the shrine is all that is left of an immense, far deeper cistern. Many of the ways in that quarter, and so on down the slope, are built over what used to be courses, carrying the water down through the city."

"Still, but there is no outlet to a tunnel at the shrine, not that I ever saw, and I once lived in that quarter — had a room there, at least."

Cantello looks sidelong at Galidern, doggedly munching. "I have been told that there is a concealed doorway, in the niche behind the standing stone. Halidern can tell us more; a relative of his is the shrine-keeper, not true?"

"Asgal. One of my mother's kin," the boy allows.

Hodd barks a laugh. "Why not, in a realm where thieves and worse on horseback are guardians of the law? Who was bribed?"

Instead of protesting, Galidern grins broadly. It appears that the smugglers maintain a token secrecy by emerging from the tunnel, or entering it that end, only after dark, a procedure Cantello means to follow.

"You," he tells Galidern, "may remain with your kinsman, till it is safe for you to return — " handing the boy the coveted key.

Hodd tells Cantello, "But, you know, you have an old friend - some sort of relative, if you believe him — who has his place near there. Fane Restil."

More is said on this subject, but can be most effectively revealed in the consequent activities. The tunnel party finishes its small meal and moves on; behind them in the dark a couple of rats appear to clean up their crumbs.

Near the Coldiron Vale, an angry Nidlaam turns on Tarfal, mounted next to him. Four hundred men have waited out the afternoon in futile ambush, and a thorough sweep of the country south and east has found nothing. "You were sent to dupe me."

"No. There must have been some change of plans."

"Your companions guessed your treachery, and told you a false plan. You were sent unknowing to dupe me."

"My treachery?"

"What would you call it? You were vouchsafed a sudden vision, is it, of the greatness and justice of our Regent, his fitness to be king, and in an eyeblink had returned to your proper allegiance? Or perhaps you became convinced even Cantello the Peerless could not give us a queen, and then — " his tone becomes a taunt — "the girl would not undress for you — "

"She has whored herself for smugglers' spawn."

"Hush! or everyone will be convinced she's our true queen." If the charge is true, at least one element of the story is still missing for Nidlaam; Tarfal came to Coldiron guided by what might be ungratefully called smugglers' spawn, and the most likely explanation is an alliance between rancorous lovers of Idolema, refused and repudiated; why the woman — not much more than a girl — would ever sleep with this Dernlo is the only mystery, not one he is compelled to solve. There are more urgent concerns.

"Before this touching conversion to Corvan's cause — "

"I became convinced, I told you, that the slut is not Idolema."

"Certainly, of course. But before, you were part of all the plots, to keep her concealed, to produce her at the last possible moment — all your illustrious house was, and our Lord Lumatt of Tarne, all this I know and have long known — "

"I was no more than a listener."

"I don't care," with an abrupt hardening of tone. "After our regent is fully our king, the nobles are going to have to explain themselves, and that enquiry Corvan will leave to me; there will be no appeal from my decisions." He is not abashed to let his relish for the prospect be seen. "What I must know now is, *what was the plan*? Not this supposed journey to the fen country; if by whatever means the claimant was to reach Hallabreg, what then? Who are the allies there? What is the plan?"

Most of Tarfal's slow answer is disappointingly vague — or encouragingly so, if it fairly represents the sketchiness of the preparations by the so-called Loyalists — more misplaced loyalty than thought, Nidlaam concludes, unknowingly echoing Hodd Scorner. "There is an officer with the Royal Guard," the youth offers, "Geddo?"

He knows the man, and has suspected his sympathies, though, short of outright proof, the Guard has been outside his reach. "Tell me."

VIII

Having once (see the chapter before last) breezily flouted critical convention, I take it that we are so far steeped and stewed in error that while no recovered virtue can redeem us, no new sin, equally, can worsen the case; like other chastities, strict point of view, once gone, is vain to regret, unrewarding to resume.

In Hallabreg, then, the old south side, where, clambering the skirts of the Myrin, the streets narrow and branch, often mounting into winding flights of uneven stone steps, interspersed with cobbled steeps, the houses, few of any size, balance (and somewhat precariously, by the look of it) any inconvenience in their command of a magnificent view of the lower city, the wide and fertile Valley of the Great Hallas, the green-grey downs beyond.

One of the larger structures, resting on a wider level where a shoulderblade of rock juts to create a kind of cove, is the tavern owned by Fane Restill — an inn, he prefers to call it, but while he could (but is seldom asked to) find or create overnight accommodation for perhaps half a dozen, there is no stable in this place where horses hardly ever come (they tether their own pair of sturdy donkeys in the small yard), and such food as is readily available is drink-shop rather than inn fare — coarse bread and cold sausage, strong cheese, pickled onions and eggs.

Restil, a large-framed man with little fat on his muscled body, has always thought he should be short-legged and rotund with florid, fleshy features; his real face, bony and at a glance forbidding, has been an impediment to his ambition of being seen as the genial and welcoming host of an inn bursting with good fellowship, a home away from home for men of every condition. Originally following his father's trade of rough-sawyer, he acquired the place, changing its brooding name, *The Eyrie,* to the friendlier *Wayside House,* when, shortly after their marriage, his bride, Nelanda, received an unexpected legacy; the tavern still is in legal fact hers. After twenty-four years, four children (the first and third, with Nelanda, help run the tavern) and much shared experience, title should no longer matter very much, but may come to (quite soon). Earlier, Nelanda used to try to achieve some sort of reconciliation between her husband's aspirations and the reality they were given, suggesting that granted its size and situation, obscure ways from any frequented roads, to dream of its becoming the inn of his desires was ridiculous, and that they must either find fresh capital, in part by selling this place, and invest in a larger house in a busier spot (a move she grimly opposed), or else acknowledge that a neighborhood drink-shop was all they would ever have. Though childbearing and a lifelong passion for fresh-baked bread have thickened Nelanda's form, she is a small woman, her head scarcely reaching to Fane's clefted chin, but though he could carry her tucked under one arm as he often does a fresh keg of spirits, her husband is afraid of her — of her tongue, mostly, which wounds with the much same intimidating sting as the succession of fresh-tied birches his mother (also a little woman) applied with a never-dulled enthusiasm throughout his boyhood; above everything he fears Nelanda's excoriating ridicule, though not quite enough ever to abandon altogether his pretensions to hospitable grandeur.

What saves them from bitter enmity, and even maintains belief, their own as well as that of observers, in a reasonable partnership with a foundation of genuine affection, is Nelanda's strategic acumen in exercising her ascendancy only in private, never — or hardly ever — interfering with the parade of tales, jokes and current observations with which Restil maintains his chuckling public authority, presiding over a crowded, or more often adequately peopled tavern with as much lordly affability as his mien permits.

They are having a good week. Old New Year is always a festival time, but this year, with a coronation added, Hallabreg, despite the onerous and time-consuming checkpoints on all the roads, where travellers must submit over and again to excessive and not overgentle interrogation and even searches, is filled with visitors from every part of the realm. Something between shrewdness and prudence has let Restil profit from the crowds; his (and Nelanda's) decision not to raise prices, as most of the more central taverns have, was at least as much based on the reflection that the backbone of his business is and will continue to be with locals, who know very well what everything should cost, but many of the visitors have stretched their resources to the limit in making this journey, and rumor of a hostelry where a mug of beer can still be had for a sensible price has caused many who would not normally stray far from the river to mount the steep hill in search of the *Wayside*.

In the chattering din of the main room, Restil, elbows propped on the high counter, is in talk with one of these bargain-hunters, a man on the brink of middle age, round-shouldered, plainly clad and with an uneventful face, at the same time faintly familiar-seeming and wholly unmemorable. He has introduced himself as Kellan, a horse-dealer from the north.

"And the names," he says. "Everyone of note anywhere in the realm has come, at Corvan's urging, so they say."

"As well they might, now we are to have a king again."

A fair-haired man, an easterner by his accent, offers, "They say Cantello will be here. Cantello! When was he last in Hallabreg?"

Restil gives his knowing grin. "Stands to reason, doesn't it? Regent or king you'd want a Cantello on your side, if not by your side."

Kellan hums apparent understanding. "In my country, you hear talk not everybody is ready for Corvan's kinging."

"Talk," Restil interjects, before the fair-haired one can speak. "There's always a lot of talk."

Just behind, slicing blood-sausage, his wife is shocked. All the regulars must know by heart Fane Restil's handful of stories about his encounters with fame; she has heard, probably a couple of hundred times, how he (as she very well remembers independently, if with some differences of detail and emphasis) served the late king, Dairemid, a mug of beer on a warm summer's day, he having made pilgrimage, to give thanks for the safe birth of his daughter. to the nearby Shrine of the Pure Water — oddly named, since while several freshets spring here and there from the mounting rocks, there is no sign of water at the shrine, only a worn, man-high column of flint. Nelanda could recite word-for-word the unvaried climax and conclusion, how when Dairemid tried to pay for the drink, Restil declined his money, saying it was reward enough to stay the king's thirst on such a day, "and the king said, very well, then I wish to buy this tankard, to be a keepsake, so he gives me a gold piece, five whole marks, for a stone mug, mind you, and he wrapped it in his kerchief, you'd have thought the mug itself was pure gold. I won't soon forget that."

Amazing, then, that mention of Cantello the Peerless has not set off her husband's intimate recollections, mainly from childhood; their fathers had business connections, and Fane is almost (doubly almost) related to Cantello, whose father's second wife (his mother having died young) was, if Nelanda has it right, Fane's mother's former sister-in-law — his uncle's widow, but near enough for Fane to become proprietary when telling of Cantello's boyhood appearances in Hallabreg, his incomparable skill at games and less celebrated mastery of languages and lore; the tale of how the hero-to-be set right a well-known scholar on the Paranopan succession is almost as familiar as Dairemid's extravagantly-purchased tankard. Somewhat more obscurely, he has also had dealings with the lesser, still-famous Hodd Scorner, whose name is automatically associated with Cantello's. None of this is being given a fresh airing, and Nelanda wonders whether her man is developing a new tactic, where he modestly waits to be coaxed into revealing his lofty connections. But when she prompts loudly, "Wasn't it Cantello you once lent your quarter-staff to?" he waves it off, muttering, "All a long time ago."

Kellan says, "Is anyone still making tales about the lost princess?"

"Not likely she'd ever be forgotten, lost or found," the light-haired man says. Perhaps forty, he has the face of worn but inextinguishable boyhood — a foolish face, Restil decides, and the man is showing himself a fool.

"If she was going to be found," chimes in one of the regulars, Orde, the local baker, "She would have been found before now, wouldn't she? seven years it's been, all the law asks for."

Bude, another regular, puts on a face of informed cunning. "There might be those," he begins, "Who don't want — "

"Who wanted the peppered eggs?" Restil loudly interrupts, swivelling to snatch a platter from the work-table, and mouthing *Nidlaam's spy* at his bewildered wife. Notwithstanding her immediate skepticism, he has no doubt; Kellan, if that's his name, is here to pick up hints of what he would call sedition.

There has been plenty of Loyalist sentiment in most outlying parts of the capital, surprisingly so, perhaps; the landless and luckless had been Dairemid's greatest admirers, those nearest the palace most critical, but with Corvan the opposite is true — and the difference cannot be accounted for in new hardships suffered by the poor over the seven years of the Regency. In one thing, indeed, Corvan's arrival, or his promotion of Baron Nidlaam, has brought an unintended benefit, since many of the petty bullies and their lawless followings, who in some quarters formerly lorded it over their tiny chosen fiefs, intimidating shopkeepers, taking goods and young women at will, injuring those who sought legal redress (or, worse, their wives or children), are now enlisted in the Black Guard, which ranges too widely in the realm to be a frequent threat to inconspicuous townspeople.

Understandably, with his kindly memories of Dairemid, Restil has had Loyalist sympathies himself, but is in this a realist; the reappearance of Idolema is now beyond imagining, and a crowned Corvan, free from the slight restraints of the High Council, a virtual certainty; above all, Restil does not want the *Wayside* identified as a Loyalist meeting-place, a hotbed of treason. Caution here runs counter to his temperament; in his dreams he would love to see himself at the heart of perilous intrigue, living by passwords and two-in-the-morning meetings, but to join in, or even countenance a conspiracy with no chance of success would be — to use Nelanda's favorite word for his impractical schemes — stupid. Stupider still to permit the impression that his harmless place is habituated by such conspirators.

"But Idolema," Kellan persists, when the food has been claimed. "Here, too, you say, she still has her advocates?"

"I don't know about *advocates* — " the fair-haired easterner, with unassertive calm. "If alive, she is in law — "

"When they say, Idolema, they really mean Omelda," loudly proclaims the woman of that name (not often heard, however). "Why not, I'd make a fine princess. I'd know how to keep a privy council happy, let me tell you."

Orde cackles. "And the Royal Guard, I don't doubt."

"They'd better keep their weapons edged for me."

General laughter, but Restil wags a warning finger. Though nothing exists to forbid it, wives, except with one or two of the oldest regulars, are seldom seen here, and certainly no unaccompanied women of any decent repute, so that speculative visits of the two local whores (part-timers, actually, both with other more reliable sources of support) does not harm and may sometimes help everyone's business. But Lilac (Omelda's working name), no longer in her springtime, increasingly tends to confuse the object of her calls with a growing fondness for drink, beer when she is paying, brandy with a client, past, potential or firmly engaged, and Restil, much more so his wife, is doubtful about the commercial benefits of a drunken and loudly opinionated whore.

Against all prediction, the putative horse-dealer evidently likes what he sees and hears; after a quick dumb-show with Restil, indicating that he intends to take possession of a small table just vacated, he summons billowy Lilac with the immemorial beckon of a rotated chin, and she joins him, shedding the holiday raucousness, replacing it with a well-rehearsed, lidded allure. "Your first time in Hallabreg, handsome?" Restil overhears, and is able to resume fretting over his own concerns, while continuing to serve drink with his best attempt at a friendly face.

Tomorrow, he's going to have to replenish his stocks; the beer should last out the week, but food is running low. The money coming in would be enough to get him out of trouble, if he could invent a way to abstract as much as seventy marks without Nelanda noticing. Seventy marks! The wide pocket on his apron is heavy with coins, but when they close about midnight, she'll supervise, as always, its emptying on the counter, and she and Nanda, their first-born, will merge it with the contents of the cashbox, and make small stacks of each denomination, till the day's take is determined; Nelanda might not have an accurate estimate, but a shortfall of seventy marks, in a total unlikely to surpass a hundred and odds, thirty, would hardly pass unnoticed. The coronation is tomorrow, the day after a celebratory holiday; the *Wayside* can count on perhaps three more days of this prosperity; it might be he could contrive to tuck away about twenty marks a day, and make up the rest by taking out more than is actually needed for buying bread and other supplies — it occurs to him that he might hide an unopened keg of brandy behind beer-barrels in the storeroom, and pretend to need another.

There is no plan, no matter how far-fetched, that can include the possibility of confession, of throwing himself on his wife's mercy; in this class of trouble, she has none, and to open himself to the full force of her scorn is a horror beyond contemplation — hers and Nanda's; their daughter, though her looks, unfortunately, are a gaunter version of Restil's own cragginess, is altogether her mother's girl, and at twenty-two, with no prospect of marriage, an able apprentice — or perhaps by now, a journeywoman — in Nelanda's well-honed craft of belittlement. Merely the thought of exposing himself to that twinned tirade makes his head ache.

Bitterly, he reflects that Nelanda, in a way, is responsible for this mess. A competent woman, in many ways admirable, there may be some truth in her self-evident belief that but for her he and his inn would have failed long ago, but her claim on all their successes and apportionment to him of everything that might have wrecked them are what makes it the more necessary to his self-respect that he look for a success she could have no part in — as she would say, to go behind her back.

The brewer, Darwat, supplier for practically all of the *Way-side*'s excellent beer, a friend for more than twenty years, had plans after last summer for increasing his output, acquiring a new malting

in the Downs country — a malting new to him; it is an ancient building, and came on the market only with the extinction of the family
that had owned it for more than a century, the last brewer dying
childless. For this, Darwat needed to borrow, and asked Restil to act
as a guarantor in the amount of seven hundred marks. Without consulting or, right up till now, even informing Nelanda, he agreed,
looking forward gleefully to when he could tell her that in return for
the favor, Darwat, as soon as he cleared his debts, was to supply
Restil's beer at a price one-fifth lower, which would mean, he calculated, more than an added mark of profit on every cask.

Nothing went wrong — that was the souring fact, nothing at
all went wrong. Darwat purchased large additional stocks of barley,
and it is true the price was high after a weak harvest; his original
little brewery within the city had been able to use the common car-
rier where tavern-keepers had not taken away their own purchases,
but now he found it necessary to acquire a dray, and to keep a team
of horses, and he also required extra help, and a large new stock of
casking supplies, all of which led to his failure to make the first
quarterly payment (of twelve) on his loan. He remained one payment in arrears through the second installment, but (as explained last
week, in a near-tearfully apologetic meeting with Nestil) for the
forthcoming spring festivities was obliged to extend credit to the
taverns for the added quantities of beer they laid in; it was, as he
said, either that or lose the business, and the taverners, after all,
would easily be able to settle up when the customers started crowd-
ing in. But Darwat's outlay in brewing the quantities called for once
more left him without funds for his third repayment, and this default
led to a stern demand and worse threat against the guarantor.

Not having been forewarned by Darwat at the time the
demand came, Restil was stunned to silence. Never believing it
would come to that, he had pledged his tavern — impossibly so,
since he was never its proprietor, and now, unless perhaps he can
appease the creditor by supplying not less than one quarterly installment, his lie will be exposed, a worse prospect even than that of losing the *Wayside*; he'll be thrown in prison for his fraud. He has no
hope, if hope is the wanted word, that Nelanda will do other than
deny the tavern can be seized for his debt, produce the evidence of

her separate ownership, doom him to imprisonment. If it is a choice between that and losing the tavern, she is surely right.

Absurdly, it is all a question of two or three days, not above a week; by the day after tomorrow the city's hostelries will be awash in money, and Darwat, as he has promised, can make the rounds collecting his debts, which amount to far more than enough to pay off both delinquent installments, but the lender, Ospant, a dour man. a general merchant with court connections, related to the Master of Finance on the High Council, has extended his last grace period, and will act unless he has his payment on the day following the coronation. He has made witheringly plain that he has no ambition to keep a hillside drink-shop, and regards the place only as a negotiable asset.

Only faintly, in the churn of anxiety, Restil acknowledges he should be glad that what ought to be his worst nightmare will not come true; his wife and family are not going to be left destitute by his folly; Nelanda will repudiate the debt, and a thoroughly discredited Restil will be seized and punished — unless he can persuade Ospant to accept the seventy marks not yet acquired.

Trivial concerns, maybe, while the future of a realm hangs on a thread, while Nidlaam and Cantello duel, a young girl (slender but by all accounts not shapeless) splashes water on her face to drive out drowsiness, and a never-complacent Regent for the hundredth time strokes the lush fur collar on the kingly robe hung ready in his personal suite, for the thousandth time assuring himself that it is too late now for the elusive Idolema to reappear. Yet we should not forget that there are always otherwise-preoccupied people, lots of them, with little or no attention to spare for the historical moments that dominate our chronicles; empires tremble, usurpers usurp, decisive battles grind to a finish, but even when we say, the city took up arms, the whole country rose, the entire continent went to war, there are many, most, in fact, who did no such thing, many who were only marginally conscious of these grand events. Hungry people wonder dully where food can be found, young men and young women yearn obsessively, one for another, poets address song-birds and describe cherry-trees, the larcenous plot and the vengeful sharpen, the bereaved mourn, the put-upon madden, children play and bicker, hobble home with wounded knees, ungraspable life ebbs away from the ancient, and there are the sick whose whole world is present pain; agreed history is a sort of election from which more than half have always abstained.

The results still stand; we are bound by a plurality; if the questions we address do not concern (are not acknowledged to concern) the majority, they are certainly those which affect far more than any competing condition or choice; one event that (take my word for it) can change the lives of thousands, must outweigh a thousand different happenings, each of them affecting two or three. But while we resume and seek to resolve the big story, perhaps now we'll remain peripherally aware of other only slightly intersecting life and lives stumbling on.

But besides that really, really praiseworthy slice of fashionably diffused compassion (like rice-fields, flooded over acres, inches deep) Restil's agony helps explain why, when the tavern is cleared and closed, the take duly counted, all but a grudging minimum of candles and lamps extinguished, he is by himself in the storeroom, calling up an unintelligible reassurance in answer to his wife's descending demand for him to come to bed. When he does, if rechallenged on his doings, he will allege a sudden concern over his supply of brandy. Exact inversion of the truth, that he was hunting for a cask concealed behind the beer, will explain if she has heard the noise of shifting barrels. On top of the small puncheon of brandy now invisible, he has stacked and covered with a bit of rag the fourteen marks he was able to risk withholding when surrendering the evening's cash (not without his daughter's remark that she thought they had done better); tomorrow, surely, when business is at its height, he'll be able to abstract more, making more than one visit to fetch beer, leaving some of his take each time.

Again, Nelanda calls out, and this time the tone of his reply contains, perhaps, a hint of tentative reprimand; what is in her head, to be bawling her discontents when they have paying guests in the house — the horse-man, Kellan, after completing his transactions with Lilac, apparently to the satisfaction of his appetites and her financial needs, has decided to keep overnight the room he hired for an hour, and the next-door small bedroom has been taken by the fair-haired easterner, whose name is Valmar, occupation unstated. The entire arrangement makes Restil uneasy, but he is certainly in no position to decline added income.

"Fane Restil — " the voice, hushed but firm, coming from the darkness by the outside door, makes him start, almost to leave his boots. His hand goes to the short hardwood truncheon, kept always on a short loop hooked to his belt. His body is between the small rushlight and the source of the voice; among the possibilities jumbling through his mind is the improbable idea that Darwat, the brewer, has come to tell him he has paid off his back-debt.

"I am Cantello." Not touching a weapon, he moves into a patch of dim light. According to Hodd, this Restil likes to boast of his early connections with subsequent fame, but while Cantello recalls childhood times at Hallabreg, he has no physical memory of this man, who must have changed greatly; Cantello's unconsidered expectations were of someone rather short and soft, with features to match, and he cannot guess where this tall angularity comes from.

"They said you would be in Hallabreg — we were talking about you. Sir." The man is peering uncertainly, and his words come out in a tumbling rush that betrays his attempt to be casual. "I was just looking over my stock, never been so busy, so many here for the." A missing noun is supplied by a gesture.

"You have beds free?"

A pause, then, "For you, sir, here?"

"For me and some others. We do not wish to be seen." Idolema with the remaining two men is in the dark of little court-yard, not ten paces away.

"But they say the king — Corvan, the Regent, who will be king — they say he summoned you."

"We are here on other business. Four, and we need beds for the night."

"Is this to do with — "

"The coronation, yes."

"You know the Black Guard — "

"What?"

"They'll be everywhere in the morning, sir. Twice, the last two mornings, they've come at dawn to ask who's sleeping here."

"Tomorrow, I think, they'll have other business, watching the streets. In any case, you'll tell them nothing. You're going to help us." Curiously, Restil already has no real choice; he must know that the presence of clandestine visitors, invited or not, puts him in jeopardy. But the man, Cantello perceives, has some other unease of his own, connected with this belated vigil in his storeroom.

"I wish — " plaintively, "You would find some other place."

"I would wish for some other time, in some other realm. Come — " The door behind him opens, and Hodd slides in, followed by the others.

"There are men in the street with lanterns, Black Guard, maybe."

"Is this all of you? Better bar the door," Restil says, and scurries away up a short flight of wooden stairs. In the tavern's main space, he sees to it that his windows are all shuttered, and the front door secured, but after his brief bout of activity returns to nervous indecision.

"This is what I mean, they are everywhere, and I am under suspicion. There are men staying here, and one of them is a spy for Nidlaam. Not," he appends judiciously, "That I have done anything to interest Nidlaam."

"This spy introduced himself?"

In the dim lighting, Restil peers. "Hodd? You, too?"

"Still watering your beer, Fane?"

Restil scowls, but the presence of Hodd appears to convince him he is not among enthusiasts for Corvan. "The one who called himself a horse-dealer may be a spy, I was sure of it; he seemed to be fishing for Loyalists all evening, but then lovely Lilac got his attention. Our local bed-creaser," he unnecessarily explains (no mother would ever give her daughter such a name, Rose, Daisy, Peach, Lily, Poppy, for generations adopted by Lilac's calling). "No harm in her, and she would have nothing for any spy, other than what he paid for, so now I don't know. Before that, Kellan got a nibble out of the easterner, wanting to know, was there still talk about the Princess Idolema — "

"Were those his words? — " young Sab's abrupt urgency is odd, and the taverner gives him a puzzled look.

"He had some strange turn of phrase, like, `is anyone still making tales — ' and before I could stop him, this Valmar blurts out-- "

"*Not likely she'd be forgotten, lost or found,*" Sab supplies.

"You were here?" Restil, bewildered.

"They are both Loyalists," Sab tells Cantello. "Those are the sign and countersign."

"Here?" Restil wonders, blinking.

A child's question, as asked, but with, after all, a point to make; this is an out-of-the-way spot for Loyalists conspirators to be meeting; Cantello does not see how anyone could have guessed his route into Hallabreg. It may only mean that Idolema has far more active support than supposed, and that all over the city similar connections are being made.

Hodd suggests, "If these signs and countersigns have been spread about far and wide, might some of Nidlaam's human hounds not have learned them?"

"It's late in the day to concern ourselves with spies," Cantello says. "Nor do I know why they should be spying here, so late in the day, when that game is already lost or won."

"Just what I thought to myself, sir," Restil agrees.

"The same," Cantello observes, "Can be said for Loyalist conspirators — what can be their object now? They must," sardonically, "be looking for miraculous intervention."

Hodd knows what he means. "Aye, tiptoe around, exchanging passwords, and hope something happens, but don't so much as stick your tongue out at the Black Guard. They'll still want praise for having helped, when the Lady Idolema is raised."

"Is she alive after all, then?" Restil demands.

"She is here," Idolema says, from near the doorway — a more than hackneyed dramatic device, but life, from time to time, takes a fancy to acting out clichés, and in this case gets a push in that direction from Idolema's astute timing; since the last moments before emerging from the tunnel she has been clad in a simple grey robe she carried in her pack, and although no taller is a great deal more plausible a figure; Restil, not doubting for an instant, bows his head.

"I gave a drink once to your father when he was thirsty, lady."

"When I was newborn," she says, smiling. "I know the story well; he prized the pewter tankard you gave him."

"Nothing but a common stone mug," Restil mutters. "For which he paid me well, overwell."

"He kept it always."

Though impatiently, Cantello finds encouragement here; a moment ago this man was insistently proclaiming his neutrality, separating himself from the active Loyalists; if Idolema's appearance can so quickly resolve his doubts, there is hope it can do the same for many.

"Your guests must be wakened, then," he decides. "They may, after all, have the ghost of a plan, or some information we can use. Sab, you know the words, you may even know the men."

"They'll take fright, I don't doubt, being roused at this hour," Restil half-objects, but with Sab following he makes for the main staircase. Before they get there, a short-legged, plump woman, evidently Restil's wife, appears at the top, and comes down to the mid-flight landing. She is in a long nightgown of deep blue, with an overmantle in a lighter shade, her head covered with a kind of linen helmet. She is not pleased.

"What is this?" she demands. "We're closed. Closed." she makes a two-handed gesture as if to push out the intruders, then turns to her husband. "You mean to be up all night — "

"It's all right," her husband says. "You should go back to bed. The less you know — "

"Are you altogether stupid? You know they have promised a whipping for anyone caught this week selling drink past midnight. Perhaps you don't care, but you want to see your wife and children flogged with whips — "

"This is my business, no affair of yours." Perhaps the presence of the girl reawakes in Restil some echo of that long-mislaid spirit that led him to boldly thrust cold beer unasked at a king. "Go back to bed. Go. Back. To. Bed — " at the third try hitting the needed note of command. Nelanda, affronted, tries to stare him down, in which, Cantello judges, she is normally successful, but whether her husband has recovered lost steel, or recognizes a position from which retreat would be fatal, he remains unmoved. After an agelong five seconds, she, though with a demonstrative puff of exasperation, turns away defeated, and remounts the stair.

"Wait," Cantello tells Restin, having reconsidered. Asking again about the bedrooms that are free, he is told that there are two, one much like those already occupied, the other "the best room," somewhat larger and better-furnished.

"Sab, you and Hodd will take one, and I will be in the other with the lady. But for now — " turning to her, "you had better be out of sight, at least till we know more about these others. Hodd, you will guard Idolema."

"The old signal for `all safe,'"

"Wouldn't it be better — " the girl begins.

"Nothing we do, lady," Cantello repeats, but with a show of deference, for Restin's sake, "Has any object, unless we keep you from harm."

Admirably, she avoids further dispute, and with Hodd is led upstairs by Restin, followed by Sab, who will wake the presumed Loyalist conspirators.

Lone brooding in the dim-lit beer-shop, many troubling things written in Cantello's seasoned face, you know the scene. He has reached the juncture where foresight, as it has to, fails. In his mind he had been searching for some unsupected, hidden way by which Idolema could be wormed into reach of Corvan's ceremony, always recognizing the element of childishness in the idea. When small, he had lived some years in a house on the edge of its village, its rearward herb-garden hemmed by a dense band of bushes and stunted trees, beyond which was tough-grassed heathland mounting to green hills. More than one established if far from completely unobstructed path found a way through the thickets, but to Cantello as a boy there was an awed and sensuous excitement in finding (in part, making) a new way, a secret way, snaking beneath low branches, pushing through apparently impassable leafage, dodging brambles and nettles, though not always mud, emerging in some faintly unexpected place. But the secrecy, the adventure, the grown Cantello conceded, were entirely his, it was, all the wild possibilities of childhood were, like the wide end of a funnel, tapering down to the same small destination, the secret way only a diversion, winding back to the predictable. If his task were Nidlaam's, to assure Corvan's orderly elevation, he, too, might scour the realm in search of the hidden competitor, but would above all make sure the narrow end of the funnel was stopped up; all stratagems for unveiling Idolema must come down to penetrating the defenses of the coronation ceremony.

With the landlord, Sab returns, ushering the other two overnight guests; he as it happened had no need to wake either, finding them in talk together in Kellan's room. Evidently his use of the proper password has reassured them, as does their recognition of Cantello; the straw-headed man, indeed, gives something like a whoop of joy. The other, the bland-faced man with the accent of a northerner, Kellan, is first to explain himself.

"I came here seeking men like Valmar, who are everywhere in the city — not all, of course, with his connections."

This is a prompt, and Valmar explains. "My wife's brother is an officer of the Royal Guard, not Nidlaam's lot, the real soldiers. He — like many, he still wonders if the Lady Idolema might not reappear, even now."

"Geddo?" the name Tarfal belatedly supplied.

"You know him?"

"I have been informed he has Loyalist sympathies."

"What of that? Half or more of the Guard — the Earl Armid himself, so is said, still gives his first allegiance to his old oath."

"But you can't count on that," Kellan puts in, his tone quarrelsome. "Nothing's going to stop him taking a new oath tomorrow, unless the true heir arrives."

"She will, she will," fervently, then with an anguished appeal to Cantello, "Won't she?"

Caution still is needed. "What makes you think I know?"

Valmar looks both blank and stricken. "We were told — "

The older and darker man is less prone to distress. "Word coming from the south, with old Tarbul's name fixed to it, said that the lady would come to Hallabreg, aided by one far-famed — that would be you, sir. Course, we never dreamed we'd find you here."

Cantello imagines what Hodd would say to this, and supplies it himself: "We are touched by Tarbul's confidence." The more sourly considering that this optimistic message must have been sent at a time when Tarbul could not know Cantello and Idolema had so much as met — as he still could not; word that Cantello had been intercepted by Suliwat's contingent of the Black Guard must have spread through Lesser Ault, and in any event his last words with the old warrior had given no encouragement to plans including him.

His grimace further panics Valmar. "Are you saying, then, that it's all a lie? We took all these risks, made all our plans, and Tarbul was just inventing it all?"

"No. no," Restin says soothingly. "She's here, the lady, now, under this very roof. Spoken with her royal highness, I have, not ten minutes ago — " At this point, it strikes him that he may be saying too much, and he breaks off, with a guilty glance for Cantello.

At times like this it is impossible to be certain of anyone; unlike Restin he does not think Valmar a fool, though he has a way of abruptly shuttering up his face, as if withdrawing into vacancy — or contemplation. Yet, of the two Cantello mistrusts the putative horse-dealer the more, and oddly the very act that seems to have caused the inn-keeper to relax his vigilance, the man's congress with the hired woman, is to Cantello the most suspicious. Urgent bodily dictates are not unknown to Cantello, and the man may be merely a sensualist, excited, maybe, by the idea of conspiracy, as with others danger has been known to stimulate the bowels, the kidneys, even an appetite for food, but granted there may be, as he says, Loyalist schemers in every one of the city's hostelries, trying to catch some hint of Idolema's whereabouts, it is strange for this one, having found Valmar with an exchange of sign and countersign, to end his final night's watch with this Lilac, who would hardly have anything to tell him. About Idolema, that is; a spy for Nidlaam, concluding he was no longer likely to hear word of the lost princess, might consider the local whore an excellent source of information on neighborhood loyalties; no doubt, once safely crowned, Corvan intends, through Nidlaam's brutes, to root out all disaffection, and these last hours of uncertainty would seem an excellent time for finding potential treason. But too late, Cantello resolves, for any report of Idolema's whereabouts to go beyond these walls.

"She is here," he agrees.

"Then we can — it can still — " in his excitement, Valmar discovers a bad stammer, and has to start again, swallowing much spittle. "Forgive me if you have some other plan — "

"What do you have?"

The man looks from face to face, needing confirmation it is his turn to speak, perhaps uncertain of where to begin. "It is the ceremony tomorrow," he at last offers.

Sab says, "And how it can be interrupted, yes."

"Well. You know the front of the palace?"

"The rear, you mean," Cantello supposes. "The front looks out on the walled grounds."

"What everybody calls the front, then, on the square." Although indeed an easterner in origin, from Farther Nid, Valmar has been four years in Hallabreg, and knows the city well. "For tomorrow, they have taken out the railings, and there is a platform built out from the tall windows there, right out into the square itself, and not more than, say, breast-high."

"Not that," Restin amends, putting out a flat hand level with the top of his thigh. "A child, a child of seven, could rest his chin there."

Valmar shows some animation, and more intelligence than hitherto. "Of course, they want, they need, our king-to-be needs his investing to be seen by as many as can be, and that's where, as they must, they make themselves most vulnerable — the crowd there that thera will be."

Restin demurs; every way into the square is to be guarded, everyone stopped and searched for weapons; "It's been put out that you'll need to start early to be sure of finding a place. Course, I'll be here," he adds.

Valmar agrees; there will be soldiers stationed two armslengths apart, all about the edges of the platform, according to Geddo, whose company has the southerly side — "but, you know, there is that big building that juts out into the square, that side."

"The Old Wool Market," Restin supplies. "Disused for a lifetime, talk of pulling it down before it can fall down. A pity, it was once a fine bit of work."

"Well, but my brother-in-law has the guarding of that place, too; it is the one spot where there's a way into the square the Black

Guard doesn't control. There's a little entrance, just an ordinary door, in Shoat's Alley, just off the Millway. It was bricked up inside when Nidlaam's men made their inspection, but now it is not."

This, then, was the entire Loyalist plan; Idolema was to be found, having reached Hallabreg by some means neither known nor imagined, and smuggled into the Old Wool Market on the morning of the investiture, to emerge and declare herself at the right moment; Cantello is glad Hodd is not here to offer one of his corrosive comments. For reasons already touched on, a plan depending on the staunch sympathies of Armid's guard, or any part of it, would be his own last choice, but time, now, is running out, and nothing better is on display.

"If Geddo's men are on watch now, you could go there while it's still dark." Restin's suggestion, and not without some self-serving cunning; Cantello has no doubt he would be happier without any of his overnight guests.

"That's crazy," Valmar says, mildly enough. "Anything moving tonight will be stopped by the guards; at first light the throngs will make better cover than darkness; they'll only halt those wanting to enter the square." He will go, he suggests, very early, to make sure everything is prepared, and when he returns the others can start.

"However — " Kellan objects. His part in this — what his part in any plan was ever to be — is hard to see, but he attempts a contribution, saying he at least should go now, and make his stealthy way to the *Great Hallas*, not the river, but the large hostelry on its near bank, where a number of Loyalists from his province have beds; by these means word of Idolema's imminence can start secretly to circulate and spread among supporters first thing.

"No," Cantello rules. "You had better stay."

"I know how to dodge the patrols — to talk my way past them, if it comes to that, which it won't."

"It's an unnecessary risk. Your Loyalists, you say, are still looking for some miracle, and we can give them one, prepared or not."

"But knowing what to look for — "

"You will stay here with us." The tone of incontrovertible command Cantello seldom resorts to, and Kellan's answering glare soon falters.

He chuckles unconvincingly. "As you wish, master; we are all in your hands."

"True."

On that, the meeting peters out, Cantello still wishing for a better plan, unable to invent one. As host, Restin stands at the foot of the stairs, ushering his guests to their beds, before following.

The tapped-out signal brings Hodd to the door, still cautious, blade in hand. "How did it go? We have a plan?"

Having outlined the salient points of the discussion for both him and a large-eyed, attentive Idolema, Cantello has a murmur of reassurance for her, then draws Hodd outside, pulling the door to.

"What then? We march out there in broad daylight with the Black Guard everywhere, and saunter down to this Wool Market place?"

"I hate a plan that becomes the plan because there is nothing else. It may be that the throngs in the streets will be enough to give us cover."

After a skeptical grimace, his friend puts on a face of patient suffering. "With you, it always ends up with some lunacy; why should this be different?"

"Tonight, I shall be in here, with the girl," Cantello says. "In the chair, with a sword ready," he emphasizes. with an answering grin aiming a light punch at the shoulder of lewdly grinning Hodd. "How are you for sleep?"

"You know me. We'll be up and moving in, what, four hours, five? Let the cub have his rest."

"We need a good sword on the stairs, to keep watch against anyone going out." Cantello shrugs. "Or, I suppose, coming in, but especially, going out."

Hodd nods. "Which one is it?"

"I would say the northerner, Kellan. Not anyone can be fully trusted where the rewards of treachery may be so great — Fane himself, for all we know, may need money."

"Do you understand that?" Hodd is suddenly almost comically querulous. "They give you a bag of gold, or, what, some position in the world, and what have you got, having turned sewer-rat? Like that boy; where will he look for his lost manhood, when his great-grandfather spits on him?"

"He may have kept faith. I wish I had been able to counsel him — " a nagging ache for Cantello.

"We use what we're given."

IX

"Your pardon, I shall not leave your side tonight."

"Then we shall have to share the bed," the girl says with an impossible but steadfast neutrality. Having shed the grey gown, she is unselfconsciously (but to him, fascinatingly) in a plain white shift; somewhere, since her resumption of woman's dress, her eyes, which is obviously impossible, or perhaps sentimental illusion, have become larger and more incontrovertibly violet.

"You take it, lady, I shan't sleep. For a few hours; we must be ready to leave at daybreak." Quickly, he outlines his intentions. In the muted candlelight, her shoulders and arms have the soft gleam of quietly extravagant youth.

"What?" she questions, to his dark gaze.

"Do we have it right?" (Throughout what follows, Cantello's insistence on sticking to business is to be understood as a defense, increasingly desperate, against the recreational appeal of moist skin and lissome limbs; on her preferences, his chances of resistance, no further bets can be accepted, but as a premise the tactic allows us a great deal of otherwise-improbable exposition.) "The Royal Guard, a banner blown in the breeze, till they have sworn a new oath. Besides, it was Tarfal who gave me the name of Geddo. Earlier, he had started to tell me about how they would proceed, once you had been brought to Hallabreg; I cut him short, believing I could hear it when the time came, and now I wonder whether this Valmar's plan is the same."

She says gravely, "I wonder about the men who were gathered at Mitfell — "

Puzzled by this leap, he grimaces. "We have nearer concerns. That was always a foolish gathering, a gesture — what object could there be in bringing together forty, sixty, two hundred armed men? Your way here could never be by force of arms; I said from the first they could be useful only as a decoy, and perhaps they have helped keep Nidlaam's attention in the wrong place."

"But you see, there are men, fathers and sons both, from families I have stayed with, who have been good to me — friends, almost foster-families; they have taken great risks for my sake."

Cantello judiciously refrains from correcting this judgment; no doubt some genuine affection did spring up, but the dangers were braved, not out of love for her, but in the hope that her preservation might help them to a more tolerable realm than any ruled by Corvan. He says, "If they behave sensibly, avoid open battle — "

She frowns, returning to the puzzle of Cantello's strategy. "The message you sent, by way of Tarfal and the smuggler's son — you advised them to stay away from actual fighting?"

"As I would hope they know to do, without any advice — even if my message was never delivered."

"You believe it might not be?" swiftly, trying to seize a point.

"No journey can be certain, as things are. Some are worth risking."

She frowns. "Cantello; when you pledged your help, I said I would follow your orders, as I have. I never promised not to ask questions."

"What is your question, then?"

"Why you endorsed that strange pairing — alliance, if it is one, Tarfal with the other." Again not naming Dernlo.

"It was a mistake, but when I sent them, I couldn't know we might be caught up in the same plan Tarfal had knowledge of." Whether, that is, the plan has been betrayed to Nidlaam, and the Old Wool Market turned into a trap.

"You wanted to use his treachery to distract Nidlaam?"

"I wanted to remove possible treachery from amongst us, and use it to our advantage if real. Tarfal was unreliable, after — " he cannot finish.

"After I would not let him in my bed?"

The subject is painful, but Cantello recognizes, though does not welcome, the cue for questions he must ask. "Did — does Dernlo believe you to be Idolema?"

Perhaps flustered by recall of the dark time when she shared that dour man's bed, she unnecessarily shakes out and refolds her dress for the morning. "Does it matter what Dernlo thought?"

"It might. He and Tarfal had a long day together for talk. Does he?"

"Why? That's a strange choice of words. I told you they must have guessed my importance. You yourself all but admitted it, both to Dernlo and to his father."

"As you say, Dernak has a shrewdness about what's near him; he may have guessed beyond guesses. He likes to see himself as fearless, though he knows I know better, but even he would hardly dare let his son make a bed-partner out of what he saw as the late king's lost daughter."

"It was a strange time, when nothing could be relied on — another time, he might not have dared it, but then, he did."

"No," Cantello says, incontrovertibly, watching her.

She continues smoothing the robe, not meeting his eyes. "Why *no*?"

"Because you are not Idolema." It is said. There is no thunder-roll or shaking of the earth, only a shaken girl imposing all the semblance of calm she can invent.

To her credit (as he judges it), she does not waste their time with imperious assertions, but unwilling to concede, asks, loftily enough, "What makes you imagine I am not Idolema? Is Cantello, with everything else, a judge of such things?"

"There are a dozen or more small points — " not rising to the bait, keeping his own voice conversational. "Someone has schooled you well, or some two or three, chiefly Nila, I suppose, with Tarbul's kin, but — who was the old serving-woman who helped smuggle Idolema away after Dairemid's death?"

"Chora, you mean? she is still alive, though ancient now. Why?"

"A servant born of servants, who, familiar enough with royalty's elbow, can never see with the eye of royalty. Or hear with its ear; there was a complaint you made about the rooks in the sycamores by the palace disturbing your rest, a nice touch, but those sycamores and that rookery are some way beyond the end of the servants' wing; no princess has ever been disturbed by their dawn debate."

"No grown man," she reminds him, "Has ever heard that whistle you used to tame the wilder-hounds."

"You made a mistake with Restil, also, with that pewter tankard; whoever told you the story missed its point, that Dairemid tactfully bestowed a reward by giving gold for something worthless; fortunately our host was too busy fawning to make anything of it. Then, too, you did not refute me when I mentioned — invented — Dairemid's inability to sing the simplest tune; no one who heard it, surely not the daughter he must have often lulled to sleep, could fail to remember Dairemid's sweet tenor voice."

"It is all a long time ago. Childhood memories are easily displaced, when one lives as I have since."

"Idolema," he says, quite sure he is not addressing her, "Was past eleven when Dairemid was killed; these are not the memories of infancy."

"There on the scarp, I believed I was talking with a friend, not facing a test."

"Again," ignoring the bitter thrust, "The swans that nest on the Little Hallas where it flows through the palace grounds are a unique breed, of a pale-blue shade seen nowhere else, but you said nothing when I recalled their pure whiteness. Old Tarbul, I noted at

Ault, is color-blind; when he described for me the leader of the Black Guard contingent, Suliwat, mentioned the man's mop of hair, but not that it was a flaming red, though it was the first trait anyone with normal sight would notice. There is that danger in anything he may have recalled for you."

"I have seldom spoken long with Tarbul."

"Also, you seem to me younger than eighteen."

"And these niggles lead you to conclude I cannot be the princess?"

Almost, faced by her distress, he gives it up as pointless; her real identity, in fact, is unlikely to affect his actions. "For the most part, you see, I don't care, but I must wonder what it is, this journey of ours — am I perhaps the decoy, after all? Is the real Idolema to be brought in by some other means, while Corvan's attention is on us? I would like to know these things before making the final step, since that would mean the Loyalist scheme has your death as part of it. Yours and mine."

"No — " coming swiftly to a decision. "Idolema is dead."

A lengthy, weighty silence; loss of royal standing does nothing to alter his desire to learn her bright skin with his fingers. "I am sorry," she says.

"For what?"

"That you had to be deceived."

He brushes it away with a gesture. "And the Loyalists chose you to replace her."

"A few of them did, more than four years ago."

"They chose well. You are like her — or a good deal like what she might have grown to; very few would ever question that you are she."

"In exile, she lacked friends near her age; I was the house-keeper's daughter, her chosen companion whenever she came to Tarne, and everyone there noted the likeness. Well, I am her cousin, not one she would ever have acknowledged. My mother was no one, a servant; my true father, so she has always maintained, is the Baron Falnis."

"Eltow Falnis is father, chances are, to many unacknowledged children."

"Yes, but then he himself — his mother was, in her youth, famously a coquette. The then-baron, my supposed grandfather, was newly married to her, when the king, Dairo, Dairemid's father, was at Falnough for the hunting."

"Dairo. They call him the Good, now, but like many another enthusiast of the chase, he was noted for his hunting from bed to bed as well."

"Who would dare tell him what was out of season? The next midsummer, my father was born, accepted as heir to the Barony. He did not particularly resemble those of the royal house, but when he in turn was of an age to indulge his appetites, one of his unsanctified children, as she grew, was thought by many to look a great deal like the young Princess Idolema — who was, if all the tales and hints were true, and my father indeed Dairemid's half-brother, my first cousin. Her death, four years ago, was unrecorded, or called mine, and Idolema went into my grave."

"How did she die?"

"She was sickly, I had been told, from the first day away from the palace, and I never really knew her to be well; colds and fevers, stomach troubles, and she was easily tired; her weight was less, I was told, at fifteen, when she died, than when she was eleven — it had been more than a year since last I saw her; by then, with the fear I might easily be mistaken for her, I was also kept in hiding, moving from place to place, but always apart from Idolema — even then, I suppose, somebody had the idea that one or the other of us should survive. According to my mother, she died of her birth."

After cogitation, Cantello nods; like reading fairy-tales, being born a princess is poor preparation for life as it really is outside that nursed and groomed and coddled cell; she would have been among that small minority who have never been cold in winter, always had water, and warmed water, for washing, dined off dishes kept clean, eating only taintless food — a perquisite of work in royal kitchens is all the food judged blemished in some way, fruit and vegetables with spots of rot or overripe, meat and milk and butter beginning to smell too mature, bread showing specks of green, all normal conditions for the hungry most of the world, and certainly no reason for waste. It is true that in the realm at large, more than half the children born never attain a tenth birthday, but that very mortality means the tougher survive; Idomela went into exile with scant defenses, for when the great houses became unsafe for her, against fleas and lice, flies and worms, the bites of rats, the omnipresence of dirt and ordure — many, even, who struggle to exclude these things (and exceptions are commoner than you would suppose) are often defeated by the scarcity of clean water, most of which by far has to be fetched on shoulders from a well or flowing stream none too near. Suddenly exposed to anything like those conditions, the princess would be like a tortoise with no shell.

Abruptly, Cantello laughs. "Then this money I am carrying comes from your father."

"He believes, my uncle; he knows nothing about the change; I was never at Falnough, not since I was three; he saw me as I now am only after Idolema had died, and her he had hardly seen since she was an infant."

Having, at whatever cost, banished one worry, Cantello has a new one to ponder. "Who does know about the substitution? How many?"

"Only a few — fewer, now. Last year in Tarne several of the original entourage were captured and killed. Others have died."

"The House Tarbul — does Tarfal know?" The knowledge might very well bear on his confident attempt to climb in her bed, and his aggrieved citing of her time with Dernlo: Tarfal might consider his lineage not only better than that of a smuggler's son, but superior to hers.

"He hinted so. Is he a traitor?"

Cantello declines to be deflected. "Rumors, in any event, are going to linger. If you came to be accepted as queen, how were you going to make yourself safe, at any time, from denunciation?"

"Most of the handful who do know have helped in the deception, and would be in no position to challenge my elevation as rightful queen."

"What about your mother?"

"She always taught me to believe I was something more than a servant's child; this now is fulfillment of her dream. You have met her."

"Nila?" The only possibility, but for once Cantello is genuinely astonished. "She has learned her part well; I took her for a lackland relative of the Earl's."

"She had many years to study it; there was once such a kinswoman in that Tarne household."

"But — " He wants to say something about Nila's manner with her daughter, the prideful deference of a waiting-gentlewoman, her prim disapproval when the girl dismissed her to talk alone with Cantello, the restrained emotion of their farewell.

It is understood. "As you saw her, she is no different in private with me; by now I think she has almost forgotten I am not Idolema. That belief pleases her far better than the truth. Besides, no one near my mother, or who knew me growing up, would see any advantage to betraying me."

Not possibly true. "Some might threaten it, desiring money or position."

"Extortion? They would hardly dare; the Loyalists, most of whom genuinely and fiercely believe in me as the proper heir, can be not much less fearsome than Nidlaam and his Black Guard."

This brings a grim smile to his face: if Idolema is dead, then Corvan, however cruel, however unapt, is, so far as law can recognize, undoubted king, and here this girl calmly accepts a counterterror to help maintain a rule of no perceptible legitimacy.

"And do you think these Loyalist bullies — Loyalist! you must admit the term now has a certain irony to it — can they, any more than Corvan's lackeys, compel me through fear?"

"No," simply. "You are Cantello. I don't know what you mean to do, now your suspicions are confirmed. Without your help, then, obviously, I am dead and it is finished; Corvan will be king."

Cantello, chin resting on clasped hands, ponders aloud. "It is hard to imagine that anyone could be worse than Corvan, with his Nidlaam; I think you would be a great deal better, better-prepared, it may be, than most who come to power through their birth, and never think about the use of that power. You spoke of friends, and facing a test — "

"That was my fear — " seeming about to excuse her moment of anger.

"No, but you must understand that for someone who comes forward to make the claims you do everything now is a test. Most, perhaps, many even who till now have accepted Corvan, would want you to be the lawful heir, but even among those there would be be some doubters. When, knowingly or not, they test you with recollections of Idolema's childhood, it is better to risk giving offense with a failure of memory than to take what may be a false bait."

"Yes, but about the pure-white swans; I had that same story from Idolema herself." Her eyes widen. "Or was that your own trick?"

"Hardly needed," he apologizes. "But the less you remember of former times, the safer you'll be,"

Does she notice that the conditional has gradually vanished from his syntax, to indicate a decision made? "I know, I know. I'll be careful — " like making him a promise to help keep his support, but introducing a new note of intimacy.

Wanting to kiss her, excoriating his own adolescent volatility, Cantello again drags himself back to dispassionate summation. "Once this realm believed the line of Dairemid had been restored, your sons his grandsons, then it would be so — well, if your likely surmise about your father's fathering is true, they will be no less the old king's great-grandsons than if you were Idolema. In blood, if both the fatherings could be proved, your right is scarcely less, once we admit the claims of bastardy, than that of Corvan, who is equally your cousin."

"Exactly what Tarbul says."

"In any case, with other dynasties in other times, queens have had lovers, and the Heir not much resembled the king; another generation passes, and it doesn't matter." A grin. "Maybe better for the realm; perhaps you could never be perfectly safe from those who know your secret, but they can make us safe from you. If you were truly Idomela, once acclaimed, you could govern as the passing fancy took you. Now, it seems no rule could be as bad as Corvan's, but all history teaches us never to hail someone's mildness and benevolence, till he has the power to be otherwise; the powerless have to love justice; it's their only hope, but the powerful can as easily dispense with as dispense it."

An answering smile. "As is — "

"As is, you undoubtedly possess what was always Idolema's most persuasive quality — you are not Corvan." This gets a mocking gesture of gratitude from the girl, but Cantello scarcely responds. "The desire of so many to be rid of Corvan can, I think, carry you to the throne, and no one but his cronies will raise any question about your genuineness — unless your rule becomes as oppressive as his."

"Can you believe it ever could?" Again letting her eyes flash fire.

"I am not the best judge." His supply of dissimulation is now very near its end.

"Who has had a better chance of judging me?"

"Well," he rashly ripostes, "but who is more in love with you?"

She is startled. "In love? In *love*?"

"Forgive me; call it unsaid."

"In love? With me?"

"Why shouldn't I be?"

"I thought you saw me as a stupid child, a nuisance, at best a duty."

"I might have seen Idolema so; the dangers she faced were on her own account. If, as I judge, you are without personal ambition, you are the bravest woman I have known." She is, it seems, barely seventeen.

"Braver than the Lady of Synta? — " very swift to challenge; every woman knows who is her rival.

"She was not so much brave as dauntingly resourceful, but yes, braver even than Modran, her lover, who headed her bodyguard, and was called the Mad, for her reckless defiance of death. That is a sort of courage, granted, but one that can't be separated from stupidity — that is, all said, blindness to all danger rather than true courage. Your nerve is not that; you see dangers, fear them, and go on — "

"Still afraid."

"That's what bravery is, the only courage we should praise — admire. The rest — " he makes almost a brusque gesture — "is obvious."

"What *rest*?" — now almost flirtatiously; she knows the answer but wants to hear it.

"If I did not love your spirit — any man would find plenty to admire; your eyes, your sudden smile (it comes now) — don't make me say too much; your slender legs, your breasts, your belly, how you move, like some confident cat — " confirming love meanwhile invents new aspects of it; what he praises he sees and desires, and words become caresses, though still no more than their hands have met.

Remembering, with an effort, his original theme: "Don't ask me, of all men, for cold assessments of your future."

Too late; her eyes are soft and shining, and her voice tremulous. "What — what an extraordinary man you are, still; I thought you had no more to surprise me, and now — " with a tender irony — "you give up your command, put power in my hands; you must have been here before — "

"Not here, no; this is different, only itself."

"But you're no boy; you must know you can want a woman and still be master, as Dernlo was, and Tarfal wished to be, but when you say, love — "

"I should not have said it, but speaking it includes trust, 'I trust you not to abuse this power I surrender.'"

"Does it, truly?"

"It might, and perhaps always should; we should all be prudent with the limited resources we have to invest, and not love till we're sure of safety — " Debate, debate, when, no less than her, he desires touching, exploration.

"Not *say* we love. That might be possible."

"For someone else. For me, I've been left for dead too many times; I've no calculation left for my own life. Do with it what amuses you."

A long silence, filled with half-glances and half-evasions. "I suppose we had better make love together, while there's time."

A joy, familiar but always new, can be found in his observation that her laconic phrasing is an ineffectual mask for a genuine, warming readiness: he can exult in its existence while resisting its demands. "I think not. There's nothing I could want more, but I'm not yet insane."

"What could be saner than to bring our bodies together, now, when for just this moment we can? Please don't deny us this. Within a few hours, I shall almost certainly be dead."

"Only if they first kill me."

"Let's give it up," with a passionate if hopeless conviction. "We could leave, find a quiet place — go abroad, even. What do I owe the realm — and you, you have given much more than can ever be repaid; there are people in Eremia or Maegland who will hear about the terrors of Corvan's reign like tales of long ago and never miss a meal. Why not? Why must we be the conscience of our people?"

"I can't answer that."

"There's no victory for me. If, by some remote chance, our plan works, I shall be queen. You think I want that? I am, they told me, the one chance of saving the realm from Corvan, from Nidlaam; this is the burden I've been given — for myself, I would want a quiet life, ordinary friends, a little comfort, love if I'm lucky, otherwise a good father for my children. Now, my own body will be an *instrument of alliance* — " she clamps her teeth down hard on her lower lip. "Pardon me. Till I saw the chance of a moment's happiness, I never pitied myself."

Still carefully, he moves to her, grasping a safer elbow, while brushing the hair back from her forehead. "Fear is permissible," he murmurs.

"You see, I shall have to betroth myself, soon marry where political advantage lies, and prudence will keep me faithful. In either case, this is my last chance to choose. To have the joy of choice."

"If you succeed — " it remains obvious to drowning Cantello he must, for too many good reasons, continue to resist this. Without real conviction, he takes shelter behind ramparts already shown as penetrable. "What will you do with them, Corvan, Nidlaam and their packs?"

"Corvan will swear allegiance, what choice has he?"

"But with Nidlaam at his ear, will plot to displace you."

"No, no, Nidlaam must go. Most others can be excused as obeying the only rightful ruler they know, but we can't have a place for Nidlaam's cruelties."

"Then you will have to send him into exile — "

"Or have him executed. Why are you doing this?"

" — and to do either, overcome and disarm his Guard. The Earl of Lasth, wherever he stands now, will be important to you from the start; his armed men, rather. The other nobles, too, some of which are already yours, Lumatt of Tarne, Eltow Falnis, but with the Black Guard Corvan could launch, bring off and consolidate a counter-insurrection while the barons are assembling their forces, and that will mean civil war. To forestall that, you must have the Royal Guard."

"But even before Armid," shyly, "I'll need you, guiding me. Why shouldn't we be lovers, too?"

"It may be," he allows with an extreme reluctance, never comfortable with the notion of an official post, "You'll need me, for a time at least, by your side — "

"To advise only, if you can make me queen," she adds, with a sudden — to him, not unwelcome — grasp of authority. "Then, praise or blame will be mine, so I must train myself to be the final yes or no."

" — but for us to sleep together then would be worse than imprudent; it could unmake everything. To say I want you is absurd understatement — but to bed once, and then to see each other, and hunger for the rest of our lives?" Intellectually, he can admit this may be hyperbole, but it doesn't seem so, with the willing woman still unboarded.

"It makes no difference — or yes, perhaps it does, if it is just once, or just a few times, then it can always be a wonder."

He grins ruefully. "So we always contrive to believe — I can believe it now, but that's my greed for you, willing to make up and accept any story. A very long time ago, there was a woman I wanted and knew I could never have — have, in the sense of join my life to — "

"A married woman?"

"I had to destroy her, end her power."

"Oh. That woman, still." She contrives a note of boredom.

"And the blood whining in my veins persuaded me that there could be no danger in enjoying her for a time, for a week, that it would be foolish not to; nothing else would be changed, and I would have had that wondrous week. As I did."

"I am glad for you — " sourly, retroactively jealous.

"My dear not-Idolema — "

"My name was Aretta." Almost the name he had invented for her, when she herself was only his invention.

" — you're a thousand times her worth; I don't for a moment wish her back. Still, she has haunted half my life. My choice to sleep with her meant her destruction was also mine — not through witchcraft, through self-loathing." Something of rote, here; he has revisited the episode so many times, and now it has changed, in a moment, into a tale, nearly a fiction.

"You think that to lie with me will make you hate yourself?"

"I think it might make me hate whoever comes after me."

"Perhaps no one will."

He shakes his head. "You say yourself, you cannot make your throne safe without marriage and an heir." The self-evident can still cause extraordinary pain when spoken.

"And you, great Cantello, will keep your life safe by turning me into another of your creatures kept everlastingly perfect, in a tomb of amber. With a blade in your hand or an enemy in front of you, you are brave, no less brave than Hodd, whose courage you praise. But you're going to make me remember a coward."

A huge, forced chuckle. "To be successful, a coward has to make himself proof against taunts."

"Don't laugh at me. I can't bear it if you think I'm a silly girl."

He is, on the contrary, admiring her cogency. "I am laughing at me."

From outside, the landing, voices come, not loud but with a carrying intensity of tone. Cantello makes a face and turns back to the door, opening it in time to hear Hodd, referring to his bared sword, say, "I have this right." What this is answer to is easily reconstructed; the other man is Kellan, outer jacket on, satchel in hand.

"We are allies, not enemies," he tells Hodd.

"And being so," Cantello speaks immediately behind him, causing him to start and swivel, "We keep to an agreed plan. No one leaves here before morning."

"Not that far off morning now," Kellan says with a precarious jocularity. "I still believe — "

"Your beliefs do not interest me."

"What makes you our captain?"

"Force. I have the men and the weapons. Seen, they should not, as I prefer, have to be used. Either you will go back to your room, and remain there till I say, or I shall have you bound. Choose now."

Looking exasperated, the man wearily shakes his head. "We are all working for the same thing, aren't we? — what can we hope for, where friends threaten friends?"

Grimly bright, Hodd says, "We must debate that tomorrow." His blade, an armslength from Kellan's groin, has never wavered.

"Very well," the man capitulates. "Heroes will have their way." He turns, goes into his room, and firmly shuts the door.

"Window?"

Hodd shakes his head, and leans his sword against him so he can hold up hands to measure a small square. "Opens on the court-yard; young Galidern couldn't worm through it."

"By morning," pondering, "it shouldn't matter."

"We could kill him."

"Since he knows that, we shouldn't have to." They nod to each other, and part.

He has been gone for minutes, and comes back to a reversed world, his parsimonious caution unreal, the sober fact a chance for shared joy: in the renewed thought that Nidlaam may already know about the Old Wool Market (robbing Kellan's attempted excursion of its presumed objective), Cantello has glimpsed his own mortality, and with an inward smile predicted he would not go to his death wishing he had been chaster.

"What is it?" Aretta is seated on the bed.

"Nothing important.   You should try for some sleep." Honorable to the end.

Absorbedly, she picks at loose strands on the tattered counterpane.   "Do you know how many men I have been bedded by? One."

"Him?" Cantello doesn't know whether distaste (for Dernlo) or compassion (for Aretta) comes uppermost, but any frayed remnant of patient resolve is swamped in muddled but purposeful emotion. A step in her direction, she stands to receive him, and in his swift, close embrace of her there is no space for ambiguity.   Her lips, beneath the surface somewhat roughened by weather, are even softer than his imaginings.

She knows.   "Even a queen, I think, once in her life, should be able to bed with a man she has chosen."

"What about conception?" a final prudency, between kisses.

She shakes her head.   "Not while the moon is so slender — " a phrasing, practical in intent, to waken deep echoes at some other, mythic level.

But the seeming imperative need to mate is all in the present, like pain, or cold, which, while they can be provided-for or complained about, are far less than fully imaginable when absent; the specific urgency, regarded in prospect or retrospect is absurdly exaggerated; nothing is easier than not to take a woman's body next week, than not to have yesterday — the reason why we can be wiser for and more censorious of others than ourselves; anyone can make the sensible, the prudent, the self-preserving choice in imagination, especially for someone else.   With ourselves, in what a thesaurus might lead us to call the estrus of the moment, it is choice that apes irrelevance.

This is not to take sides. The scales for weighing Cantello's grave concern (now fled) for future well-being against Aretta's understandable grab at ephemeral fulfillment have not been designed, but times arrive when further debate is like the (possibly anxious) hesitancy of corks bobbing on the outer rim of a vortex by which, whatever their world-view, they are going to be seized, spun and swallowed.

As it is now, and (as we all agree) about time, too. Would I could borrow the word-processor, the hyperventilating readership, of the author of *Passion's Proud Torment*, and fourteen other titles, plots guaranteed identical (see mail-order coupon inside back cover), to be telling how erect were the breasts of coy Kimberley as she felt the hard rod of Mario's manhood press against her; you can't just make this stuff up, you know — but what is it in the end but overcooked zoology? informationally akin to interesting data about the distended throat of a mating male grouse: if worth describing at all, human copulation has to be about the juxtaposition of singular personalities, not species-wide body parts, universal endocrine activity.

And so, though Aretta's breasts were erect as anything, and the rod of Cantello as reliably rigid as the dumbest dildo, though she accepted him with a grateful gasp, and they yielded, as the style manual says, to a glad frenzy, she speaking his name a great many times, yes, yes, all that, the altered calms between ecstasies (more than a couple, hers extravagant) are what should command the attention of serious folk.

Early, she was bright-eyed with discovery; before her new life as Idolema, there had been a maid — one of her own class, as was then — claiming considerable experience, who raptly informed her there was no sensation in life to come near the pleasures of a shared bed, an assessment not confirmed for Aretta, relegated to a tall tale, till now. "I knew I would love being made love to by you," she says. "But not this much."

Equally of her youth is the unanxious but concerned aware-
ness of his experience; "You must show me how to please you
better," after having been very pleased herself more than once. "I
would like to be as good as any woman you have had, be remembered so."

There is no time, is his first thought; she is speaking like a
bride with months, years ahead for mutual learnings — and then he
says, and means it, "Nothing could please me more than to be here
with you." For many reasons, and even at her proposed level, which
invites him to judge her as he would a whore, he is still marvelling at
the strength of her legs, and yet, their smoothness.

"But a man needs to be able to brag — about how a woman
did cunning things, to leave him emptied."

"I love you, that's enough."

But love, or for unbelievers, the sentimental-sensual intox-
icant that furnishes its illusion, loves to level, even to counterchange,
disparity in age; at some later time she has recalled with delighted
mock-contrition how, at their first meeting, she offered exactly this
as a bribe for his assistance, how he had saved her humiliation with a
rebuke that was also flattery. Quite abruptly, with a low moan,
perhaps of compassion, she puts her hand against his cheek. "My
poor Cantello — " and this is very nearly maternal. "You must
always be Cantello."

"If we win today, you will always be Queen Idolema."

"Yes," wanly, then, "But that's not the same. I can still be
silly sometimes, lose my temper, change my mind, make mistakes
— only the title is perfect, the queen can be flawed and still queen."

"But I am silly and bad-tempered too, and make mistakes
sometimes."

With no loss of affection, she rejects the parallel. "No —
not to the world. Oh, with me, perhaps, if we could be lovers; I
would like to give you that, more than anything."

"However it ends, this adventure is my last." Far better than Hodd, he considers, he has a chance of settling into obscurity; for well over a year, till dragged back into the realm's sorrows, his life had been contentedly without event, and could be so again, with minor adjustments to earn or grow subsistence. Could have been so again, he amends, confronting the uncertainties just ahead, and the unthinkable certainty, in victory or defeat, of losing Aretta.

Who seems almost blithe in her grave determinism. "Haven't all your adventures been your last? Not even a Cantello can cease to be himself."

In the end, unwillingly she dozes, and he, against every precept of a responsible lifetime. dozes briefly too. Waking with a stab of guilt quickly lost in wellbeing, then in world-embracing gratitude, he wakes her with kisses.

"Our host promised milk and bread fresh from the oven."

"I could eat a loaf." She is already gnawing at his knuckles.

"You were right; nothing matters now."

"Oh, no," deeply sensuous. "Everything matters now."

Even in this early dim, when they are somewhat washed and, with heroic mutual self-denial, dressed, they are, flank to flank, contained in such a roseate bubble of satisfaction and desire it seems to him that everyone will guess how the night was passed. Yet as they assemble, Sab rested and eager, Valmar absorbedly over-concerned with mud on his boots, Kellan subdued and sulking, only Hodd appears to notice, and his shrewd eyes meet Cantello's in an amusement that appears more comradely than lascivious, and might, with anyone else, provoke suspicions of a covert sentimentality.

"As it happens, they paid handsomely," Restil, chinking coins, tells his skeptical wife. It is nearing noon, the drinkshop, like the entire quarter, virtually deserted, the quiet here on the hillside emphasized rather than broken into by the sounds that well up from the city below, dull mutter of crowds like distant thunder, with the occasional flash of a child's high-pitched cry or a whinnying horse.

"What do you call, handsomely?"

"Gave me twenty marks," he lies, an almost unprecedented event.

"Never!"

"Then I must have dreamt it," he says, producing and laying four gold pieces. one at a time, on the counter. As expected, Nelanda at once sweeps them up. Let her; he has sixteen more of the same concealed, and is at this moment the master of more wealth than ever in all the years of their marriage, more fortune than most men will command in a lifetime. Deep in his belly he feels a gratifying throb; this is how it should be for a man. not dependent on what his woman grudges out. He will have enough and over to pay off Ospant, particularly if, as he intends, he again holds back some of tonight's earnings. By then, his customers will be drinking to the crowning of their monarch, now minutes away. If Idolema, Restil can modestly, quite openly, lay claim to some part in her coming, while if she fails and they hail King Corvan, no one need ever know the girl spent her last night here; the conspirators will no doubt be fled or dead. In either case, Restil should be free of his most urgent worries.

"With some foresight," his daughter Nanda, lurking, comments, "We might have had this price every night the past ten days."

"You'd better quiet about it," Restil says, allowing some menace in it. "At the same rate, your bed should cost you thirty-five marks a week; do you think the little work you do here is worth such a wage?" When Darwat repays him, as he'll be able to in a few days, Restil will possess something near a hundred marks; a skilled craftsman does well to clear ten or twelve for a week's toil.

"Oh, yes, and where would you be — " Nanda begins, exactly her mother's tone.

"Be quiet," Nelanda orders. "Your father is right." Again, wholly new.

X

Hours before — deplore, and rightly, this awkwardly artificial back-eddy in time, but then excuse it on the grounds that it would
be even lamer to interrupt what obviously must be the climax of our
main tale to round off Fane Restil's small epic — the assorted company remained gathered at the scrubbed table in the private dining
room, an increasingly anxious Restil coming and going, uncertain of
how long he could keep his wife away, afraid of another morning
visit from the Black Guard.

Though they had wakened early, it was scarcely ahead of the
city. Orde, the baker across the way, preceded them, and the
evidence, bread, hot from his ovens, made a welcome breakfast.
First to venture cautiously into the street, Valmar, is back well within
the hour allowed him, with no good news; he has been unable to
speak with his brother-in-law, Geddo, and Black Guard in the nearby
Millway, though apparently at this early hour mainly loitering, made
it too risky for him to try the door in Shoat's Alley. He has had to
pass and repass another company of the Guard who have used
hurdles to set up a makeshift gateway near the foot of the Myrin,
giving them the story that he was trying to fetch a midwife, his wife
having started her labor, but failed to find the woman at home.
Having made this report, he performs his curious trick of withdrawing behind a face emptied of all expression.

The surly Kellan has been as restless as their host. He was
prevented from going out into the courtyard to breathe, he alleged,
the morning air, and is at a guess surreptitiously gnawing at a twig of
strockan small enough to be kept in his mouth. Now he lunges for a
new opportunity. "There," he tells Cantello. "We need more help, as
I said. If I could take word to my friends by the river, they might be
able to distract the men in the Millway."

"How?" Hodd breaks in. "Are there tumblers among them?
Jugglers?"

"Engage them in talk. Half a dozen of us together would certainly be challenged, and could be slow to identify ourselves."

"Your ideas do not improve," Cantello, with heavy irony.

Annoyance, quite possibly genuine. "How long have you had sole charge of this conspiracy? Many of us — Valmar, here, and I could name many others — have worked and planned for months and years, and now it must be one more of Cantello's great, lonely feats — by whose authority?"

"By mine," says the woman they will call Idolema. "There will be rewards — for those who have kept faith — " this with marked emphasis. "No one, least of all Cantello himself, would wish to claim all the credit for success — success indeed is only possible if many voices, many bodies, give me their support. But Cantello is now our only strategist. I say so." With an openness as generally imprudent as it is joyful to him, she takes his hand, gazing into his eyes with a resolute tenderness no one could misinterpret. Stirring stuff, this.

"But, lady," the man ventures. "Others, surely, may have parts to contribute?"

"Kellan," Cantello, sternly, inspired, perhaps, by his lover's splendid example of candor. "It is our considered opinion that you are one of Nidlaam's spies. If — " elbowing aside the man's protest, as well as a shocked interjection from Valmar — "If we are mistaken, I ask your pardon, but you must see there is nothing you can do to unconvince us."

"There are a dozen, a hundred staunch Loyalists who would tell you — "

"No doubt, and that would necessarily be true for any successful spy. I would dislike having to kill you on no more than suspicion, but if you want to stay alive, you must go or stay as I order; I cannot risk the enterprise on doubts and quibbles. You are going off nowhere on your own."

"Lady," the man appeals. "This is a great wrong — is this the justice your rule will stand for?"

"One death, perhaps unmerited — " young Sab has taken time to recover from his shock and probable disappointment at what amounts to Idolema's, *his* Idolema's declaration of her love, but now he rallies. "One? If Corvan is crowned, there will be hundreds, as there have already been scores." This, for Cantello, has a special poignancy coming from his late friend's only surviving child. Who adds, "If our success might depend on it, any of us would kill a suspected spy of Nidlaam's without a blink. Has he a weapon? — " of Valmar, who is nearest the man.

"He showed me a knife, last night," quite bewildered. "I spoke very freely with him, as I thought he did with me; he has the names of friends, the places we meet."

"If Corvan is crowned," Cantello promises, "This man will not live to betray you."

As Kellan tries to resume his protestations, Hodd saunters round the table to stand, a hand outstretched; with the absence of a sword, an exact repeat of last night's confrontation. "Knife," he says.

"I cannot be unarmed."

"Unarmed, disarmed, take your pick."

Kellan's jacket is almost knee-length; his hand goes inside to what must be a thigh-front sheath, and he starts to ease out the knife. Hodd's head is slightly cocked to one side, and it is plain to Cantello he actually wants the man to attempt an attack — but since there is practically no doubt about how that would end, even without unaided Hodd touching a weapon, it is only cold-blooded execution given a saving pretense of combat.

"Put it on the table," Cantello intervenes, before its appearance can bring the crisis; there is still a remote chance the man is no spy.

"Masters, please — " Restil, in the doorway. "No fighting and killing, not in my house."

Kellan extracts the knife, a good hunter's blade, and does as told, saying, with a jocularity he doesn't pretend is anything but artificial, "I hope you have some of this — this warmaking, left for our enemies."

It is the jittery Restil who explains a way, using back-alleys, that the barrier at the foot of the hill can be avoided, bringing them down not far from the other end of Shoat's Alley from the Millway; no doubt his eagerness to see the backs of his guests is part of his expressed confidence they can go unobserved by soldiery. Yet, having paid Restil the very generous sum agreed with Aretta, Cantello cautiously leads the entire party out into a clear morning, a cool breeze surging out of the northwest. They are six, and to make them less notable he has decided they should stroll, in two groups some paces apart, he with Valmar and Idolema (as he must school himself to name her), while Hodd and Sab have the glum Kellan between them; his suspect presence is an unwanted complication, but if not killed out of hand, he certainly can't be left behind, only a minute or two away from the chance of betraying them to the Black Guard; he has been grimly warned by Hodd that he will be dead in an instant, if he does anything to attract attention. If their weapons are seen, they will in any case be challenged, and Cantello with Sab and Hodd are cloaked to conceal their swords, nothing out of the way for such a chill morning, but Hodd has lamented the necessity of leaving off his bow. The girl, too, is wrapped, in a shabby mantle supplied by Restin, one left behind, he said, by some guest long past; with a kerchief over her hair, she is not strikingly different from the many country girls who must be in Hallabreg for the festival.

Already, Valmar notes, far more people are up and about; from down below, unseen as they pass steeply down a high-walled alley, voices sound, particularly the shouts of children, and the rattle of hoofs on stone, rumble of wheels, the many mysterious noises of a crowded city coming to life.

On their back-way, they encounter only a few, nodding and wishing good day, not the subject of undue curiosity, coming in minutes to the head of an uneven and dilapidated stone stair. Unencumbered sunlight is at its foot, where the way levels and widens, cobbled.

Cantello pauses.   "Remain here," he says, mainly for Idolema. "Sab?" He wishes Hodd to stay beside Kellan.

With the youth, he descends the crumbling stair. Planted behind the rightward wall, a tall rowan overhangs its foot, and the level here, as Restil told, is the mere stump of a street, closed in to the left by small, close-set houses. To the right, perhaps sixty paces, it opens on a more frequented road, which ought to be Pilgrim Course, not far from where it merges into the Millway. Clumps of men, women and children, all in holiday mood and garb, are making their way down with no haste, and a pony ambles by with its slumped rider.

Cantello turns and signals Hodd to follow. "The small alley-way," to Sab, pointing, "is there, by the houses — " hardly discernible unless told what to look for.

When Valmar descends, he knows where they are, very close to their goal; the high, square flat-roofed building of which the upper windows and cornice are visible beyond the near houses is, he says, the Old Wool Market, the short side, its end; the structure is far longer than it is wide, its farther end jutting well out into Palace Square.

Wasting no time crossing the quiet street, they go single file in the narrow footpath, which is no more than fifty paces long, and opens on a way not much wider, rutted, and littered with refuse. From where they are, crouched between two dwellings, they can look across to the weathered stone of the Old Wool Market, with its slightly recessed, long-unpainted small back door. Beyond, no more than two dozen paces, the Millway seems a solid mass of people, moving for Palace Square. Or facing that way, craning necks for a view ahead; very little movement can be seen, and it must be that just out of sight, the Guard is manning another of its makeshift gates, and carefully searching for concealed weapons — not to say a disguised princess — before letting anyone into the square.

There is, as Sab mutters, no chance of reaching the door unseen; while the entrance to Shoat's Alley is narrow, the tedium of waiting causes some to look idly around; two small boys are briefly just inside the alley, before a slight edging forward in the crowd makes them dart back to rejoin presumed parents.

"Seen is not always noticed," Cantello says.   "Valmar?" — indicating he will be the one to cut across and try the door, since he has the best chance of being recognized by Geddo, if he is there.

The man, no willing apprentice hero, nods resignedly, puts the tip of his tongue briefly between dry lips, bends to brush once more with his fingertips at the dried mud on a boot, and darts across, evidently deluded that to do so in a half-crouch makes him less vis- ible; "The fool should saunter," Hodd blackly comments.

At the small door, Valmar raps and pushes in quick succes- sion. As the result of one or both, it opens inward, and part of a man's figure is briefly and dimly visible. Valmar turns to signal all is well, Cantello's breathing resumes, and the man vanishes inside.

"Sab, you and Idolema," Cantello says, not wishing to go in a single conspicuous crowd. "No need of haste." Astonishing him (a stoic understatement), Aretta turns to kiss his cheek and murmur, "Always," before setting out with Sab, in the proper casual manner.

They reach the door, and are admitted. "Hodd — take Kennar with you."

They go, and as they pass the door, a man comes into the alley from the Millway, one of the Black Guard, sword in hand. Tentatively, apparently alerted by some report of unexplained doings here, he approaches the Old Wool Market, doing his best to keep watch in all directions. Arriving at the door, he can hardly fail to notice that it is an inch or two short of fully closed. He looks over his shoulder, a young man, indecisive, but certain he should summon help.

An enterprise hangs on a fraying thread. Cantello crossing the way like an uncaged tiger, swords the man through the belly, catching at the same time at his waist, so that he can bundle the dying man in through the doorway and out of sight. "Bar the door," he orders, as he lets the convulsing body slide from his blade to the flagged floor.

Someone does so. A large, murky space, all windows either bricked up or boarded over, with bright needles of light penetrating here and there. Cantello's companions are gathered near him, and there are others, men of the Royal Guard at their most ceremonial, tunics braided in gold, ornate high-crested helms. One wearing an officer's sash, after bending over the downed man to be sure his wound is mortal, straightens to say, "I am Geddo." The face, so far as can be made out, is broad and open, perhaps showing signs of anxiety.

"I am Cantello. Here is your queen — " correctly deducing there has been no time for that announcement.

"Madam — " the officer has a rasp in his voice, making him sound on the edge of anger, which he is certainly not. "A day for this realm, the best day this realm has seen for seven years and more. Many of us, more than can be told — our joy, that is to say, we have worked and hoped for this, and now — "

"Let us hear — " Cantello's interruption is equally a rescue, "How this day is to be made wonderful."

The plan is simple, boldly based on the untested supposition that the mere appearance of Idolema will carry the day; without saying so Cantello supposes that her public revealing would, if no more, force Corvan to postpone his own elevation while her claims can be examined. That will be a bad-tempered, brawling episode with allies aligning themselves, in the end decided less on evidence than by the swords each side can command; no doubt in all the realm it is Idolema who will win more support — or Corvan find more enemies — but as he told her last night, here at the center it might yet be a struggle between Royal Guard and Black Guard, settled before any of the provincial forces can enter the fight. How much of the Royal Guard might choose Corvan is beyond any guessing; not all, obviously, are like Geddo, enthusiasts for the lost princess.

The floor of the Old Wool Market, Geddo explains, rises on a virtually imperceptible incline, the large double-door that is its main entrance opening on broad stone steps, placing it practically on a level with, though some distance from, the platform constructed for the coronation. There are, naturally, guards posted, Geddo's own men, to keep spectators from mounting the steps. If, when the ceremonies begin, Idolema is positioned just inside those doors, at the moment when the traditional invitation to any challenge is uttered, they can be thrust open, and the rightful queen emerge, hailed as such by her retinue, a cry he predicts will be taken up enthusiastically by the crowd; Geddo's view, not quite Cantello's, is that Corvan will have no choice but to yield.

By wary habit, he and Hodd prowl the large space, looking at everything, and Geddo goes with them. Though high, the ceiling, as their eyes adjust to the dim, is obviously inadequate to account for the building's full height, and an exposed iron staircase somewhere near the middle of its length is said to lead to what was the main storage space. Beside the front steps, Geddo explains, is a bay where wagons would come, so that bales of wool could be lowered; the device for this, with gears and pulleys, has long vanished, but the open platform can still be seen, high above the square. Again, men of the Royal Guard are posted there, at the last moment forbidden by a nervous Corvan to carry bows. Not even the Black Guard, according to Geddo, will have archers in the square, such is Corvan's fear of treachery, but the news is welcome to Cantello; one of Nidlaam's creatures, armed with a bow, could be a danger when Idolema is first revealed.

With probably more than an hour left till the ceremonies begin, more than twice that before her moment arrives, Cantello decrees that Idolema, for her safety, can wait on that upper level, its single access, the iron staircase, where two at most can go abreast, more easily defended than the open spaces below — evidently, as she remarks, the incoming bales of wool must also have been hoisted there by the outside winch. Geddo himself, with a trusted subordinate, will be stationed at the foot of the stair, Hodd and Sab seat themselves higher up, while Cantello as ever remains with the girl, the woman, his woman (for another hour). Geddo's kinsman, Valmar, will slip out to join the crowd in the square, where his voice can help ignite the acclaim at Idolema's appearance, while Kellan, still protesting, has been put in the care of the guard, with instructions to keep him close.

Above, it is somewhat lighter, and, for the same reason, a few unregarded gaps in the stopping-up of the unglazed windows, noticeably more chilly; Aretta shudders and draws her worn cloak closer.

Suddenly she gives a reproachful laugh. "Pale blue swans."

The laugh ends in a yawn. "We had our night," he says. Perhaps their only one.

"We had our night," in hushed wonder.

Corvan, now, through the glamoury of verbiage and our established disdain for imposed unities, seen in extended closeup for the first time, is angry. A couple of hours away from being a king, when he should be surrounded by a nearer circle of dressers and hairdressers perfecting his appearance, an outer ring of attendants and sycophants, all in their various ways currying favor, he is closeted instead with overbearing Nidlaam, who, for all his utility, never seems to bring anything but bad, or at best disturbing news, along with unheard-of demands for wider powers. Now, at this brink, he is asking for permission, written permission, to strike at elements of the Royal Guard, arrest some of its officers — an attempt likely to cause bloodshed — and to do so without so much as informing its captain, Armid.

"You could turn my coronation into a pitched battle between your men and his — for what? You told me Palace Square would be secure."

Nidlaam, having hoped to get his way with heavy-handed hints, reluctantly recognizes that Corvan's willed obtuseness mandates plain speaking.

"Those charged with guarding the Old Wool Market — I believe they may have the supposed Idolema in their midst." The king-to-be hates to hear the name mentioned, but when it has to be alternates between a scornful conviction she must be dead, and the irascible stipulation she be hunted down with no more excuses.

Nidlaam cannot believe Corvan's hesitation. Dark-faced, frowning, his resplendent ceremonial dress still to be completed, the prize he has to have in earnest jeopardy, he amazingly wants to change the subject.

"We intend to advance overlordship of Coldiron to a full earldom."

At such a time, does he expect abject gratitude? Besides, this promotion is not the one Nidlaam wants. "With your indulgence, lord, I would rather it remain a barony; the Coldiron Vale would be like a toy earldom."

"You reject a rise in rank?"

"That, pardon me, I have not said. When your power is perfected, lord, it will be possible to proceed against some who have worked against this moment. With prisoners already in my keeping, and new informants eager to display their allegiance, a conviction for treason against Lord Lumatt is within reach; the Earldom of Tarne would become vacant with his conviction."

Corvan blinks. "You would want to be Earl of Tarne and Baron Coldiron, both at once?"

"There are precedents."

True, there are, and warning ones. With the wealth of those southern fiefs added to his present strength, Nidlaam could become a rival in power to the king, and while he has always displayed a ferocious loyalty to Corvan's cause, that same ruthlessness is daunting to contemplate as a weapon at Corvan's own throat. Nor is the arrest and conviction of the powerful and influential Lumatt the simple matter of evidence that Nidlaam pretends.

"We shall see." Corvan is, as often, pondering which of the nobility can be nurtured as an alternative to, and check upon, this man, whose talent and zest for making himself feared should be less needed, as the people learn to love their king, as surely they will, once the disloyal have been dealt with.

Without in any way minimizing Nidlaam's capacity for wickedness, nor his manifold unpleasant traits, it must be recorded that until this moment he has scarcely imagined himself as anything more than the king's right hand — one unanatomically capable of independent action, and using his power to influence Corvan's policies, but always the ruler's intimidating lieutenant. It is Corvan's hesitation, and the guessed reason for it, that causes just what it fears, the sudden leap of greater ambition. Though not an earl born, and with no near relationship to the ruling house, his lineage, bristling with cognate titles and wholly sanctified by marriage through a dozen generations, is surely superior to Corvan's, whose mother was an obscure provincial merchant's younger daughter seduced by Dairemid's laughable younger brother, who contrived to get himself killed in a foolish horse-chase before he had fathered any legitimate offspring. Through the kindness of the old king, Dairo — or perhaps his remorse, he having proposed the fatal game as a diversion — Corvan, not formally adopted, was brought up at court, very nearly as a prince. Nevertheless, older men and women remember that, deprived of his mother, constantly encountering reminders of the disparity between his foreseeable future and that of his uncle, Dairimid (as later, that of his infant cousin, Idolema), he very early became a rancid and brooding boy, with a capacity for spite limited only by his lack of boldness. Poison, Nidlaam reflects, recalling the more-than-suspicious circumstances that brought Corvan unpredictably to power, would be just the weapon of such a boy and such a man.

For Corvan, the same edgy uncertainties lurk in the authorization Nidlaam is seeking; the Royal Guard under Armid of Lasth may have been less unquestioningly biddable than he would have wished, may indeed be adulterated with some lingering so-called Loyalist sympathies, but if Nidlaam is allowed to prune, thin out and at the last uproot that force, nothing will stand between the king and the Black Guard, which is to say Nidlaam's ambitions. Other kings in other times have become mere ornamental puppets, prisoners of their captains, and between the two Corvan, with no warrior reputation of his own to bind warriors to him, is easier with Armid's bland unconcern than with Nidlaam's brutal effectiveness — which he will for a time continue to rely on. Despite rank and effortless popularity, Armid, though he has sometimes lost his temper over the other's excess of zeal, is too vain, too lazily self-satisfied ever to be a threat.

"By your leave, lord, time — " almost visibly thrusting aside distraction to push his warrant once more under Corvan's nose.

"This must be taken care of, and discreetly, before the ceremonies begin."

"A quarter-hour should be enough; Geddo can have no more than a dozen men with him." Nidlaam has his best, his hearth-company, at hand.

"If you start this, you had better have this so-called Idolema to show, or plain evidence this Geldo — "

"Geddo, sir."

"Well, that he planned what you say."

"I think I can promise his full confession, after a few days at Coldiron." Though Nidlaam has long been aware of the man's unreliability, his confidence here rests largely on information from Tarfal, but while the youth was duped in the question of Idolema's route into Hallabreg — still unknown — Nidlaam believes he has it right this time; by report, Geddo's men guarding the Old Wool Market are certainly prepared for something. Geddo, however, is like the hare or hedgehog sometimes incidentally trapped with a stag or boar; Nidlaam, fearing new agonizing by Corvan, added curbs on his freedom of action, has said nothing about the probable involvement and possible presence of Cantello. Of Cantello! Nidlaam has in his reach the power to write the final chapter in a legend.

"And Armid — " with tormenting reluctance reaching for a pen.

"Give me ten minutes to have my men in place, then summon Armid, lord, tell him of the treason, and what steps we have taken; instruct him the Royal Guard is not to interfere. This is a case where he cannot stand on the integrity of his men; it will be, and properly, out of his hands."

"And properly," Corvan echoes. He signs the warrant.

A new reign must not begin in gossip; with Aretta-Idolema seated on a rough wooden bench, Cantello, rather than sitting beside

---

her, her hands in his, as they both would prefer, speaks with Frant, a big-shouldered young soldier of the Royal Guard. He, of good but unrenowned birth, is adamant that by far the most of Armid's force is Loyalist in its leanings, but that Nidlaam, too, has his informers among them, the reason Geddo's conspiracy has been limited to this handful of trusted men.

"Oh," he says, with a near-reverent gaze for Idolema, "But it will be good to live in city, in a realm, freed from suspicions and fears, all the disappearances, the rumors of hidden cruelties worse than any we see. Nidlaam — "

There echoes a noise between a rap and a boom, seemingly at the front doors. From the high outside platform, another of Geddo's men comes with a badly frightened face. "Black Guard," he says. "The Black Guard is here, fifty or more. Lord Coldiron is with them."

"Stay here," Cantello tells Aretta, drawing his blade.

"Hug me."

He does, and they kiss, too. A tradition well and perhaps over-established mandates we ascribe to one or both at this crucial point utterances either of penetrating poignancy or numbing sentimentality — the difference is purely subjective, depending equally on the temperament of the reader and the plausibility of the characters — but in this instance we are rescued from the perils of invention by the touching spontaneity of Aretta, who says, "Forgive me, love."

"For what?" he says, "For completing my life?" — and then, with a little shove from the unseen stage-manager, Sab arrives, bearing what is not news.

Two of the Royal Guard still remain to protect Idolema; neither here nor for any previous action is there any apology for not conforming to fashionable revisionism, placing the woman, contrary to all but a tiny number of freakish exceptions in recorded experience, in the front of battle, blade flashing: aside from the cultural impossibilities, turning to nonsense the entire chivalric tradition, as Cantello has more than once implied, nothing could be more absurd than to risk the one life that gives any object to their exertions.

Cantello leading, the others clatter down the iron stair. Hodd has advanced to the bottom, a position abandoned by the Royal Guard men, who have mustered about Geddo, too late, it seems, to dispute the forcing of the front doors. Light streams in there, and with it a dense phalanx of well-armed men, quickly spreading to array themselves across the breadth of the hall. The small knot of Royal Guard facing them is outmatched by five to one.

"Shut the doors, and bar them," comes from Nidlaam; Cantello's first sight in years, but still not to be mistaken, a large man, not exceptionally tall, but big-shouldered and burly, with a thick neck and wrists. His thought is no doubt to insulate this confrontation from the ceremony, from the crowd waiting in the square, but possibly he does not foresee how dim this place will be without that opening. He peers, as he begins a call for instant surrender.

There is a flurry of movement among Geddo's small group, and a man breaks free, running across the twenty-five pace gap between the two forces, shouting. It is Kellan, doing his best to hail Nidlaam and denounce the traitors here, but the man next to the Baron (the impassive Glake), seeing a despairing attack, swords the man down with a single sweeping mow, and half a dozen of his company crowd around to kill and rekill the man with many thrusts. Ironic reflections omitted for the sake of narrative pace.

Some of Geddo's men are glancing back longingly to the small back entrance, now closed with heavy bars, but surely they must know, Cantello prays, that Shoat's Alley, out of sight of the crowds, will be filled with Black Guard, with no need to burst in, ready to fell them one by one as they emerge. Nidlaam's men resume a slow advance.

"Defend the stair," Hodd says, or perhaps agrees, reading Cantello's thoughts. Before the recommendation of a retreat that way can be relayed to Geddo, Nidlaam, halting, speaks again.

"I have no desire to spill more blood. Who is Geddo? So: I know that you are harboring a woman falsely claiming to be lost Idolema. We, his majesty and I, would be ready to entertain the notion you were deceived into believing this impostor was genuine, and are therefore not to be blamed, if you will simply surrender her to me."

"Clemency from Coldiron, there's something a man can trust."

Nidlaam swivels, as if noticing the stair only now. "Hodd Scorner, still championing what he does not believe in — and is that Cantello? A pity you bound up your fame with this shabby business, and brought your friend into it, too."

"Nidlaam," he calls back. "I say this only once; sheathe your weapon, and prepare to swear your proper allegiance, or you and many of your men will not outlive this day."

The threat is plainly absurd; all told the Loyalist side is fifteen or sixteen swords, while Nidlaam has more than sixty, but Cantello's is still a numinous name, and many of the Black Guard fidget uneasily, showing each other — to whatever extent perceptible in the gloom — troubled faces.

"Allegiance!" Nidlaam's loud jeer breaks into but does not entirely break the spell. "Most men grow in wisdom, but you in folly; young, you knew the meaning of allegiance, and did not pledge your sword to fraud." (While our sympathies are unchanged, it must be conceded here that, as we know, Nidlaam's charge is accurate enough, and only the awfulness of Corvan excuses our hero.)

This ritual exchange gives Cantello space for a quick exchange of glances with Hodd, who mouths, *Nidlaam*, and nods slightly. Though a sword is still in his hand, the Baron is hanging back from the actual fighting, so as to urge his men forward.

To Sab and another man behind, the one who had been mounted on the outside platform, Cantello says, "Hold the stair." As more Black Guard press forward, he and Hodd leap down to meet them, a single idea between them. There is little space for elaborate swordplay, but the two foremost of Nidlaam's men go down at once, and the force and determination of the charge takes the champions into the midst of suddenly daunted men; with no more than three mighty cuts Cantello cleaves a path to Nidlaam, Hodd turning to guard his rear, and at once engaging three of the enemy.

Geddo and most of his men seize the opportunity to fight their way, though with losses, to the foot of the stair. Confronting Cantello, Nidlaam has flankers nearby, but by and large his men hang back, or interest themselves in the other fights going on, either fearful Nidlaam will be angered by any suggestion he needs help, or else with a fine structural sense of a duel epically ordained. Still, Cantello has swiftly to deal with an attack coming from his left, and having sent that man reeling back, mortally wounded with a knife-thrust under his chin, must be quick to turn Nidlaam's long almost surreptitious thrust. The man's great strength is apparent in the fol-lowing overhead chop, shocking Cantello's wrist, but then with a sidestep, spin and pace, Cantello finds or creates the space he needs. Very rapidly he notes with dismay that Hodd is in trouble, and that Sabb, disobeying, has quit the stairs, his place instantly filled from above by one of Geddo's men, and plunged furiously into the melée with crude but telling strokes.

Once more Nidlaam attempts to surprise him; their main blades ring and slither, clash again, Nidlaam giving ground with a defense that shows skill and a powerful forearm.

It will not be adequate. "A pity," Cantello says contemp-tuously, "You cannot be made to die often enough for all your crimes."

Peripherally, he perceives a flicker of movement, feels a sharp hurt on the right side of his back, and knows he has been wounded. By Glake, who might have killed or disabled him, but for his caution, darting in to sting and retreat. He sidles, looking for a fresh opportunity. as Nidlaam is driven back. Putting him into a low defensive crouch, Cantello seizes the chance to turn angrily on the other, who backs away too tardily to save himself, and is cleanly decapitated while defending against a low thrust that never comes; astonishment is the final expression of the usually expressionless.

Cantello, feeling pain and sensing blood from the wound on his back, swivels back in time to meet a desperate new attack by Nidlaam, who with a yell launches himself into a bundling attempted rush, and as suddenly is silenced, skewered on Cantello's short-armed jab, which, jerking free, he follows with a great, triumphant backhand that rips open the man's belly, hip to hip. Grotesquely spilling a cascade of glistening guts, he crumples in a dying heap.

Events, sometimes, though not announced, as they should be, by thunderclaps or bolts of sudden silence, can be apprehended in their magnitude by some process outside the normal senses; most of the Black Guard are not watching, or can have no clear view of their double loss of leadership, yet its effect spreads like an instant contagion; everywhere they shudder back, losing heart. Keenly aware of his own hurt, and that his bleeding must be stopped, Cantello nevertheless is able to hew and intimidate his way back to where a worse-wounded Hodd is being partially supported by hard-pressed Sab, who seems untouched, and with his one free hand is wielding an inexpert sword in fearsome swipes. Together, as their enemies hesitate, Cantello and the youth are able to bear Hodd, who is conscious and determined in spite of obvious pain, back to the foot of the stair, and there a couple of Geddo's men work him up to where, for the moment, he can be seated.

"You are wounded, too, master — " in Sab's factual statement there can be detected the crumbling of one world, where heroes are invulnerable, and perhaps the forming of another, heavier one to rest on his own shoulders. "The stair can be held now — " indeed, it is packed with ready swords, facing a leaderless enemy reluctant to renew their efforts.

He means, however shyly, that Cantello should seek aid, but damaged captaincy still has work to do. Hauling himself up a couple of steps, as Geddo makes way for him, Cantello turns and stands straight. "You men," he roars out. "Your Nidlaam would not hear me, and you see I have kept my word; you have no overlord. Learn: sheathe your weapons and live to serve your queen."

These are mercenaries, not enthusiasts for any cause; there is a perceptible ebbing, with many exchanged glances. "What queen?"

calls out a tall, dishevelled but seemingly unwounded man, an under-captain, likely now to be senior officer here.

"There is only one; Idolema, daughter of Dairemid."

"She's dead," another man says.

"She is alive," the woman corrects, appearing halfway down the stair, cloak and kerchief discarded. Muffled, from the square comes the sound of fanfares, there announcing the coming of Corvan. Hodd, Cantello incidentally notes, must have managed or been assisted in the climb to the head of the stair; he is no longer visible.

A wary truce has come about.

Hodd is being tended by Valmar, who never found the opportunity, as planned, to slip out into the crowd. The odd way he has of periodically shuttering up his face is now explained; in youth he was pledged to a monkish order, the Filidians, quitting them precipitately at twenty when unable to commit himself to continued celibacy ("I met who was to be my wife"), but not before he had acquired much herb-lore and leechcraft from that healing order; he brings a schooled gentleness and a deft touch to his examination of the gaping wound in the hollow of Hodd's thigh, is able to staunch the worst of the bleeding, and to make him somewhat more comfortable, full length inside one of the compartments where individual batches of wool used to be stored.

Cantello, meanwhile, assisted by a solicitous and bravely unweeping Aretta — her last act, he foresees, with even intimate possession of that name — has stripped away his bloodied shirt, and winces as Valmar presses a piece of cloth into the wound, and with another, moistened one starts to clean away blood.

"He has the strength to heal, my lady," Valmar assures Idolema, mixed news for Cantello, who heard no such assurance in Hodd's case.

Patched, he pushes aside the man's attempt to restrain him, and stands, gesturing to young Frant. "Lend me your tunic." His own blood-blotched shirt is lain aside. The soldier grins, but it is Cantello who is asking, and for the rest of time the tunic will have a legend and a boast attached to it; he gives Cantello his helmet to hold, and willingly pulls off the tunic, then stands hugging his own elbows in sudden chill as Cantello endures a fresh jab of pain slipping it on.

Now, from the deep pocket of his discarded outer jacket he takes a small cloth-wrapped object; uncovered, it is a slender circlet of pure gold, too large a ring for a bangle. Watchful Aretta comments on its beauty, but he reads a doubt in her eyes.

"No," he reassures her, "This does not come from Synta; it is a last part of my tithe in the Hoard of Mylsturm, and once was worn by the sister-daughters of kings in Paranopa."

"You carried this with you?"

"To place upon your head. Come."

Just inside the hatchway that gives on the former loading-platform, they listen to the unaware Archmage below droning his way through the largely falsified pedigree and yet-more-disputable claims to power of Corvan, who must be kneeling by now, head bowed, awaiting the unveiling of the crown. The throng in the square is strikingly silent.

"You should be resting your wound," she whispers.

"I'll have time for that."

"Oh, love — " a sigh, a cry of pain, a wrenching wish for a different fate.

Outside, the Archmage has paused, and a murmur in the crowd means the glittering crown has been exposed and raised.

"Who knows of any impediment to this man's crowning?"

Emerging, Cantello, huge-voiced, proclaims, "The rightful heir lives. See your Queen, Idolema — " and as she comes forward, the sun, clambering above the central heights of the palace, produces an effect that in the theatre would risk being called meretricious, but here is pure and perfect drama; sunlight salutes royalty, the calmly radiant face of royalty greets the sun. The slender circlet of gold flames as Cantello holds it above her head, and places it gently on the dark hair above the fine brow. The simultaneous murmur of many voices adds up to a thunderclap, *Idolema!*

While we have plainly chosen sides, it does no harm to a reputation for all-round compassion to consider for a tiny moment the plight of (admittedly unlovable) Corvan, the crown quite literally within his grasp, as he rises from his knees, glaring up at the source of interruption he has been promised cannot come. Nidlaam has failed him; he cannot silence, much less make unspoken Cantello's unsupported claim, and is in no situation for debate; his packed audience is turning against him, and he is a long way from certain the slender young woman high above his head is not the actual lost princess he last saw at eleven, two days before his uncle's death.

Yet, this has been his realm for seven years, not to slip away unfought-for. He looks at the Archmage, tall but stooped, long-jawed and lined under his ceremonial headgear. But for him, Corvan could be king; the actual seventh anniversary of his protectorship was last week, but this censer-swinging old strategist persuaded him the coronation would be better linked to the vernal festival of Old New Year, with its theme of rebirth — and is coming forward with no help now; an opportunist to rival Corvan himself, holding the crown like a letter whose recipient has moved leaving no new address, he is gazing up at the platform where the claimant and her champion stand, perhaps weighing whether anything more like a sign from heaven is likely to occur in the foreseeable future. Most of the nobility industriously assembled from throughout the realm are equally on a knife-edge, with the duplicitous southerners, Eltow Falnis, Lumatt of Tarne, ready for open revolt, if they had their armed followings here at Hallabreg. With the noise of the spectators, largely mounting acclaim for the alleged Idolema, continuing to grow, Corvan turns to the handsome Armid of Lasth nearby; some of the Royal Guard stationed by the platform are near joining the mood of the crowd, but Armid's reputation for fairness, his general recognition, may still help achieve deadlock, a breathing-space where, as the people must understand, the validity of this pretender can be soberly evaluated — and judiciously rejected; Nidlaam, when he returns, will see to that.

"This is madness," Corvan tells Armid. An hour ago the man was piqued, near outraged, that Nidlaam had been authorized to proceed against an officer of the Royal Guard without first notifying its captain, but now he has ample proof that order was necessary.

"Or a miracle," Armid replies, and the fool unsheathes his sword, strides to the edge of the platform, and bowing his head holds up his blade two-handed, proffering it to the girl. The men of the Royal Guard roar and stamp their approval.

There is still the Council, largely Corvan's creation, seldom anything but compliant through seven years; it is unthinkable to him that this hysterical response of an untutored mob can produce an actual change of rule so long as the Council must adjudicate. No one hinders him, but very few follow as he goes back into the palace, back straight, repelling all notion of retreat.

"Your leave," Cantello murmurs. "I must look to Hodd."

"My *leave*?" in initial disbelief.

"My part is done, lady — " the still-swelling plaudits confirm it. "I no longer command."

Fighting to remain conscious, Hodd asks, "The cheers? For our side?"

"We shall have a queen."

Even in this extremity, Hodd rejects any such objective. "We won, you and me, like — "

"Always," Cantello finishes for him.

XI

Another place where resort to ritual formula would be comfortable; `And thus began the reign of Queen Idolema, told of in many songs and stories.' Curtain. Not that we're fooled; we still know that there would be complications, setbacks, disappointments, days when nothing went right, just as we might guess that not far outside the frame to that uproarious Brueghel canvas are unhappy people, hungry beggars, disappointed (incredibly, even dysfuncional) lovers, solitary dyings, but give assent to formal limits, aware that art is all choosing, as much in what to leave out.

There is, still, a difference between framing to contain and cropping so as to mislead; a biography of Bonaparte cannot conclude with his fleeting Palm Sunday, the triumphant return from Elba, editing out Waterloo and St Helena, nor the tale of Aladdin be called complete with the marriage, before his wife's disastrous acceptance of the wicked uncle's trade-in deal; without dramatic shade there is no noticeable light.

There is, besides, the question of loose ends. Within a formal frame, not every strand needs to be poked through to the back and tied; we should not be fussbudgets, like Mr Magnus (of the infallibly entertaining initials) in *Pickwick*, checking and rechecking to be sure the striped bag, the red bag, the paper parcel and the leather hat-box are all in place; has anyone ever cared about what becomes of Sparafucile after he drops off his client's sackful of Gilda, or lost sleep over the eventual fate of Osric in *Hamlet*?

Here, however, our hanging characters are no mere walk-ons; the joint or several futures of our principal pair unresolved — and there may be those in the audience who, like Cantello, want to know what happened to Tarfal the traitor; something more than a conventional coda is indicated.

It is the sixth day; as acknowledged though not willingly official advisor, he has remained at Idolema's side, helping to hold off the many who see in the accession of an inexperienced girl the opening for influence, or even bullying. A process already productive of some astonishment not quite able to show itself as offense: the southern lords, both Baron Falnis, a large, loud-voiced man with a foolish laugh. and Lumatt, Earl of Tarne, sumptuously dressed and very conscious of his dignity, obviously believed that in covertly protecting the supposed Idolema and (if somewhat ineffectually) scheming at her accession, they were grooming a puppet, a mere symbol of power through which to advance their own interests. They had not counted on her independence of spirit, nor on the number and variety of staunch allies she would instantly acquire, with Cantello to translate these strengths into practical currency, constantly assuring the queen that she does indeed have the power to disappoint, where necessary, any petitioner.

But it is a not a part he is comfortable with, and one he means to withdraw from as the queen's position becomes secure. The news of Nidlaam's death, melting-away of the Black Guard, Corvan's grudging submission, the swift arrival at Hallabreg of armed Loyalist forces, and above all overwhelming popular support have made her acceptance far simpler and swifter than once seemed possible, and today Cantello feels almost guiltlessly able to absent himself from a meeting of the reconstituted Council, presided over by the pompous but reliable and essentially innocuous Oremin, whose uncontroversial agenda for the day bored him. He is very easily bored by the details of governance, and today Idolema, to supply the necessary idea of force, can have the newly devoted Armid by her side. After seven years, the Royal Guard has at last resworn its oath of loyalty.

In the obscure corner of the palace Cantello has chosen for his quarters he is found by old Tarbul who has just last evening come to Hallabreg, now dismissing at the door the servant who has been aiding him, then doing his best to turn to a joke his evident shame that stiffening joints and general fatigue made the long ride impossible for him.

"A fat linen-merchant's fatter wife might think it great luxury to sit on pillows in the back of a wagon, while others drove the horses, am I right?"

Cantello pulls out a chair, and sees the veteran warrior seated. It is hardly more than ten days since their last meeting, but Tarbul looks far older or wearier than in the inn at Ault — or perhaps he has merely been drained of purpose; he was from the first near the center of the Loyalist scheming, and may well have seen the restoration of Idolema as his life's last great task. For which reason Cantello now offers congratulations on the success of those plans, quite content to have the old man go on believing he, Cantello, believes he has helped the authentic Idolema to her rightful place.

"Hah. Aratar's boy — young Tarfal, you know — he once said, it's easy for the old to sit making airy plans where others do the dying. He was rebuked, but it's true enough; I should be commending you. As I knew you would, you found you must help our cause, after all."

"For no better reason than seeing it was bound to fail, as proposed, the men assembled at Mitfell and no clear way to reach here."

"Reason enough for men like us. There may be choices, but you can't choose against your nature; I no more believed you at Ault than if you had told me you'd decided to give up peeing."

Obviously he desires more information, the focus of his interest easy to guess, but, not to seem too eager, introduces a less personal topic, the question of local magistracies, some vacant, others filled by what he calls "Corvan's creatures, wilder-hounds of the law."

Cantello holds up a hand. "This would be better raised with the queen herself — or with Oremin, who, with the Council, advises on policy."

"Oremin," despondently, with a sniff, but he accepts Cantello's evasion.

After a contemplative minute, "You lost your friend, Hodd? I would have judged him indestructible."

"As he did," gravely.

An understanding nod. "I never forgot I had the same organs as those I tried to kill — you know this; there's no cowardice in making survival part of your plans, am I right?"

"You see me — " at the brink, now, probably, of the reason Tarbul is here, places Cantello does not want to go with this man.

"What went wrong with the plan, so to bring about Hodd's death? The boy — he was useful to you?"

In this are various elements, the deep desire to be proud of his great-grandson, puzzlement that he is not to be found here, nor is spoken of. Tarbul must have spent the night with close kin; two of his grandsons, Aratar and Taremin, Tarfal's father and uncle respectively, are at Hallabreg, brought by Corvan for his coronation, while Tarbul's surviving son, Darval, a frayed and dissipated sixty-odd, rode in unopposed from the Mitfell camp with others of the clan when their Black Guard adversaries unaccountably withdrew.

"Hodd Scorner — " ignoring the second question — "was killed at the Old Wool Market, as were others. But for the fight they put up, Nidlaam at the last moment would have seized Idolema, and Corvan would now be king."

"And Tarfal?"

"Was not with us. I sent him from Senningtop, with a message for the Mitfell encampment."

"Through the wilderness? Never alone? Has he been heard from?"

"He is alive, and unhurt."

"Where?"

"I believe, at Coldiron still."

"Coldiron?" Bewilderment is coming uppermost. "Then he was captured? But I am told Nidlaam is dead, that you killed him, sword to sword — "

"True."

"Then why has the boy not been released?"

"He was never a prisoner — " admitting to himself that the head of the clan will have to learn the truth, and that in keeping it back he is sparing himself, not Tarbul. "Forgive me, master, I believe it was Tarfal who betrayed your plans and mine to Nidlaam, the reason for the fight that killed Hodd, among others."

"It seems to me," with deliberation, "That if anyone other than Cantello said this — you *know* this? How can you know this?"

"There is a young woman, daughter to the Eremian embassy here, who was Nidlaam's mistress, or one of them; she tells me she was at Coldiron when Tarfal came with friendship and offers of information — something already suspected." Zembra, showing little emotion over the death of Nidlaam, came to ask whether she would be allowed to retrieve from Coldiron some of her belongings, chiefly clothes — or else to test whether Cantello could be seduced; she was said to be an ardent collector of powerful men. Shrewd — or perhaps merely too vain to accept failure on any less flattering terms — she decided Cantello's indifference indicated his attachment elsewhere, and even guessed where, observing with feline irony that an experienced man might come to require better and more varied satisfaction than a novice, no matter how royal, could provide. It was, perhaps, to ameliorate that undiplomatic assessment — or soothe its souring effect on Cantello — that she offered the tale of her dinner with Nidlaam, interrupted by the arrival of Tarfal, and what came of it.

"Predicted, rather," Cantello ruefully amends. "Master, I must share the blame in all this; I saw the signs of his disaffection, and instead of taking him in hand, tried to make use of it; he was allowed too much opportunity to betray us."

"Hah. Not near as much opportunity as he had, growing up, to learn how true men behave. You say he remains at Castle Coldiron?"

"As I believe, though never a prisoner, but Nidlaam wanted him kept there as a hostage for the truth of his own stories. Now, of course, with Corvan's failure and Nidlaam's death... "

"Will the queen proceed against him?" — a tragic question, for a lifelong royalist.

"She has said nothing to me about it."

The sardonic glint in Tarbul's eye suggests he finds this answer evasive: no doubt he has been given the news that the new young queen is less malleable than might have been, and has therefore come to see the man said to have the most influence with her. He could hardly guess Cantello has in fact begun, and intends increasingly, to distance himself from any share in Idolema's official intentions. "You can perhaps indicate to her — I don't know whether she'll have time to meet with me — that if these charges against Tarfal are true, he will no longer be of our House — that she can count on our loyal support, no matter what action she takes."

Including execution, he means; there would be no reason for such an assurance otherwise.

Cantello, as he tells Tarbul, cannot imagine the queen will not gladly find time for a meeting with so distinguished a visitor, one among her earliest and staunchest advocates, but whether guessing she is uncomfortable with those who know her true origins, himself uneasy over the news of Tarfal's defection, or merely fatigued, the old man declines, summoning his servant so as to be led away on faltering legs.

Had he stayed a few more minutes, he could not have avoided an encounter with Idolema. But for stray moments, Cantello has not been alone with her since the eve of Corvan's interrupted ceremony. Now, having dismissed her escort, she has come to find him.

Idolema tells him, "The Council now agrees on a date for a new coronation." There is here a tinge of reproach for his absence from the Council, but the news is hardly reason for her rash visit. Nothing remains secret here at the palace.

"Those arrangements can safely be left to Armid." He means, security, now largely a question of keeping watch on any from the former reign with reason to fear Idolema's law. Without Corvan's need to make the coronation ostentatiously public, her ceremony, in the traditional confines of the Oratory, will be more easily protected.

"Have you given further thought to what I should do with Corvan — what would be seen as justice?"

"Two questions." He knows she is puzzled by his distancing, but this encounter makes him uneasy; together with her in a small space he cannot ignore how much he wants her. "Pure justice would mean his exile, for all the crimes he countenanced, regardless of which of them he can be shown to have committed. His permitting, at the least, permitting, release of the wilder-hounds is alone enough."

"Exile," she agrees, "Or death."

"Death by law, death as punishment, is not a thing I understand. In policy, to allow him to retire might win you more praise."

"He would need to be kept under constant watch."

A familiar shrug. "He has no power left, and no means of making any; what idiot would ally himself to one who was humiliated as he was?"

She does not pursue the point. Instead, "There are posts to be filled, those he gave his cronies."

"I have spoken this morning with Armid's lady."

"Indeed?" As before, when he told about Zembra's visit, or with his recollections of Synta's lady, a quick suggestion of bristling at perceived rivalry; Ilana, in a borderland between her blossoming youth and a graver mature charm, is an acknowledged beauty.

"And she has agreed, as her husband had already, subject to her assent, to take Sab into their household, and to coach him in some of the skills he will require, if he is to be at court." Sab himself, though thinking them rather silly, has had no objection to learning fair penmanship, courtly dance, the etiquette for a feast or a polite seduction (not so designated).

"Yes, yes — " not giving it much attention. "He must have a knighthood. But — Castle Coldiron is without a master. Would you become the new lord there?"

"I?"

"Like the castle, the barony is vacant; Nidlaam had no heir. It would mean great security for the realm for you to be there."

"No doubt."

"The living-quarters there are said to have every comfort — famously so."

"Its dying-quarters are also renowned."

"No more. Cantello, you know my heart. I could come there on a royal progress, we could be together — once or twice each year, surely, perhaps more. What is it?"

What it is is vast disappointment. He is Cantello, still Cantello, title as well as name, the only one he desires, and he does not know how she can imagine he could ever accept another. Rather, he does know, and dislikes the knowledge. "I would make the worst of barons."

"Worse than Nidlaam?" she teases.

He does not reply, and the silence stretches out tensely. Idolema, thumb to her lips, takes two reflective steps, and turns with a swish of brocades and ruffled lawns. "I naturally thought you would — in my conceit, I was certain you would take this chance for us to love — as always, I overprice myself, it seems."

"Girl, my girl — " an unexpected mode of address, but she does not check him, "I have loved you for what you are — "

"As I have you."

"And now you want to change me, put a collar on me, make me a crafted part of an ordered realm. Baron Cantello; I can hear Hodd Scorner speaking that title."

"For my sake, for the sake of what we are together? Not even for that?"

He struggles for words she can understand, rejecting the various pat replies that come; the disparity is that she believes what she loves can remain unchanged, no matter what he chooses to do, whereas he knows that one is a necessary condition of the other; he is the freedom of action he has always held and paid the price for.

"More than anything, I would want to find a way for us," he begins earnestly.

"Not anything, it seems."

"Not to become someone I am not. What would that gain?"

"Time, time together."

"Time with a stranger."

"How can you know that?" — very like a child's question, and he resists the urge to give back, How can you not?

"You said, I step outside myself; I can see what I am."

"Cantello," tenderly. "I wish we had never found a way to Hallabreg, and been forced to sit on the wrong side of the Myrin while Corvan made himself king. I wish we could live in your house beside the river, and I could give you a son."

Her need outbidding all prudence, he catches consolingly at her hand. "We can only do the best with the life we're given; you made your choice, a brave one."

"If I had known in time how you felt for me, I might have chosen otherwise."

He shifts his weight uneasily, not wishing to be high-flown. "Everywhere in this realm, your realm now, there are men and women with reason to be glad you did not."

"I don't care; I want happiness for myself — for us."

He makes a patient face. "In all my life — "

Idolema withdraws her hand. "I thought, as Lord Coldiron, you — I thought you would do this, for me. If you have made up your mind to set me in amber, I can't think of any more plans."

Though needing little sleep, that little has always come without a struggle, and to lie awake, tormented with words, is an unfamiliar, exasperating experience.

Nor is he accustomed to indecision; professionally he forms plans swiftly, if he has allies hears alternatives, argues out the best course and sleeps sound — but he has seldom had to tackle a question where there is no clear imaginable victory, where it is a choice among ills. To lose Idolema, the last treasured memory of his Aretta, is bitter to contemplate, turning to a numb and joyless prospect the life he so jealously defends, but to keep at least part of her at the cost she proposes is better only in those alluring dreams of bedding with her when she can come to him, not only bedding, being together, as in the promise of that shortened night at Fane Restil's hostelry — or, still, the promise of that, in the huge dark on Sowback Scarp, when he had talked quietly with a blanketed girl. At Coldiron, she could come to him.

For a short while: soon she must marry, a son to one of the earls to solidify her hold on the throne, or a prince from Maegland or Eremia for the sake of foreign alliance, children will come, and he would be Baron Cantello, the formerly-famed, wielding a limited power he does not desire — witness how swiftly he relinquished command when Idolema's accession was assured, when he had completed the task for which he assumed the leadership. To achieve a known and defined objective best served by those skills in which he excels, he not only accepts but insists on his primacy, but power in general, power as a persisting condition, titular power, he recoils from, whether as served or server, and his fame, his accomplishment, has made that feasible — how could she fail to see how impossible it was, to wedge him miserably into the ill-fitting niche of barony?

Abruptly he knows that she doesn't care, and doesn't blame her for it; she has come, as she was groomed for, to a prize bleak for all its glitter; she, too, has not desired power, but cannot renounce it, and so schemes at the chance of some consolatory happiness, interludes with the only chosen joy. She has tried to negotiate a bargain with her destiny, not seeing (or choosing not to care) that her solution makes him, Cantello, the male equivalent of a king's mistress.

That, too, in the end, ought not to matter; Cantello's considerable pride is not dependent on how others define him; many women, he concedes, and some men, have been willing to accept unappealing roles for the sake of love, or have done so, willing or not; put that way his refusal of the barony stands as an accusation against the generosity of his feelings, a contaminating admixture of caution; this after declaring his love with a recklessness she marvelled at, after inviting her to dispose as she saw fit with his remaining life.

Still, the last, before he escapes into sleep, is what sounds like Hodd's remembered voice. "We gave all this, to turn great Cantello into the queen's drone?"

He wakes with a solution that is logical, simple, an obvious way to everything they say they desire, Cantello and Aretta, yes, Aretta. With all this to recommend it, a lifetime's experience suggests there is practically no chance of its adoption.

She smiles to see him so early; her dark hair, skillfully dressed, is netted in silver and small amethysts, and she is in a light morning gown of a lemony shade; he does not know the origin of her sudden and extensive wardrobe, but whoever these costly and cunning garments were intended for must be very near her for height and slender girth. He loves her — that conviction can return to him with all the force and wonder of a fresh perception.

Perhaps, after all, it will suffice. They are in a drawing-room, with tall windows that look out on the palace gardens, the dark willows bowing over the bend of the Little Hallas beginning to show faint traceries of pale yellow-green in the early sunshine. At the far end, servants are clearing a breakfast table, and without taking her hand he leads her close to the windows.

"Yesterday — " a low murmur, "You spoke of making other choices, if only we had known in time we were going to fall in love."

Her expression is hard to read, but includes some surprise. "If we had known in time," she echoes.

"Why must it be too late? With Nidlaam and his bullies gone, Corvan in eclipse, all major objectives, yours and mine for the sake of the realm, are accomplished. You might step down without any reproach." Only marginally conscious of it, he is challenging her declaration, that she would far rather not be queen, to live quietly with him — the adverb not intended to rule out a good deal of untranquil passion.

Her mouth comes open, and after a silent struggle she says, "Abdicate? After all we went through, all you did to bring us here?"

"Chiefly, it was, as you yourself maintained, a question of saving the realm from Corvan as king. He can be forced to sign a renunciation of any renewed claim on the throne, in exchange for clemency."

"Well, but — who would you put in my place?"

"Hestion, it would be," he replies, choosing to ignore the new, wounding imperiousness of tone.

"Hestion," wrinkling her nose; the man has sat, saying little, at meetings of the Council. An affable, uninspiring but equally unalarming figure, not stupid, with a reputation for decency, the Fen-Warden Hestion, Earl of Halladene, is in truth nearest to the legitimate succession, and when the real Idolema died, ignoring the untenable claims of Corvan, should have become king, though he has made no such claim; his grandmother was elder sister to the old king, Dairo, and he is thus the only acknowledged surviving great-grandchild of Corimal, founder of the dynasty. He is, moreover, exactly the unthreatening man to win support, if hardly devotion, from all the contending nobility, largely through the negative quality of inspiring no fierce enmities.

She looks at, then truly envisages the prospect, and for a moment something like hope, or an appetite for adventure, is in her eyes. It ebbs like an expiring flame. "But there is so much still to be done, that cannot safely be entrusted to others, you know that. Next year — "

"In a year's time, it will be too late."

"For you? You can't keep love alive for a year?"

"For you. After a year, you will not be able to give this up."

He knows this is true, though she makes a gesture as if to flick the idea away. Soft-footed, a maidservant comes in, acknowledges Cantello with a dip of the chin, and approaches Idolema to deliver a quiet message. She stands expectantly by for some answer, delaying her disappearance into the nowhere whence she comes.

"Cantello, forgive me," Idolema says, in her public voice. "I have Oremin waiting to discuss decorations for the coronation. Let us meet later."

His mount is a good one, with the saddle and bridle, not his, but his services to the realm should surely permit him to borrow a horse unasked, without dire consquences; after he reaches home he can lead his pony to Lesser Ault, and return the horse to the cavalry station (no longer of the Black Guard) nearby. It is good to ride as of old on the highway with no fear of being accosted by threatening patrols; spring has truly arrived, the day honey and silver, the breeze not yet warm, but filled with the promise of warmth to come. Nevertheless, he takes note of darker and more continuous cloud away to the south and west.

And journeying can still be dangerous, hardly for him, but for those less capable of defending themselves, and may get worse. His one insistent wielding of borrowed influence was to urge upon Armid and the other earls commanding soldiery that the Black Guard must be disarmed, dismounted and dispersed, before any remnant bands can turn to banditry. Closely related, he also convinced them (or thinks he has) that the wilder-hounds must be hunted down and destroyed, before breeding and wider dispersal turns them into a permanent scourge — while, that is, the original, trained creatures can still be controlled by the pipes till now in the possession of Black Guard officers; a new, unbiddable generation can make not only the wilderness but the roads unsafe.

A reemphasis of this was in the private farewell letter he left, which otherwise touched lightly on general points of policy, but thereafter confined itself to an explanation, so far as it could be articulated, for his choice — his coward's choice, Idolema will call it, but he could not endure a leave-taking, face to face, quite sure, despite unspeakable pain, that his decision is the right, indeed the only one. For them both, the ruler determined actually to rule, and the man unfitted to a life as her holiday; he tried unsuccessfully to explain the irony, that if he didn't love her it might be possible, because then he would still have some life between their infrequent times together, but as it was, her proposal condemned him to joyless, lifeless months, even years, waiting for the next reunion.

It is true that his decision to break away also means a dismal period, but he is no longer a boy, to believe that he would or could mourn their parting to the end of time, just as if he died or she died the survivor, unhappy for a while, would live to love again.

But his letter ended, as he ends, in sorrow not for himself but for her. When chosen to replace dead Idolema, she must have been dismayed by the difficulties — of maintaining the deception, certainly, and of finding a way to displace Corvan, but beyond all that, the challenge of rule, of being the one to decide among differing counsels, and to bear responsibility for that choice. Never a carefree prospect for one born to those duties, and groomed from birth for their burden, and so much the more daunting for a girl whose expectations, till she was past thirteen, only reached as far as a reasonable marriage and a life of obscurity. *How did we get from there to here?* — Cantello smiles at the memory of Hodd, years ago, asking that aggrieved question; they had spent three days enjoying the famous warm baths and equally celebrated brothels at Racq, and only a short river-trip and a couple of minor battles later were wading thigh-deep through stinking mud, searching for a place they had no desire to visit.

The recollection is more germane than he first recognized, but one large difference is that Idolema, still resenting her change of condition, is, so soon, already caught up in the fascination of power, which, as Cantello knows very well, masquerades as the illusion of one's own indispensability; she is virtually a mirror for his own reason for taking up her cause, that unless he did, others would make a botch of it.

It is, perhaps, the most miserable of human conditions (we have strayed, here, a long way from the bold strokes and untrammelled resolutions of the epic tradition, but it can't be helped; we as a species can no longer confine ourselves to primary colors and diatonic harmonies), to be enthralled by what continues to be loathed; a graceful and elegant assassin wasp cased in amber can be made to represent as readily the attractions of power, with its lethal sting. He aches for the bright, naked girl who wished for ways to please him better, but knows she does, too, and can no longer be that. She would accuse him of the same, but already her love is demonstrably conditional; she is heartbreakingly young.

It might reasonably be objected that, understanding so well, Cantello, for some undetermined time, might have stayed at her side to offer his support and sympathy, but as it is he believes he could have become the greatest danger to her continued acceptance among the powers that count. To him it may seem unjust that diversion outside marriage, perhaps admired with a king, at worst earning a half-jocular shake of the head, might be enough to discredit a queen, but those who love and those who wish to rule must deal with the world as it is (and it remains true that it is women who bear the children whose parentage must admit no doubt; a king's diversions will not put a questionable heir in the palace cradle). He had already been obliged to antagonize some of those likeliest to know — some who unquestionably know — her true origins; it is easy to foresee a time when, exasperated by his continuing influence with her, one of them — Lumatt of Tarne comes to mind — becomes bold enough to challenge not only their irregular congress, but the credentials of the queen herself. She would, of course, still have many defenders, but that way leads to civil war, with unimaginable suffering and uncertain outcome; after public denunciation of Idolema, her accusers could not allow her, as she might then (too late) prefer, to abdicate and retire into obscurity. Youth, beauty, sufficient resemblance to what the real Idolema would be by now have helped bring her this far, but more, the widespread popular distrust and dislike of the man she came to supplant, and Cantello hopes she can keep in mind, as fear of any possible resurgence of Corvan fades, how precarious it is going to be, for a proving year or three. As, in another context and in other words, he warned her, to remain queen, she has to behave herself.

Nearing Grosault, the gentler promise of the day has been greyed over, and a steady rain is falling; Cantello makes a patient face and turns up the collar of his jacket; he cannot be more than an hour from a hostelry, warm drink and a good fire. Last winter, when the wind was in the northwest, too much smoke from the fireplace fogged his living quarters, and he intends to rebuild the chimney when warm weather comes. He may also unclog the old mill-race, and fashion a new wheel, not for grinding corn, but to turn a large lathe; he still possesses some of the skills from his father's trade, and can produce furnishings and other needed things of wood — wagon-axles and axe-hafts, for example — to trade for his food and other needs. He is more than content to seek no new adventures, but if adventures need him, they know where to find him. He will, as we know, begin by refusing.

www.ingramcontent.com/pod-product-compliance
Lightning Source LLC
Chambersburg PA
CBHW030247130626
46549CB00002B/428